Praise for *If I Stay* by Tamara Morgan

"Morgan is [an] author who has a great ability to create a world and players, teasing with the secondary ones and fulfilling with the primary. This is the first book in what looks like a great series about the manor household. It's stylistically an easy read that flows almost seamlessly while telling a romance with huge family implications."
—*Harlequin Junkie*

"*If I Stay* is a really sweet and fresh romance, with a good mix of fun and dramatic moments. A great start to what should be an excellent series."
—*My Written Romance*

"Ms. Morgan gives a nice start to a new series with *If I Stay*. Overall I enjoyed this nice easy read where sometimes you find that you can actually go home and find what you are looking for."
—*Romancing the Book*

**Also available from Tamara Morgan
and Carina Press**

if I Stay

TAMARA MORGAN

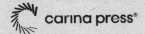

carina press®

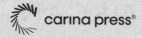

carina press®

Recycling programs
for this product may
not exist in your area.

ISBN-13: 978-0-373-00266-5

If I Stay

Copyright © 2014 by Tamara Morgan

TamaraMorgan.com

www.CarinaPress.com

Printed in U.S.A.

Dear Reader,

The idea for the Montgomery Manor series hit me sometime during the second season of *Downton Abbey*. I was lapping up the drama and gorgeous clothes (as you do), and realized that one of the biggest things missing from the show was a guaranteed Happily Ever After.

As a romance author, I take my HEAs very seriously. When I crack open the pages of a book, I want to know that love is not only possible, but guaranteed. I want to walk into the story confident that the hero and heroine will get the romance they deserve. I also want to be able to fall headfirst in love alongside them.

And there's so much to love about these two. Ryan, a former stunt driver forced to become a chauffeur due to circumstance. Amy, a nanny who relishes the chance to return to her childhood home. Both are struggling to find acceptance and a place in this world, even if it's only in the downstairs portion of Montgomery Manor.

So rest easy—this modern-day take on the upstairs/downstairs theme offers the same high drama you've come to expect from this kind of tale, but with a guaranteed HEA and plenty of laughter along the way.

The path to love might not be easy, but it's always worthwhile. I'm so happy you decided to walk it with me!

Tamara Morgan

For April, my friend and my sanity

if I Stay

ONE

"YOU CAN'T HIDE IT from me anymore, Ryan." A low feminine voice broke through the underlying buzz of the garage radio, which was set to play an unending stream of '80s butt rock. "I know what's going on here."

Ryan looked up from under the hood of the Giulietta Spider he was working on, his body tense. Even though there was no malice in that voice—or in the tall, sunny woman attached to it—he couldn't help a feeling of alarm from tingling through him. How much did she know? And what had he done to give himself away?

"Is that a fact?" he asked, forcing his lips into the semblance of a smile. When in doubt, choose reticence. It was a motto that had gotten him through many a tense situation.

"Oh, yes. I've penetrated the mysteries of your deep, dark automotive secrets at last."

This time, his smile came more naturally. "I doubt that. Remember what you said when I tried explaining how the twin camshafts work?"

"That you had a better chance of getting me to speak Greek. Backwards. After having my tongue surgically removed." Amy Sanders peeked inside the engine and wrinkled her nose, seemingly unimpressed, as she always was, with what lay underneath the hood. If she had any idea what she was looking at, it *would* have impressed her—it sure impressed the hell out of him. This particular Alfa Romeo boasted an engine made for zipping along cobbled Italian roadways, all but begged for its owner to put down the top and let go.

Sadly, all Ryan planned to do was change the oil and then take it for a sedate, low-impact journey on a fully paved side road with little traffic and no challenge. The thrills of his job never ceased to bore him.

"I'll never understand the concept of multiple car ownership." Amy cast a look over the three cars parked in a row—worth a combined half of a million dollars—and shrugged. The contents of the garage represented just a fraction of the vehicles Ryan was paid to take care of, his daily share of the Montgomery collection that rotated out of the showroom behind the house, each model more impressive than the last. "If it runs, I'm happy. If it doesn't backfire while it's running, I'm a giant bowl of ecstatic Jell-O."

Ryan wiped his hands on a rag already stained with grease and gently lowered the hood, his alarm all but forgotten. The sole threat this woman posed to him right now was on his ability to focus on work—and that was a threat he was happy to face. "The only reason your car doesn't backfire anymore is because I fixed your timing alignment last week."

"I know. I'm still appropriately gelatin-like over it." Her face broke into a wide-lipped smile, bearing testament to that statement. With bright, sparkling hazel eyes and a smattering of freckles across her nose, Amy was every inch the girl next door. The annoyingly pert, always cheerful, undeniably attractive girl next door—the one he'd never, in his almost thirty years of existence, ever actually had living nearby.

He'd had the fantasies, though. Who hadn't?

She hooked a thumb on the belt loop of her snugly fit jeans and swept an exaggerated appraisal over him. "You know, my mother always told me to marry a mechanic. Or, if I couldn't manage one of those, a plumber. She said I'd save a fortune in repair bills."

"Your mother's a wise woman. Does this mean you're finally proposing?"

"It would, but you're technically not a mechanic."

His smile faltered. "I might as well be."

Either she didn't notice the sudden shift in his mood, or she ignored it. "There you go again, turning me down and breaking my heart. But don't think that lets you off the hook. I really *have* been watching you—and I've got you figured out."

If only it were that easy. He'd had plenty of time for self-reflection in the past two years, and even *he* couldn't understand the motivation behind half the things he'd done. Stupidity, most of the time. Recklessness was pretty high up there too. In fact, the only decent thing he could have been accused of doing any time recently was maintaining a friendly distance from the woman standing opposite him.

She shifted from one foot to another, her hip jutting out in a way that made him long to run his hands all over the curve of her ass.

Forget decent. He was being downright fucking virtuous over here.

"You're ashamed of my Rabbit." Unaware of the internal battle being waged just a few feet away, Amy gave a triumphant toss of her head, her straw-colored ponytail flipping over one shoulder. "Every time I come down to the parking lot to find it, you've got me buried behind at least three town cars and a limo. I see how it is. You're putting my poor, neglected baby in a corner."

He was forced into a laugh, his hands up in mock surrender. "It's not that. I swear."

"I bring shame to your pristine garage."

"It's not my garage."

"I bring shame to your pristine reputation."

"I don't have one of those either."

"There's shame in here somewhere. I can practically taste it."

She wanted shame, did she? It wasn't that hard to find—at least not when Ryan was in the vicinity. "What if I told you I blockade your car on purpose?" The tips of his ears grew only slightly warm at the confession. "That I bury it deep in automobiles so you *have* to come find me whenever you want to drive somewhere?"

She broke into another of her wide smiles, offering it up as if her happiness was such a palpable, physical thing she had no choice but to share. This woman had been working at Montgomery Manor for only four months, and he'd already become addicted to the sight of that grin. He wanted to bask in it, roll in it, run his lips all over it.

He didn't, of course. Amy wasn't the sort of girl you kissed behind the garage and forgot about the next day. She was the sort who required staying power.

Hence the virtue. And his alarm at being found

out in the middle of what could only be called his puppy-like adoration.

"Now you're just making me blush," she teased. "Can I unbury it myself today, or is this where I bat my eyes and ask you to do it for me?"

"Nah. You're still parked on the far end of the lot. I got bored, so I washed all the staff cars this afternoon."

She stopped in the middle of pulling her keys from her purse. "All of them?"

"I got *really* bored."

"Oh, man—you should come up to the nursery for a change. I'm still praying for the day Lily and Evan nap at the same time. It's like they collaborate to create a timetable of mass destruction." Her tone belied the sense that she held the Montgomery twins in anything but affection. "Naturally, since it's my half day off, I left them as sweet and docile as lambs. They'll probably coo and simper and charm their mother into believing I have the easiest job on the face of the planet. They're wily, those two."

"I don't think I even know where the nursery is."

"It's easy. Start moving up the main stairwell. Turn right. Follow the sounds of screaming."

"Your screams, or the twins'?"

Amy decided she liked that question. "All three of us, naturally. We're thinking about starting a band. What do you think about the name *Diaper Genies?* It's got the right amount of sass."

Ryan shook his head. "I think you need to get out more."

That, sadly, was truer than she cared to admit. And from the sounds of the terrible music playing on Ryan's radio, she wasn't alone in that regard. "That reminds me—are you coming out with the rest of the staff tonight? Holly said she has a table reserved for us at O'Twohy's. We plan to drink and gossip and maybe, if the mood strikes, sing a few karaoke duets."

"Me? Nah." Ryan shook his head at her request and turned back to his work. As his work consisted of maintaining, cleaning and occasionally driving the five dozen cars and motorcycles that were Mr. Montgomery's pride and joy—not including his children, of course—Ryan presented a nice picture. A very nice picture.

Growing up, Amy had always remembered the Montgomery chauffeur as a stern, austere man who wore a dark suit when he drove and mechanic coveralls for all of life's other important moments. Ryan never wore anything but jeans and a white T-shirt, both clinging to his stocky frame and speckled with grease— and she meant that in the best way possible. The *only* way possible on a guy who looked like this one. His short blondish hair offset a pair of ears that had the tendency to protrude boyishly from the sides of his face; his nose—broken several times over—kinked at an angle that somehow managed to look rakish instead of menacing. And what she'd seen of his arms showcased crisscrossed scars and burn marks. Nothing catastrophic, mind you. Just enough to give him an edge.

Few people in their cozy town of Ransom Creek could claim such an edge. It was a place of rounded corners and cushioned falls.

"You're not much of a one for socializing, are you?" she asked.

"I like socializing just fine. But I'm not much

of a one for bars." He paused, neither smiling nor frowning, his serious intensity making her feel a bit squirmy around the edges. "Enjoy your afternoon off, Amy. You deserve it."

She watched him for a moment, wondering if there was more to that statement than met her ears, but enlightenment didn't come. The truth was—squirmy feelings and declarations of figuring this man out aside—she really *didn't* know Ryan very well. Not like she knew the other members of the staff, whose birthdays and love lives and secret wishes had been untangled in a matter of weeks. Most of them were born in November. Most of them had no love lives. And most of them wished desperately that they did.

But Ryan maintained a firm personal distance that made it difficult for her to worm her way in. He rarely joined the rest of them at lunchtime and lived in the town center instead of taking the previous chauffeur's above-garage apartment. He never came out with them when they asked. But whenever she stopped by to chat, he always set his work aside and gave her his full attention.

It was an odd mixture, to say the least.

"Thanks. I intend to." She stopped herself before she made the mistake of saying more. There was a time and a place for being a pushy busybody. The trick to being a *successfully* pushy busybody was discovering where that time and place collided. "I guess I'll see you around."

As promised, her car sat, gleaming and polished, at the edge of the parking lot. It seemed like overkill, washing a car whose body was more covered with rust than paint, but she appreciated the sentiment all the same. She might not be fast. She might not be flashy. She might be surrounded by better built models with flawless designs and heartier engines. But this was what Amy had to work with, so work with it she did.

She turned the keys in the ignition, enjoying the smooth start of an engine that, until recently, had creaked and groaned with overuse. Whatever secret mechanical tricks Ryan had performed to fix her car last week, she was pretty sure it included a lot more than a timing alignment.

As she drove by the open door to the garage, she offered him a cheerful wave goodbye, but his face had set once again into a slight frown, so she doubted he saw her.

And that was okay. She could be patient, waiting in the background for her opportunity to strike. She was exceptionally skilled at slipping by unnoticed—sometimes for years, usually in a professional capacity, at Montgomery Manor in particular. There was something about the sixty acres of rolling Connecticut countryside and the mansion, which made its stately bow at the highest crest, that rendered her all but invisible.

She turned up the radio to drown the sounds of miniature violins striking up at her one-woman pity party and rolled down her windows, determined to enjoy the scents of bluegrass and dogwood that wafted in instead.

Those were the smells of a fresh start.

Those were the smells of home.

"NO. ABSOLUTELY NOT. You're not spending your afternoon off hanging out with me." Amy's mom squinted up from where she crouched in the dirt of her garden.

In an attempt to separate her mother from some of that dirt, Amy had recently bought her one of those garden kneeling pads with matching gloves, but the gift hadn't taken. Her mom said she preferred there being no physical barriers between her and the earth—that the plants took the extra protection as a personal offense. As she also sang to the leafy greens in an effort to help them grow, Amy wasn't sure how much stock to put in that particular practice.

"Go to the city and shop," her mom commanded. "Or take a hike along the creek. Do *something.* I don't need you to babysit me. You get enough of that at work."

"That's probably true. Though I think Evan and Lily are happier to see me than you are. Or they're better at pretending, anyway."

Her mom looked up and beamed—it was obvious where her real affections lay. Her love for her own child was nothing compared to how her heart swelled for the various Montgomery offspring.

Amy plopped to the ground next to her, the thick grass serving as a comfortable cushion. Her mom had been obsessed with her yard since the day she'd moved in. It was the very first patch of grass she'd ever owned, paid for with decades of hard work. The Craftsman cottage attached to it wasn't bad either— small and functional—but the outdoor living space was her real point of pride. The spring found it awash with bright floral blooms and the fat buzzy bumble- bees they attracted.

"How are the little dears doing?" her mom asked. "I had no idea I'd miss them as much as I do."

"Oh, they're just fine. Evan is cutting a tooth, and

poor Lily feels so bad for him that she ends up doing most of the crying over it. That girl feels everything so deeply. She's going to have a rough time of it."

Her mom rocked back on her heels and gave up her spade. "She gets that from the Clare side of the family. None of the Montgomerys I raised would admit to having deep feelings. They'd rather cut their own hands off first."

Amy laughed, acknowledging the truth of that statement. If there was one thing she knew in this world, it was how the Montgomerys felt. How they acted. How they lived and loved and lost.

And won. Most of the time, they won.

Some people found it odd that she'd been hired to take care of the newest members of the Montgomery clan—born of Mr. Montgomery's painfully young second wife—after her mom stepped down a few months back. Others found it charming. Either way, most people accepted it as fate. She was practically a sister to the babies anyway. In addition to caring for the twins for the first nineteen months of their life, her mother had also served as nanny to the three older Montgomerys—now grown adults and still likely to cut off their hands before recognizing simple human emotions. Amy had been raised almost as one of the family.

Almost.

"How are the kids anyway?" her mother asked. In that context, kids referred to anything but. Monty, the eldest, was thirty-three.

"I haven't seen much of them, to be honest." Amy frowned and picked at the grass. "Monty and Jenna are constantly running around on business, and Jake hasn't set foot in the place since I've been there. Last I heard, he was in Monaco."

Her mother perked. Jake had always been her favorite. He was *everyone's* favorite, the raspberry cream among a sea of those gross date-and-almond squares. "Oh, how nice for him. He's always loved the warmer climates."

"You just mean he loves anywhere the women are scantily clad." She shrugged, hoping she looked more disinterested than she felt. Jake and his love of bikinis was no secret. Not to her, and not to anyone else who regularly visited TMZ. "I'm sure I'll run into him eventually. At Christmastime, maybe."

"Amy." The warning tone in her mother's voice was hard to miss. "Christmas is seven months from now."

"Are you telling me to start my shopping early? Have your eye on a little something sparkly? I should probably warn you now—everyone on my list is getting a photo frame made from Popsicle sticks. All the best nannies are into arts and crafts. I read it online."

"Amy." The warning was still there, louder and more insistent. "You promised me this was a temporary thing, just a fill-in until they found someone to replace me on a more permanent basis. Weren't you going to go into Hartford for an audition last week?"

"Oh, you know…" Amy waved her hand airily, hoping that by becoming vague, she could avoid having to lie.

But her mom waited. And waited. And would probably continue waiting until Amy either discovered a long-buried affinity for telling falsehoods or fossilized over.

"I didn't go, okay?" People who had disinterested, imperceptive parents had no idea how good they had it. "I'm sorry, but getting the time off was tricky, and I don't even know if dancing is what I want anymore—"

"You promised."

"I'm happy where I am."

"You promised." Her mom sighed and ran a hand through her hair—curlier than Amy's and starting to streak with gray, but with enough of a golden-brown hue to allow her to pass for an older, wiser, annoyingly interfering sister. "Sweetie, you know I love you, but I'm not about to sit quietly by for this. Not while you throw away almost twenty years of hard work and training so you can raise someone else's children."

"Why not? You did it."

Her mom's sharp intake of breath was a clear signal Amy had crossed a line. Retreat, though wise, was impossible, and she could feel her face forming into the deer-in-the-headlights grimace that always happened when she was pushed into a corner. Her best friend from high school always said it made her look crazed, as if she might eat off someone's face in an attempt to escape, but it was her natural autonomic response. Fight or flight or pray that the ground would somehow gain the ability to absorb her and render her invisible.

"I'll allow it this one time." Her mom also recognized that look, and, whether through affection or fear for her own safety, stepped down. She lifted a finger in warning. "But I reserve the right to talk about this later. You can't hide out at the Manor forever."

Amy slapped a falsely bright smile on her face. If she had anything to say about it—and one would assume she had at least *a little*—she could hide there long enough for her mom to find something else to worry about. "Deal."

"I just hope you know what you're doing," her mom said, but so quietly Amy assumed no response was required. "Well, where are you off to for the rest of the day?"

Ah. Much better. Amy could spend hours rattling off plans in an attempt to avoid more important conversations about the withered, skeletal remains of her ballet career. "I intend to indulge in an overpriced cupcake or two at that new bakery in town, and then I'm meeting some of the other staff members for dinner and drinks. Big excitement."

Her mom ignored her sarcasm. "I'm glad you're making friends. Life in that house can get pretty lonely if you don't have a support network. You should ask for more days off."

"Oh, you mean like *you* used to?" Although Amy shared her childrearing duties with a night nurse who came in five times a week, her mom hadn't been so lucky. In fact, she couldn't remember her mom ever willingly taking days—or even half days—off. They'd once gone on a weeklong vacation to the coast while the Montgomery kids attended an elite summer camp on Martha's Vineyard, but it got cut short when the camp sent Jenna home early with lice. Rich people had absolutely no capacity for handling catastrophes of the vermin kind. They sort of screamed and whirled and threw money, hoping the situation would resolve itself. Amy had distinct memories of large tubs of mayonnaise being combed through their hair and the lumpy stuffed animals that never quite regained their shape after a thorough washing.

"Do as I say, not as I do," her mother said. "You're young. You're cute. You're unfettered. Enjoy those things while you still can."

An image of the Montgomery chauffeur spun dizzyingly through her mind, his sudden, saturnine appearance as welcome as it was surprising. Ryan was also young. And cute. And, as far as she could tell, unfettered. It was a shame he insisted on maintaining such a solid distance from the rest of them, never willing to cross the unspoken line toward fellowship, friendship or, God forbid, flirtation.

"You know what? You're absolutely right."

Her mom nodded sagely. "I usually am."

Amy brushed off the seat of her jeans as she rose to her feet. That thing her mom said—about life at the Manor being lonely if you faced it alone—was true. There was nothing like the echoing resonance of someone else's success to make you feel like crap. *Especially* if you didn't do bars to take the edge off. She couldn't count the number of times she'd brooded over a mai tai at another dance audition failed, another reminder that outside of Ransom Creek, she was the center of no one's world.

And if you couldn't drink your woes away, what was the next best thing?

Amy clapped her hands, which put her on the receiving end of a warning that her loud, inappropriate noises would counteract the soothing melodies her mother had just crooned to the begonias.

Screw the plant life. She was more concerned

about human life—particularly that of her new favorite family chauffeur, and even more particularly
how she could entice him out for a night on the town.
As far as she could tell, there was only one thing in
the world a man liked better than drowning his sorrows in a good single malt.

It involved darkness. Bodies. Copious amounts
of sweat.

And lasers. Lots and lots of lasers.

TWO

RYAN GOT HOME from work at the same time every day. The same time, via the same road, with the same slow scuffle to his step. You could practically set a clock to his monotony.

He didn't used to be so predictable. Predictability had always ranked right up there with all the other—*ility* words he didn't much care for. Responsibility. Respectability. Dependability. There were a lot of those words, once you started to add them up. Which, of course, he had all the time in the world to do.

"There you are." Mrs. Grimstock, the woman who lived in the apartment directly across the hall from his, pulled open her door just enough to allow her tiny Pekingese through. "Two times around the park today, if you please. He's in a mood. He bit the mail-man."

"Sure thing, Mrs. Grimstock," he said, even though she'd already shut the door and probably couldn't hear him. "I'd love to walk your dog again."

The dog whirled around him, not making any noise other than the clack of his nails on the hall floor. That wasn't a good sign. If the creature wasn't barking, he probably hadn't been outside since the morning, when Mrs. Grimstock had cornered Ryan on his way out.

This was what he'd been reduced to. A man once courted by the top production companies in Hollywood, a man who'd only gone home to sleep and shave and even then rarely, a man who'd stared death in the face every day and come out on top—now he went home alone to walk a dog that didn't belong to him. And it wasn't even a dog after his own heart, which itched to move faster than their customary one-mile-per-hour pace. Would it have been too much to ask for Mrs. Grimstock to rescue greyhounds?

He'd gotten the plodding animal only as far as the sidewalk outside his apartment building when a bright, singsong voice called to him from the end of the block. "Can I just say that there is something about a fully grown man and a tiny dog that gets to me every time? I'm all choked up over here."

Unable to help himself, he fell into a smile. He knew he looked ridiculous holding a rhinestone leash and carrying a plastic bag, talking irritably to a dog that would have gladly traded him for a scrap of bacon. That ridiculousness was what made him frown at everyone else who dared mock him, made him gruffer than usual if someone stopped him to chat about dog parks and sanitation codes.

But there was no way not to smile at Amy. She ordered him to stand exactly where he was so she could take a picture with her camera phone.

"Oh, don't smile," she said, her voice stern. "It'll ruin the effect. This is going on my Facebook page."

He forced his lips in a downward curl. "Am I frowning enough now?"

"Hmm." She cocked her head. "Not quite. Quick. Close your eyes and think of the worst moment of your life."

That was easy. Crash and burn, his dream fizzling out in the distance.

He heard the computerized click meant to simulate a camera going off and popped his eyes open to find Amy standing right in front of him. "You must have some really terrible memories stored in there." She showed him the picture. "You look like you're about to curb stomp the next guy who insults your puppy."

He *did* look pretty grim, though he was having a hard time holding on to the sensation as Amy's fruity scent wafted all around him. She smelled like watermelon. A few days ago, it had been peaches. Either she had a fruit basket in her shower, or his attempt at self-restraint was starting to sour.

"Oh, yeah? You know a lot about curb stomping?"

"You have no idea." She gestured around her, toward the townhouse-lined street a block down, each door painted a different jewel tone, at the knitting shop across the street, at the convenience store with a fresh salad bar inside. "Don't be fooled by these sweet city streets. When the sun goes down, life gets rough. I once had to fend off a pack of tourists using nothing but a freshly baked baguette."

"Did you hit them with it?"

"No. I threw crumbs and the birds swooped down to protect me."

That was something he could readily picture. Amy resembled nothing so much as an animated princess who could call animals at will to protect her. She was friends with the ogres, champion of the fallen.

In proof of just such a thing, she knelt and began vigorously petting the dog, who acted as though he'd never before been touched by human hands, eliciting a series of ecstatic groans as he wriggled under her touch. "Oh, he's sweet. What's his name?"

"Um." Ryan had no idea. He'd been walking the dog for months and had never called it anything but Pain in My Ass. As he was reluctant to share that particular name with a woman he'd just likened to a cartoon character, he settled for saying, "He's not mine. He belongs to the woman who lives across from me."

"Aww. You walk your neighbor's dog?"

"Before you start singing my virtues, I should probably tell you it's not by choice." He recognized the telltale dance of the dog about to release every last one of his bodily fluids and started tugging him away from Amy's flower-smattered blouse. "If I don't take him out, his owner encourages him to leave presents in front of my door."

Amy's eyes flew open in surprised laughter. Ryan could only be grateful that her mouth didn't fall open too, because the dog chose that moment to lift its leg and deposit a hot, streaming line of urine all over her neckline.

He swooped to pick the animal up, but it was too late. The best he could do was point the dog in the opposite direction and wait for him to finish.

"That motherfucking little bastard."

It was his turn to be surprised. "What did you just say?"

"Your neighbor's dog." She stood hunched, holding her shirt away from her body. The unmistakable trail of yellow along white silk would have wrested an immediate apology from his lips, but she was laughing too hard to let him get a word in. "That little shithead did it on purpose. He was waiting for me to get close enough so he could land his mark."

Ryan could only listen, fascinated, as Amy's sweet pink lips continued spilling a litany of curses that would have done a construction crew proud. Damn, but that woman had a mouth on her. It pursed and beckoned and drew him in.

"I know I've already imposed in coming by unannounced like this," that same mouth continued, oblivious to the sensations it produced, "but I don't suppose you have a shirt I could borrow?"

He forced himself to blink and viewed her frame with a detachment he was far from feeling. No amount of personal avowals that he wouldn't get sucked in to this place, wouldn't grow attached, could change the way the sight of her affected him. She was tall for a woman, so much so that she stood on eye level with him, and slender in an athletic sort of way— evidenced by the fact that she was constantly moving, always active. Taken alone, these things endowed her with more than enough appeal to speak to Ryan's baser parts, but either nature or the marvels of modern medicine had also seen fit to grace her with an incredible rack.

There. He admitted it. He liked the way Amy—the sweet, pee-covered nanny—filled out a shirt.

"I can probably rustle up something," he said doubtfully. "But my clothes aren't nearly as pretty as yours."

"As long as you didn't recently use them as a urinal, I think it's a step up."

The dog wriggled in his grasp, eager to get down, but as the creature had long since reached empty,

Ryan decided its participation in the evening's events was done. "Come on up. You can meet Mrs. Grimstock and show her what her dog did."

"Maybe *she* has a shirt I can borrow."

"I've never seen Mrs. Grimstock in anything but a robe and slippers—the same ones she wears every day. Don't get your hopes up."

Amy loped up the stairs after Ryan, making faces at the fluffy white face peeking over his shoulder. It was a good thing the dog gave her a pretext for coming upstairs and snooping around Ryan's apartment, or she might be in a much worse mood right now. She'd walked up and down the block about three times, trying to decide whether or not her highhanded change of plans for the night would be met with his approval or his anger.

Well, now he couldn't be angry. She had pee in her hair. In situations of comparative irritation, hair pee always won.

The apartment building where Ryan lived wasn't quite what she'd expected when she'd weaseled the address out of the Montgomerys' housekeeper, a grouchy but efficient man who, despite having no military affiliations whatsoever, went by the name of Sarge. For some reason, she'd envisioned Ryan set up in some kind of bachelor-pad haven full of remote control doors and mirrors placed at creepy angles. It was probably because he'd chosen not to live at Montgomery Manor—she assumed his place would have to be pretty wicked to turn down free room and board.

Maybe there was *some* charm in the warped wood stairs and the way each doorstep boasted its own colorful welcome mat, and at this time of the evening, a delicious generic food smell pervaded the air. Of course, it wasn't three thousand square feet overlooking the Montgomery Manor tennis courts. *That* was a view to which she'd always been partial.

Ryan knocked loudly on a white door with a doormat instructing all comers to *Go Away.*

"How charming," Amy said, pointing at it. "I think I'm beginning to like Mrs. Grimstock already."

Ryan grinned. "Nope. It's me you like. I gave that to her last Christmas."

She didn't have time to respond as a grizzled, white-haired woman with the most enormous breasts she'd ever seen pulled the door open. True to Ryan's promise, she wore a robe that, though crafted in a lovely pink terrycloth, probably wasn't much better than Amy's urine-soaked shirt in terms of general cleanliness.

Mrs. Grimstock closed one eye as she took in the pair of them, hesitatingly taking her dog back. "You weren't gone long enough for two park loops."

"That's because your dog mistook my friend here for a fire hydrant."

"So?"

"She's very upset."

"She doesn't look upset."

"She's really good at hiding it."

Amy laughed and immediately slapped her hand over her mouth. She was ruining Ryan's man-in-charge moment here, but she couldn't help it. She and ill-timed laughter had something of a longstanding relationship.

"She's also slightly hysterical," Ryan added, wrapping an arm around her waist and pulling her from the doorway. His arm was strong and friendly—exactly as she'd imagined it would be. Strong, friendly arms were the best kind. "I better get her somewhere safe. And clean."

"By the way, what's the dog's name?" Amy couldn't help asking as he led her away. She liked to know the names of everyone who'd christened her with his bodily fluids. It was something of a life goal.

"Beau." Mrs. Grimstock's puffy cheeks lifted in what Amy assumed was a smile. "It's short for Beauregard."

Ryan ushered Amy through his front door before she had a chance to say more. She was pleased to note on the way in that he had a much more cheerful, if slightly out-of-season doormat showcasing a Thanksgiving turkey.

His apartment was also the mansplosion of expensive electronics and leather she'd hoped for, all crammed into a space so tiny it practically swelled at the seams. She loved it when guys gave in to the somber call of stainless steel and mirrored surfaces. It was as though they couldn't help themselves, inexplicably drawn to the shiny.

"Nice." She nodded at the perfectly gleaming kitchen counters, at an island holding nothing but a half-full glass of water. "I'm pretty sure I've seen your apartment in a movie before."

Ryan looked around, a heavy crease in his brows. There was a scar at the edge of his right one, long and jagged and cutting a half-inch path of hair. She hadn't noticed that one before. "You have? Which movie?"

"Oh, you know. Just every one ever made with a bachelor character in it. Fifty bucks says you have a hidden dartboard somewhere in here. I'm guessing it's inside that cupboard over there."

Chagrin was a good but subtle look on Ryan. His ears flushed with color as he scrubbed a hand along the back of his neck. "How could you possibly know that?"

"I watch a lot of movies. And based on your apartment, I'm guessing you do too."

"It's not that bad."

"Is the dartboard electronic?"

"Ye-es."

She nodded once. "It's bad."

Ryan's shoulders shook as he gave in to a self-deprecating laugh. "I'm getting you a clean shirt. You can poke around in corners and pass more judgments on my lifestyle while I'm gone."

"Not one of your shiny clubbing shirts, please."

"Ha!" He clapped once, triumphant. "I got you there. I don't have any shiny clubbing shirts."

"Of course you do. Dozens of them. You leave the top two buttons undone and put gel in your chest hair so it curls over the top."

He turned and moved toward the back of the apartment, where she could just make out a shiny gray comforter and a bed that was much too large for a single person living alone. "You're a strange woman, Amy Sanders."

"I'm not the one who combs my chest hair!" she yelled back, and was rewarded with a thump on the wall next to her head. Neighbors. Yet another reason life in the Manor would be so much better than this. Why live next to strangers when he could take up residence right down the hall from her?

Ryan clearly had no idea what he was missing.

Ryan rummaged in his drawer until he found a re-
spectably clean T-shirt that wasn't stained around
the edges with motor oil. He had a better wardrobe
than this—not quite at the shiny clubbing shirt level,
though there might have been a sparkle or two involved—but no way in hell he was pulling those out.
There was no need to give the woman in his living
room any more ammunition than she already had
against him. He didn't care how much he might want
to rip off her shirt and lather up her skin with his own
hands. Almost two years he'd been living in Ransom
Creek, and he'd managed not to let anyone this close.

Five more minutes, and he was pretty sure Amy
would have his Social Security number and the exact
dollar amount on his last tax return. She got under his
skin in a way that felt so comfortable, so inoffensive,
she could take up residence there forever and he'd be
perfectly content to let her.

"I hope you're a big fan of Metallica." He emerged
from the bedroom and handed her the shirt.

"Oooh, I am." She held it up and laughed to see
the band name in monolith size lit up with lightning.
It was one wolf howling at the moon short of tragic.
"Back in ballet school, we did a performance to a
symphonic version of one of their albums."

He grabbed the bottom of the shirt, refusing to let
go. "If that's the only version you've heard, I want
my shirt back. You can wear dog pee."

She tugged. "It counts. We even had a fireworks
display. Our stage director got third-degree burns."

"Bodily harm does not a Metallica fan make."

"Bodily harm is what's going to happen if you

don't point me toward the bathroom right this minute."

Laughing, Ryan let go. Amy was the sort of woman who wouldn't lift a hand to kill a mosquito. "It's through the bedroom. Follow the trail to all my expensive hair care products."

As she sprang in that direction, she ran her fingers playfully through his hair. He wore it military-short, a relic of his stunt driving days, and the twitch of her fingers against his scalp felt intimate—the kind of intimacy that acted like a reflex on his body, putting all of his parts on instant, twitching alert. He struggled to send those parts a message of overriding calm.

Down, boy. That line you're straining to cross right there is a finish line.

No matter how strong the temptation, he wouldn't get tangled up with this sweet, generous woman only to toss her aside when he finally got the call. His agent back in Hollywood was so close to getting him behind the wheel of a stunt car again. Three more months, tops. He was sure of it.

"Liar," she teased. "Your hair feels like you use baby shampoo."

And on that pronouncement—quelling, quashing and sadly true—she whisked through his room to clean up and change. It was only then that he realized how strange it was for her to appear outside his home like this. Although his apartment was located near the center of the downtown area, a location chosen for its proximity to anything and anyone, no one at work knew where to find him.

It was an odd combination of housing prerequisites, he knew. He didn't want to live in isolation—

needed the thump of people coming and going, the irate neighbors who left passive aggressive notes on his door—but he also didn't want to constantly be thinking of Montgomery Manor.

In retrospect, that had been an unattainable goal. He couldn't walk five feet from his door without being reminded, in some way, of the fifty-room mansion on the outskirts of town. The Montgomerys owned this place, ruled it, blanketed it with the money and their protection. It was a little bit unnerving—especially since no one he encountered seemed to think it odd. But how could they? The hotelier family employed at least one member of every household in the county. They were practically living in a serfdom.

"There. Now I'm an official Metallica fan." Amy emerged from the bathroom feeling only slightly ridiculous. She was cleaner and, as far as she could detect, smelled much better. But men's T-shirts never fit her quite right. They were always too tight across the chest, too wide everywhere else—and Lord knew their logo placement could use a little work. In this particular instance, the band name stretched tightly over her breasts, flashing lightning at the peak of each nipple.

"Still doesn't count as being a fan." Ryan paused, and she could see the sweep of his eyes as he took her in, lightning bolts and all. It would have been a stretch to say she felt a tingle of electricity at each tip, though the sensations weren't too far off. "But the shirt looks much better on you than it ever did on me."

"That's because I have boobs."

His eyes widened as he choked on his shock. "I wasn't going to say that."

"I know. It was very gentlemanly of you." Since she *finally* seemed to have pushed him off guard, now seemed as good a time as any to spill the reason she'd stopped by. "And as long as you're in the mood to be polite, I might as well confess to stalking you."

His eyes got even wider.

"Don't get too excited—I stalk an alarming amount of people. This guy who works at the gas station down on Fourth had to take a restraining order out on me in high school. I couldn't help myself. He looked *exactly* like a young Robert Redford."

Ryan turned his head in profile. "I've been told I look like a young Robert Redford."

"You do not. You look like Tom Hardy and Daniel Craig had a secret love child."

"Is that good?"

It was *very* good, especially when paired with his strong, friendly arms. But there was no need to show her whole hand here. Or to make herself appear even more ridiculous than she already did. "Fishing for compliments? Shame on you."

"A man has his pride."

"He also has a mirror." She paused a beat, not wanting to lose their friendly momentum. "Unless you need me to write a poem to your dreamy eyes, I think we should address the issue of my hunting you down at your home. It's about the bar plans."

His attitude shifted as if on a dime. Gone was the playful banter, the Tom Hardy smile, the focus on her boobs. His arms crossed and he actually had the nerve to square his stance and glare at her. *Glare*. Please. She was a nanny now. No one out-glared the nanny.

"You don't have to come if you don't want to, but we've decided to meet at the laser tag place out on Hiawatha Road instead. They have terrible snack bar pizza and their pop machine has been broken for decades so only the root beer nozzle works, but there's this boys' soccer team that meets there every Sunday. They're a bunch of whiny punks. Slaughtering them would make me happy in more ways than I can count."

The arms came down, a hint of his smile returned. "You want me to come play laser tag?"

"Only if you promise to take out as many twelve-year-olds as you can. I'm putting together a team of mercenaries, and we could use a good man like you. You look as if you know your way around a toy gun and chemically manufactured fog."

"What happened to the bar idea?"

She shrugged. "It's boring. Uninspired."

"Then why aren't you looking me in the eye?"

Darn it. She really needed to get better at lying. People who wore their hearts and their thoughts and the contents of their stomach on their sleeves were at a real disadvantage in this world.

"I was inspired to choose an alternate venue."

His mouth firmed in a thin line. "One that doesn't serve alcohol?"

"Oh, they serve alcohol. But you have to bring fifty dollars in cash and be prepared to meet the manager out behind the dumpster." She would not list how many times she'd undergone just such a feat. It was *a lot*. "And all you can expect to get for your fifty bucks is a jug of Carlo Rossi that I'm pretty sure he waters down. It's not worth it, trust me."

Ryan cracked a smile. "Sounds like you had quite the wayward youth."

"I did. And most of it occurred behind that dumpster, now that I think about it."

"Not with the manager, I hope?"

It was her turn to fall into a grin. See? Ryan wasn't such a difficult man to coax into a good mood. Holly had been wrong when she'd said he'd probably shut the door in her face and tell her to mind her own damn business. Such language. And from such a tiny, perky woman.

"Ew. No. He was old back when I was a teenager. He looks like the Crypt Keeper now." That elicited another smile from him. "So will you come? The staff only gets a shared day off every two weeks or so. We like to make the most of it."

"Only if you tell me the truth. Did you change the location so I'd be more likely to come?"

There was no way to tiptoe around it. "Yes."

"Because of what I said about not doing bars?"

"Yes."

"And do you know *why* I don't do bars?"

She refused to look away as the intensity in his voice deepened. Although she was an only child, she'd grown up in a household where money and power were secondary only to personal strength. If she'd wanted to be treated as an equal to the Montgomery children, she'd had to earn it by holding her own, standing her ground, doing all those things that made her sound like a tree or a soldier rather than the inferior, gangly nanny's daughter she really was.

"I can make an educated guess," she said.

He neither confirmed nor denied her guess—
which was just as well, as she hadn't put it into words.
She might excel at overstepping people's boundaries,
but she did have enough tact not to call a man an al-
coholic to his face.

"Do the others know?"

She wasn't quite sure how to answer that. Of
course everyone had theories about Ryan's antiso-
cial behavior—and what caused it. A former Hollywood stuntman didn't descend upon Ransom Creek
with a chip on his shoulder and a scowl across his face
without some kind of backstory filling in the cracks.
She'd heard every hypothesis from drugs and a tragic
love affair to international espionage.

It was probably the Daniel Craig ears that ac-
counted for that last one.

But she just shrugged, showing him how little anyone at Montgomery Manor cared for that sort of thing.
They all had baggage. Holly Santos, Mrs. Montgomery's personal chef, refused to mention how she came
to meet the illustrious lady of the house, no matter
how many hints they dropped. Alex Morris, the ex-
military head of the family's security detail, had a
dishonorable discharge on his record that prevented
him from finding work anywhere else. And Amy,
well, she'd given up her place on a touring ballet company to return to the bosom of her childhood home.

At least, that was the story she told.

"No one is going to point in your face and laugh,
if that's what you're afraid of." She perched on the
edge of his couch, looking up at him. "And even if

they did, so what? You don't strike me as the type to care about a little friendly gossip."

"Friendly gossip is an oxymoron."

She ignored the grouchiness in his voice and gestured toward the Metallica shirt. "Thank you for the change of clothes. It's probably better than the white blouse I was wearing anyway. The dark color and sweet lightning bolts will blend in with the black lights. Those sneaky preteens won't be able to see me coming."

"Or they'll just gape at your chest and you can win that way."

Triumph. Once the boob references were back, it was pretty much a guaranteed victory. "So you'll come? If it helps, I'll let you gape at my chest before the game."

He flushed, and she could see his struggle not to take her up on the offer right that second. She could sense it too, her nipples tingling at the idea of being so overtly ogled—and by a man who didn't seem to care about ogling anything but cars. But his controlled gruffness won out, and he finally gave in, her breasts remaining sadly unmolested.

"There's no need to resort to bribery. You can count me in. Let's go kick some twelve-year-old ass."

Amy fell into a mock swoon to hide her delight—and her boobs' lingering disappointment. "My hero."

THREE

"I'LL RUN POINT." Alex, the Montgomerys' beefy lead security guard, a man who looked like he bench-pressed small children in his free time, made a series of hand gestures that none of them understood. "I want Ryan and Philip covering me from the rear. Amy and Holly, you two flank. You need to be stuck to my sides like a pair of burrs."

"Question." Amy lifted her hand.

Ryan waited patiently with the others to hear what she had to say—none of them finding this situation as odd as it must appear on the outside. The laser tag facility smelled, predictably, of stale adolescent sweat and burnt popcorn. It had once been painted bright purple and black, but time had worn away the best of the color, leaving the entire facility looking like a Halloween mask left out in the sun.

The sad backdrop had nothing on them, though. There were a total of five of them from the Manor here to play, each one strapped into plastic chest-and back-plates that fit a little too snugly over their adult-sized frames. He felt uncomfortable and silly. And the back of his neck was wet with spitballs the annoying soccer team kids kept shooting across the waiting area.

Goddammit. This was war.

"Yes?" Alex barked. "What is it?"

"Why do Holly and I have to flank? That sounds like the wimpy, leftover job—the one you made up just to give to the girls."

Alex frowned, and the sight of it was so powerful Ryan felt his spine straightening in response. If that man hadn't run an entire militia in his previous life, Ryan would be deeply surprised. "Fine. Prove me wrong. Shoot Ryan in the head from where you stand."

"I'd rather shoot you. You're the one being misogynistic."

"Amy, if you can hit either one of us anywhere above the waist, I'll let you take the whole damn operation over."

She screwed up her face in concentration and raised her gun. Ryan laughingly lifted his hands in defense, but she was intent on proving her point. "Hold still, Ryan. I'm about to end you."

She fired, and he could see the flash of red as her shot aimed far wide of his head and landed somewhere near the back wall. "Crap buckets!" she cried. "I'd have been better off aiming at the ceiling. Fine. I'll flank you. But I don't see what good that's going to do except shield you from getting yourself shot. You're basically transforming me and Holly into body armor."

Alex winked. "And I'm sure you'll be excellent at it."

They didn't have time to argue after that. The starting alarm—a rooster's crow—sounded, and they filed out of the waiting area toward the oversized warehouse space like a troop heading into battle. According to the tired-looking, unamused guy running the show, they had exactly sixty seconds to get in place before their targets would be activated and all bets were off.

They moved as a collective group for the first sixty-five seconds. Unfortunately, as soon as the lights went dark, the adolescent taunting started. Amy's restraint, which hadn't been very reliable to start with, went up like a wisp of the fake fog kicking in. She took off after an undersized boy with his hair hanging in his eyes, her vows to teach him manners if it was the last thing she did echoing throughout the warehouse. Holly, also taking exception to his liberal use of various parts of the female anatomy as insults, wasn't far behind.

"Pwned you, noob," a kid shouted from the rear. Turning, Ryan got ready to fire back, but Alex had already landed a perfect shot and was moving on to take out every person within a twenty-foot radius.

"Change of plans," Alex commanded. He was dressed all in black, making him difficult to distinguish among the low lights, moving with a kind of stealth that was unsettling. This was not a man Ryan would choose to cross on a real battlefield, that was for sure. "I'm single-handedly nailing every last one of these bastards if it kills me."

It was soon proven that Alex was a man of his word. Philip, one of the owners of the landscaping company the Montgomerys kept on retainer, had the kind of lean, wiry strength that would have come in handy when they rounded a corner and stepped into an ambush, but he soon abandoned them to the noble call of the ladies trapped behind a mirror on the bottom floor. Left alone, Ryan and Alex stood back to back, moving steadily toward higher ground and picking off everyone they could see. Only the occasional vibration of his chest plate signaled a hit.

Somewhere in this, there was an inappropriate comment about grown-ass adults playing with vibrating kids' toys, but Ryan didn't bother trying to find it.

He was too busy having fun.

With only minimal casualties, they reached a perch that was safely recessed from most of the kids, allowing them a chance to chat amid all the slaughter.

"Fuck yes." Alex hit the loudest of the soccer kids right in the chest and lowered his weapon. "I'm kissing Amy on the mouth as soon as this is over. With tongue. I can't tell you how good it feels to pick up a gun again."

"You don't carry?" Ryan had never understood what—or who—it was the Montgomerys needed protecting from, but it had never been a secret that Alex and the handful of rotating security guards were very much a physical presence at the house.

"Oh, man. I wish. Mr. Montgomery forbids firearms. It's one of the things I hate most about this job." Alex nodded to their rear.

Ryan aimed at a blinking light and fired, triumphant at the sound of a cracked voice calling him names he wouldn't dare repeat. "No guns? Then what the hell do you do if there's a break-in or attack?"

Alex leaned down just enough to lift the leg of his military-grade cargo pants, allowing Ryan to catch a flash of a knife strapped to his calf.

"I carry about eight of these babies on my person at all times."

"I can see how that might be effective."

Alex laughed. "So is being the only six-foot-three black man in a town of bankers and housewives. Mr. Montgomery knew what he was about when he hired me."

Too bad no one else did. Ryan only knew enough about Alex's military past to recognize that putting down a gun to run point on a security team as elite as it was unnecessary probably wasn't part of the man's master life plan. He'd wager the job had been foisted on him, slapped down as the only recourse in an increasingly depressing career path.

In other words, not all that different from Ryan's own.

"Seems to me you'd want to avoid casual warfare like this," he said. "Stay away from temptation and all that."

"You think? Kind of like a former stunt driver keeping his distance from all those sweet racecars of Mr. Montgomery's?" He nodded. "To your left. Nine o'clock."

Fair enough. He fired.

"Do you ever miss it?" Alex gestured toward the back, and they moved as one to a hidden alcove near an emergency exit. "The explosions? The speed? The crashes?"

"Hell, yes." The words rose to his lips before he could stop them.

For the longest time, Ryan had done a pretty decent job of not wallowing over his past mistakes, focused instead on keeping his head down and his nose clean, waiting for the day he could get his life back. It was impossible to get through the day otherwise. He couldn't count the number of times he'd felt the purr of Mr. Montgomery's prize Ferrari 458 revving to life underneath him and felt actual physical pain at taking it down the street at a sedate thirty-five miles per hour. Both he and the car wept at the injustice of it, of the meeting of his hands and its leather-padded steering wheel in an agonizingly slow dance that reduced asphalt kick-up and accidental pings.

But his patience with idling was rapidly nearing its end. It wouldn't be fair to hold Amy accountable for his dissatisfaction with life in Ransom Creek, but there was no denying she played a role. Since the moment she'd arrived, filling the Manor with her laughter and cheer and great rack, she'd awakened feelings long dormant inside him—feelings that went beyond sexual desire. He wanted action. He wanted more than this limbo that encapsulated him. He wanted to start moving again.

But none of that was happening in a laser tag facility, and Alex Morris, bad-ass bodyguard to the elite, was the wrong man to open up to. Ryan shrugged and did his best to make light of the situation.

"How could I not miss it? It was a dream job for any man with a pulse. What if I offered to let you take out one of Mr. Montgomery's cars and race it along the Los Angeles River at a hundred and forty miles per hour, no questions asked? What would you give up for that kind of speed?"

Alex didn't even pause. "My right nut. My left nut. Both my nuts wrapped in a bow."

"Exactly."

Alex gave him a nod of complete understanding, and Ryan felt a sudden overwhelming kinship with the man. After seeing how many shots Alex picked off without even blinking, it was clear the man was sitting on a well of untapped potential. Wasted, weeping, perfectly aimed potential.

The rooster crowed again as the lights came on, revealing their war zone to be nothing more than a stained, dirty cement block and a handful of overgrown youths whose voices had yet to change. It seemed fitting somehow, that their adrenaline would ebb away to leave only the sad vestiges of a game they were too old to be playing in the first place.

"Do you think you'll ever go back?" Alex asked, blinking his eyes, one then the other, as they adjusted to the lights.

"I sure fucking hope so," Ryan said.

"Sucks, man. I know just how you feel." And with that, Alex thwapped him heavily on the back and leaped over a retaining wall toward the exit, pumping his fist in victory at Philip.

Ryan followed slowly, chewing on the conversation, savoring the bitterness it left behind. Hope was such a fleeting thing to hinge a life on, but it was all he had.

Every single insurance agent he'd approached after the accident—and still approached every few months, hoping for a backdoor policy that would clear him for work again—had turned him down. But he kept approaching. Every movie production company he'd called, offering to sign a contract—any contract—that would clear them of responsibility for injuries incurred on the job had politely declined. But he kept asking.

They all said the same thing, that no one was willing to take a risk on the stunt driver who'd crashed a half-million dollar car into a freeway overpass on the job, his blood alcohol level teetering somewhere near the point-two level. A liability, they called him. A drunkard. Burned out. Finished. Done.

But he didn't *feel* done. He wasn't ready to give up and reconcile himself to a life of *Driving Miss Daisy*. Ransom Creek was the end of the line for a man like him. The bottom of the barrel.

The bottom of the barrel was definitely not where he'd envisioned spending the rest of his life.

Ryan caught up with Amy, who was red-faced and laughing, her bangs plastered to her forehead with sweat and what looked like war paint. He had no idea where the paint had come from but knew better than to question it. If anyone carried spare war paint in her pockets, it would be her.

"I hope you and Alex put on a better show than we did," she said. "My trigger was stuck and I got cornered."

"I'm pretty sure Alex made a clean sweep of it. That man has some scary shooting skills."

She waggled her eyebrows. "Why do you think I invited him? Come on. I'll buy us some six-hour-old celebratory pizza. Then maybe I can whoop your butt at pinball. I may not be very good at laser tag, but I'm a wizard at pinball."

He followed her out, forcing himself to focus on the here and now. Amy, here. Her kind gesture in setting this night up, now.

He was lucky to be around people who cared enough to change their plans to suit his weaknesses. Luckier to have a job. Even luckier still to be alive. That had to count for something.

One of these days, he'd figure out what.

AMY SAT IN the middle of a circle of brightly colored plastic blocks, building a tower that defied the laws of gravity. She'd swear that ninety percent of her days were spent building things out of unrelated objects. Mountains out of mashed sweet potatoes. Forts out of pillows. She thought she might try a house of cards tomorrow, but chances were Evan would want to help and demolish the whole thing.

He was destructive, that boy. And sweet little Lily did everything her brother wanted of her, even if that meant knocking down the beautiful creations they made and sobbing her heart out at the senseless loss of it all.

Amy's heart pinged for the poor child. She knew all too well what it meant to feel too much, to want so hard to please. Even with a gazillionaire family and what had to be the most gorgeous pair of blue eyes in existence, that girl was in for a world of hurt someday.

"More blocks, Amy! More!" Evan clapped his hands and watched, rapt, as she stood on her tiptoes to get a blue block on top of the red one.

"Yellow, red, blue," she chanted. "What comes next?"

"Lellow," Lily solemnly replied. Amy dropped a kiss on her strawberry-blond curls in reward for her diligence.

She'd made patterns out of the three primary colors as she went, so she figured it counted as a learning game. Mrs. Montgomery—*Serena*, she insisted Amy call her—was a big proponent of adding an educational component to every second of every day. The woman had been against hiring Amy right from the start, as she admittedly had no training in early childhood education. Three years of hurried high school studies shoved in around a rigorous dance schedule made her an expert on absolutely nothing at all, but she had one undeniable advantage in the nanny arena: family.

As a second wife, married to the head of the family just three years earlier, Serena didn't share Mr. Montgomery's sense of loyalty when it came to things like this. She'd wanted her children to learn French and dress all in white and get into the best preschools before they were even born, but Mr. Montgomery would have no more turned Amy down for a job than he would have disowned one of his children. Mr. Montgomery was practically a father to her, and had been since the day her mom had been hired here. He trusted her to raise his second crop of children, and that was good enough to silence even Serena's protests.

No one crossed John Montgomery the Second once a decision was made. She doubted anyone had ever tried.

"Now here's a sight I never thought to enjoy."

Amy stopped, suspended mid-tiptoe, unable to move. She could hear the squeals of Evan and Lily as they gave up their engineering futures to run to the legs of the half brother they barely knew but unquestionably adored. They never reacted that way when Monty came around to say hello—he was the sort of man who was powerful and generous to the point of perfection, the guy everyone worshipped as a leader but sort of cringed from as a man.

At least, Amy had always done that. He'd once caught her in the kitchen stealing sugar flowers from the top of a cake destined for Jenna's eighth birthday party. Instead of yelling at her or going straight to the cook with tales of her infamy, he'd just offered his grim, thirteen-year-old smile and said, "I know you didn't mean to do wrong, Amy. Want me to make you some cocoa instead?"

But Jake?

He wouldn't have stolen sugar flowers alongside her—he would have found them a pair of forks and helped her to eat the entire top tier. And most of the second.

She turned slowly, doing her best to slow the nervous leap of her heart, to school her features into those of a calm, reasonable young woman meeting an old friend for the first time in eight years.

It didn't work.

With a squeal that cast Evan's and Lily's into the shade, her good intentions imploded in on themselves. She launched herself across the room and into Jake's arms. His arms were waiting for just such a thing, and he lifted her in an impromptu twirl around the nursery. Of necessity, it was a short twirl, and he let out a soft grunt as he deposited her safely out of reach of her two charges.

"Geez, Amy. You got heavy."

"Maybe you got weak," she countered, feeling breathless.

She took a moment to straighten her lace tank top and appraise the now-grown man opposite her, and realized her words couldn't possibly be true. Of course Jake Montgomery hadn't gotten weak. He looked taller, more self-assured, with actual muscle packed inside his once-lanky frame. Like all the

Montgomerys, he wore his signature red hair with pride, the dark auburn strands standing up in a casual, windblown sweep above his impeccable bone structure and the charming, freckle-smattered visage she knew so well.

"I take it back." He licked his lips as he took her in, his own exploration similarly unabashed. "You didn't get heavy. You got…full. Christ, Amy. Why didn't you tell me? Or at least text me a few pictures?"

She felt hot annoyance sweep through her at his words, a feeling quite at odds with her expectations. Ever since she'd returned to the Manor, she'd lived in anticipation of this moment. Jake and Amy, against the world. Jake and Amy, all grown up. Yes, maybe even Jake and Amy, these happy golden years. Stranger things had happened.

But the real thing was both better and worse than her imaginings. Better, because he was real and he was *here*. Not off seducing socialites with perfectly cascading locks and large trust funds, or racing around the world on a yacht run by a crew of able-bodied men—actually here, so close she could touch him.

And worse, because it was impossible not to remember the boy she'd once been so close to he was like a second skin. The boy she remembered would have laughed off the idea of well-coiffed heiresses or living anywhere but his beloved Connecticut. The boy she remembered would have never looked at her with that cold, suggestive gleam in his eye.

"What finally brings you home?" she asked, shaking herself off. This sense of disappointment was her own fault for building him up for so long, for housing him in a castle built on air. Of *course* he'd changed in eight years. She certainly had. "Your dad must be so glad to see you again."

"He's not," Jake said, his eyes going flat. "I've been summoned home for rustication."

"You mean vacation?"

"I mean punishment. I'm supposed to retrench and rebuild my reputation. Apparently, he objects to my high profile way of living."

"Maybe he just misses you."

"Perhaps." His reticence said more on the subject than he probably realized. "But I didn't come all the way down to the nursery wing to talk about that. You, Amy. *You.* I want to hear all about you dancing your way across Europe with twenty other women. Particularly the other women. Did you all sleep together in a giant bed covered with satin pillows, sweaty and exhausted from your labors? You did, didn't you? I can tell by the way your face is growing red."

Suddenly aware that they had an audience, she swooped to pick up the twins, admonishing them for holding so tightly to Jake's pants, their sticky, grubby hands ruining the perfect creases of his slacks.

"I can tell that your brother and I are about to have a highly inappropriate conversation, yes, we are," she cooed to the twins, grateful to have a distraction. "And the last time I said something inappropriate, you repeated it verbatim to your mother and almost got me fired, yes, you did. Which means it's…naptime!"

Most of what she said was interpreted as gibberish, but both of the kids recognized *naptime* as the most evil word of all creation and began squirming to get out of her arms. Jake's honest laughter—a piece of childhood that tugged at the bottom of her heart—sounded at her back.

"I didn't think you'd been here long enough to get on Serena's bad side already. What did you say to set her off?"

"Good try," she called over her shoulder. "But I'm not falling for that one. These two are sponges for vulgarity. They won't spout a single one of the vocab words we work on, but a tiny reference to the act of copulation slips out, and all of a sudden it's perfect pronunciation and nuance."

"What I wouldn't give to have seen Serena's face when one of her little angels dropped the F-bomb."

"Stick around for a few more days and you'll probably get the chance. I'm not exactly her top choice when it comes to her children."

Getting Evan and Lily to their respective cribs for naptime was a bit like wrestling alligators. Or what she imagined wrestling alligators was like, assuming the reptiles had lungs like a pair of long-distance runners and a recently acquired ability to climb in and out of their cribs. No sooner did Lily get settled in than Evan was suddenly darting between Amy's legs in an attempt to escape the confines of their shared bedroom. If she tended to Evan first, Lily would get one leg out of her crib and realize how far she was from the ground. Vertigo kicked in and so did her panic.

A strong male helping hand would have done wonders in soothing temperaments and smoothing blankets, but she didn't ask Jake for assistance. And of course he didn't offer. Being a half brother at the age of thirty wasn't part of the image he projected to the world. Rich playboys stayed as far away from dirty diapers as possible, lest the female population get the wrong idea about their intentions.

Amy emerged from the bedroom about twenty minutes later, frazzled and exhausted, sure Jake would have wandered off in pursuit of more entertaining activities. So she was surprised to find him seated in the gliding rocker instead, flipping through a children's book with a frown on his face.

She paused in the doorway, watching him read, her heart catching in her throat as memories assailed her from all sides. And not just the squishy, girly ones that existed mostly in her head. There were some real ones in there too. Jake teaching her to ride a bike. Jake coolly wrapping an arm around her and daring the eighth-grade bully to lay a finger on his property. Jake struggling to remain strong when his father didn't show up, once again, for his birthday party.

"That one always makes me cry," she said once he got to the end. "When the mom crawls into her son's window and tells him how much she loves him? I sob. We're talking buckets of snot. It's not pretty."

Jake tossed the book aside. "Are you joking? This is the creepiest thing I've ever read."

"It's not creepy," she protested. She grabbed the book from its spine-damaging position on the floor and returned it to the shelf. *Love You Forever* was a classic—right up there with *Where the Wild Things Are* and every Dr. Seuss ever written. "I'm a connoisseur of toddler literature these days. It's sweet."

"If my mom had ever tried to spy on me in the middle of the night anytime past the age of eighteen, she'd have been in for a pretty nasty surprise. Several of them. Often at the same time."

She knew. She'd read the articles. "But you're not a sweet, devoted father carrying on the family name. You're a sleazebag. It's a completely different situation."

Once again, Jake fell into a real laugh, and she thought she saw some of the ice in his eyes soften to true regard. "Oh, Amy. I don't know how I managed to survive this world without you. No one is quite as good at putting me in my place as you are."

"It seems like you did perfectly fine on your own," she said sweetly. "As long as you measure survival in numbers of sex tapes released and sexually transmitted diseases avoided."

He pointed at her, still smiling. "You got judgmental."

"I grew up. These two things aren't unrelated."

"Little Amy Sanders." He shook his head and swore under his breath. She knew before he did that he was going to pull her in for another hug, and she did nothing to stop him. This embrace held none of the enthusiasm of the earlier twirl, and she was pretty sure he was using the chest-on-chest advantage to make a more lasting assessment of her growth, but it felt good to be in his arms just the same.

He smelled crisp and expensive, his arms strong against her back, his hand firm as it slipped down...

"Jake!" She backed away and closed her arms over her chest. His douchebag undertones were seriously ruining the moment here.

"What?" he asked with faux innocence.

"Sheesh. You could at least pretend to be subtle about it."

"Why? Do you want me to say I find you hideous? Pretend you haven't always been the best thing about this godforsaken place?"

She had to give credit where credit was due—he was really good at that, and it was easy to see why legions of ladyparts quivered whenever he walked into a room. Her own only girded against the assault. She wasn't about to take his compliments lying down.

"That's a good try, but I'm not part of your international harem." She pulled out her best nanny glare. "I'm happy to see you again, Jake—you know I am— but you don't get to ravish me with sweet words and expect me to roll over. If you want to get at this, you'll need to try some wooing first."

He arched a brow, accepting the challenge as it was intended. "I can woo. Wooing is my specialty."

"Your specialty is making women feel like crap so they're willing to sink to pretty much any level of depravity by the time you finally throw them your bone."

He tipped his head back and barked a laugh. "I'll tell you this—if I'd have known how much fun it would be having you around again, I'd have hunted you down ages ago."

Here, at least, she was back to some solid footing. She had a few coals begging to have this man dragged over them. "About that."

His casual smile slipped. "Please don't talk to me in that tone of voice. I get enough of it from my family."

"Don't worry—I'm not going to make you feel

bad for running away from home." Lord knew she understood the impetus. "I know what your life is now, what with all that money to spend and women to delight, but it's really crappy of you not to at least call my mom every now and then. You missed her retirement party."

His smile faltered but didn't disappear. "I would've come, but it wasn't great timing. My publicist wanted me to keep a low profile after that incident with the eighteen-year-old."

"Seventeen."

"It was her birthday. There were caveats." As if realizing she wasn't going to let him off the hook for this one, Jake dropped the act, the casual grace slushing out through his feet, leaving him a hunched, resigned—but still undeniably attractive—man. "Shit, Amy. I'm sorry. It didn't even occur to me that she'd want me there."

"She always loved you more than Monty and Jenna, you know," Amy said. "And I'm pretty sure she *still* likes you better than me. She says she once offered your dad a trade."

"I'm surprised he didn't take her up on it."

"It never would have worked. You're every inch a Montgomery."

His eyes roamed over her again, treading heavily and staking claims. "And you're very clearly not."

"Just visit her, okay?" She didn't care how many googly eyes he made at her—she intended to remain firm. The last thing he needed was another adoring female falling at his feet. What he needed was a not-so-adoring one wielding a hammer to his head. "She doesn't like to talk about it, but her fibromyalgia prevents her from getting out of the house much anymore, and I know she'd love to see you. You don't even have to stay for very long."

He nodded once, and Amy felt a whoosh of satisfaction move through her. She hadn't realized how much this particular request meant to her until it crossed her lips. The Manor had been her mother's life for so many years, her presence so ingrained in these walls you could still see remnants of her—the decorative yardstick where her careful hand tracked each child's annual progress, the tiled wall above the play kitchen where they'd all put their handprints. Being cut off from here was hard for her.

"I'll visit her soon," Jake promised. He licked his lips, his tongue tracing a slow and careful path. He had unfairly lovely lips for a man. It was a good thing his eyelashes were short and an almost invisible red, or she'd have rolled over and given up on the spot. "But you have to give me something in return."

"This isn't a negotiation."

"No, this is me asking you out."

She burst out laughing. Okay, so it probably wasn't the best response to hearing the words many women would have donated organs for, but it was the best she could do on short notice.

"I see you haven't lost your misguided sense of humor. That's not the reaction I normally get from the ladies."

"I know you don't. That's what makes it so funny."

A look of pain crossed his face, so brief she might have imagined it. "Not everything you read about in the gossip magazines is true."

"No, but if even half of it is, you hardly need another woman slain and devastated at your feet. *Especially* the family nanny. Can you imagine what your father would say?"

"He'd be furious." Jake grabbed her hand and held it aloft, stopping just short of kissing it as he pondered her words. "You're right. He'd be absolutely furious."

The sound of an irate squall from the next room stopped him from saying more.

"Shit. They didn't sleep for very long, did they?"

She released a chuckle. "Oh, please. They haven't fallen asleep yet. That's the sound of the first of many gauntlets being thrown."

"Then you deserve a night off. A *real* night off." This time, he did brush his lips against the surface of her hand, taking a moment to peek up at her with a question lingering in his eyes. It was so cheesy an actual snort escaped her.

She clapped her free hand over her mouth to muffle the rest of her laughter, but the damage had already been done. "I'm sorry, Jake. But your face. Does that really work on the women you date?"

He scowled. "Most of them."

"Don't look so grumpy. I'm willing to accept your terms." When he broke into self-satisfied triumph, she lifted a warning finger. "But on one condition."

"Name it and it's yours. I'll fly you to Paris. Rome. Morocco, if that's what you want."

He would, too. "Please don't pull the whole Jake-Montgomery-Smooth-Operator act on me. I'm not one of your groupies."

"You could be."

There was no mistaking his meaning. She withdrew her hand. "No. I can't. And if you think I'm going to sit there and let you ply me with thousand-dollar wine and cheap compliments, you're sadly mistaken. We're not going out on a date. You and I are going to catch up on old times and have a chat about your personal standards. I've got a few things to say about the way you treat women."

"You're really killing the mood here, Amy."

"And call my mom first. She has things to say about the way you treat women too."

He backed quickly toward the door as the twins' shouts grew louder. "She's welcome to say them, but you're both headed for disappointment. A leopard doesn't change his spots."

"No." Amy prepared to head into the bedroom for battle. "But he can be skinned alive."

FOUR

"I'll NEED ONE of the Ferraris tonight." Jake Montgomery sat on top of the hood of a Rolls Royce, seemingly immune to the fact that he was damaging the body with his skinny, well-groomed ass. "The red one. No. The white. It's classier. Shine her up and top her off, my good man."

Ryan didn't bother to stretch his face into a smile. He might willingly participate in the modern-day serving class for Mr. Montgomery's sake—didn't mind Monty as a human being— but no way in hell was he going to bend over and take it from the wastrel middle son.

The reasons were slippery and hard for him to get his hands on, but there was just something about this guy he couldn't stand.

"Sorry," he said, doing a piss-poor job of hiding his contempt. "No one takes those out without permission. Not even you."

Especially you, he didn't have to say. Throughout the course of Ryan's employment here, Jake had been around long enough to ding, dent and crash no fewer than half a dozen of his father's prized possessions. The first time, he'd tried blaming it on Ryan—had even gone so far as to hint that alcohol had been involved.

That had only happened once.

One of Ryan's lesser-known Hollywood skills was his ability to throw a showy punch—one that looked good, sounded better, but didn't do anything to mar an actor's perfect, irreplaceable face. He didn't think Jake cared to find out what would happen if he actually landed the next one.

"Come on. Help a guy out, would you?" Jake extended his arm, ostensibly to shake Ryan's hand, really to slip a fifty-dollar bill into his palm. As they were the only two people in the garage, the attempt at secrecy was ludicrous. "I'll be extra careful. I'm going to have some precious cargo riding with me tonight, if you know what I mean."

Ryan didn't take his hand. He knew exactly what kind of cargo Jake would want to woo with a fast car that wasn't his own, and a woman like that would make him *more* reckless, not less.

"Sorry, Mr. Montgomery," he said, emphasizing the title. "I have strict orders. You get the keys when you get clearance from up high. And *only* when you get clearance from up high."

Some of the smug veneer wiped off Jake's face, making him look exactly like a kid denied a candy bar. Ryan had no idea what women saw in the guy. He was disgustingly rich, yes. Dressed in the expensive Italian suits that made the most out of a man, sure. And there was something to be said about a thick head of hair that stood so tall birds could nest in it. But Ryan would rather lose his job and end up working at a car wash than break a rule to make Jake's life any more of a cakewalk than it already was.

"You don't have to be such a prick about it. You might have my dad standing behind you right now, but believe me when I say that his support can disappear faster than a schoolgirl cries. I'm something of an expert on the subject."

"I bet you are. That face probably makes a lot of schoolgirls cry."

As the insult sank in, a look of genuine pleasure spread across Jake's face. He hopped off the car. "You're funny, Ryan the Car Man. I still think you're a prick, but I like that about you. So it's a no go on all the cars? Not even a Roadster?"

"Sorry. Your lady friend will have to pick *you* up this time around."

Jake looked out the garage door toward the parking lot and frowned. Curious, Ryan followed the path of his gaze to where it skimmed over his own Honda motorcycle to stop on Amy's worn red Rabbit.

No. It wasn't possible.

"No. Not possible," Jake said, taking the words right from Ryan's mouth. "Her car doesn't exactly lend itself to romance, does it?"

"You're going out with Amy?" Ryan struggled to remain calm. He knew it was none of his business who she dated—or when, or why, or how—but it was impossible to quell his mounting sense of outrage. He'd nobly resisted the urge to ask her out himself because he refused to be *that guy* where she was concerned. He wouldn't be the asshole who toyed with her only to leave town the next day, the jerk who never looked farther than the end of his dick.

But Jake was one hundred percent walking, talking dick. There literally wasn't anything else there.

Is this what she's wanted all along?

"Oh, do you know the nanny?" Jake ran his hand

over the curved hood of the Rolls Royce, lingering almost obscenely on the winged form of the hood ornament.

A wrench that Ryan had been in the middle of wiping down clattered noisily to the ground. "Isn't it against some kind of law to date the help?"

"Who? Amy?" Jake laughed and retrieved the fallen tool. It took all of Ryan's self-control to take it from his outstretched hand without smashing it into something. "Nah. She's practically family."

"How is that better?"

Jake winked. "Family I haven't seen in a very long time. Family I may have unjustly overlooked the first time around."

There were so many things wrong with that statement, Ryan couldn't begin keeping track. "I can't picture Mrs. Montgomery loving the idea of her children's caregiver stepping out with you for a night on the town."

"No. Nor my father." The leering look on Jake's face was replaced by a slow, creeping smile that made the hair on Ryan's neck stand on end. "In fact, I can't think of anything he'd hate more. It's a large part of the charm."

Ryan's chest constricted. He'd watch hell freeze over before he'd stand by and let Jake take advantage of Amy like that. In fact, he'd chauffeur them himself before he'd see any harm come to her.

"I have an idea," Ryan said, latching on to that thought with a fierceness that scared him. "Why don't you take her in one of the town cars?"

"You'd let me drive one out?"

"No." He most certainly would not. "But I'd be happy to drive you anywhere you want to go."

Jake blinked a few times before understanding dawned. By the time he snapped his fingers in agreement, Ryan knew it was a done deal, and he was able to breathe normally again.

"That's perfect," Jake said. "Having you drive us around leaves me to focus my attentions on more important matters."

He didn't have to ask what those important matters were.

The fifty-dollar bill made its way into Jake's palm again. "I know my dad usually lets you know a couple days in advance when your driving services will be needed after hours, but…"

"Not a problem." Ryan refused to take the money. Even if he did have plans for the night that didn't involve Mrs. Grimstock's dog and a *Die Hard* marathon, he'd have been all too willing to cancel for a good cause.

Protecting Amy was a damn good cause.

"Will we be heading into New York?" he asked, genuinely curious. If it had been *his* date with Amy, he'd take her somewhere fun—like miniature golf or one of those themed restaurants where everyone watched jousting as they feasted on joints of meat. She'd love something like that.

"Probably. I'll get you a more detailed itinerary later." Jake consulted his phone and turned away. Now that Ryan's assistance had been offered and payment rejected, he'd clearly been relegated back to the status of No One Important. "Don't mention this to anyone and bring the car around back at six-thirty sharp. Oh, and dress the part, would you? See if you can find a cap."

Ryan cast a glance over his clothes. On the occasions he escorted Mr. Montgomery or one of his visiting moguls around Ransom Creek or out to New York, he usually put on black slacks and a white button-down shirt. Nothing fancy, but enough that he appeared suitably dignified to take the rich, powerful men and women of the world where they needed to go.

Most of the time, he was practically invisible. A nobody. A vassal. Yet despite the indignities of that position, not once had anyone suggested he lower himself enough to wear a hat.

He bit back a growl as he watched Jake's retreating form. He wasn't wearing a fucking cap.

AMY LEANED FORWARD and hooked her arms around the front seat, surveying Ryan with a grin. Dressed up for once, he looked stiff and uncomfortable and like there was a fifty percent chance he might drive the car over the nearest cliff.

Truth be told, she also felt stiff and uncomfortable and a little bit in the mood for cliff-diving. Having waited most of her life for a chance at some romantic, one-on-one time with Jake Montgomery, she should have been over the moon that he'd pulled out all his regular finesse. Champagne waiting in the car, mysterious plans he refused to divulge, a stiff and disapproving chauffeur. It was straight out of a movie.

But now that she was here, she kind of wished she was in her jeans playing laser tag with Ryan instead.

Even if he *was* looking at her as if he'd like to take a real laser to her head right about now.

"You don't have to do this, you know," she said. "Whatever he threatened you with, it can't possibly be worse than spending your Friday night sitting alone in a car while we eat an overpriced meal somewhere fancy."

"It's no problem," he said stiffly. "It's my job."

But it wasn't—not really. Like her, Ryan worked for Mr. Montgomery, not the family as a whole. Mr. Montgomery was very good at making sure his staff knew their rights as well as their responsibilities. For example, she had the right to go out in the evening, provided that Sheryl, the night nurse, had arrived and she wasn't needed elsewhere in the house. Of course, she also had the responsibility to know she was probably in over her head going out with Jake Montgomery—even if it was in the name of reform.

Never mind that Jake was so far out of her socioeconomic league she might as well be a sloth. Oh, no, the real problem here was that he was the type of guy who dove deep in the dating pool. His form was impeccable. He swam in the nude.

Amy flailed in the kiddie pool in a wetsuit with those big puffy armbands keeping her afloat. She was doomed.

She nodded out to where Jake was pacing back and forth, a phone pressed to his ear. "How long do you think it's going to take him to finish his call?"

As the call had been going on for almost ten minutes already, she was growing bored and a little bit restless. Ignoring the fact that her short black dress made athletic feats difficult, she climbed over the armrest and settled in the front passenger seat.

"What are you doing?" Ryan asked, a look of horror crossing his face as she adjusted her skirt back into place.

"There's nothing to do back there. Want to ask twenty questions?"

"No."

"Play hangman?"

"No."

"Chat about carburetors?"

"No."

"Sit here in sullen silence and pretend we don't know each other?"

He relaxed into a half smile. "That sounds perfect, thanks."

She shifted so that she faced him, the leather seat squeaking under her thighs. There was no way for bare flesh and supple cow skin to meet without a symphony of indiscreet noises rising up. At least not where her bare flesh was concerned.

"The chauffeur the Montgomerys had when I was growing up used to carry a bag of activities to keep him busy during his downtime. He had books and magazines and a sketchpad—he was incredible at drawing people. He could capture the little things in ways that gave a picture life. A sad pull at the mouth, a distinct freckle on the arm. I used to love watching him."

"I don't draw."

"He also always had candy. I bet you don't have any candy."

"Is that why you climbed up here? Because you

thought I might have a chocolate bar hidden in the glove compartment?"

She put a hand on her stomach, which let out a loud gurgle in response. "I'd love you forever if you did. I'm starving."

His eyes flicked over her, taking in the tight, bandage-like dress and the only slightly swelled stomach that was contained within it. She didn't use to have quite so many swelled parts—had, in fact, been required to maintain a strict diet once upon a time— but her exercise regime these days revolved around the occasional roll on a playroom floor. The lack of structure was taking its toll on her physique in the squishiest possible way.

"I know what you're thinking—and that's not it. I'm not in the habit of starving myself for the sake of vanity."

"I'm glad to hear it. You look amazing just the way you are."

She couldn't tell if he was being sincere or pandering to her fragile, feminine ego—but either way, her fragile, feminine ego appreciated it. Giving in to the impulse of the moment, she leaned over and dropped a kiss on his cheek. He was scratchy and warm and, if the speed with which he jumped away was any indication, not the least bit appreciative of her impulses.

"That was sweet of you," she said, flustered. Here she was, fawning over a man who'd never shown anything more than a friendly interest in her. *Cool it, sister.* If she wasn't careful, she was going to scare him away altogether. "But I wasn't putting myself down. I just didn't have time for lunch. Serena had Lily's ears pierced today."

Ryan blinked slowly, struggling not to react to Amy's proximity. It wasn't that he couldn't handle a peck on the cheek without losing his shit, but so many of the things she did caught him off guard. Dressing up so that she looked exactly like her wide-smiled, cheerful self and somehow untouchable at the same time. Climbing over seats in heels so tall they could fell a man. Kissing him for a compliment that didn't even begin to capture her vitality.

It was hard to anticipate what was coming next.

"How are starvation and ear piercing related?" he asked gruffly.

"Oh, I'll tell you, but first you have to close your eyes."

Ryan snapped his eyes shut, happy to comply. Any opportunity to hide his emotions from this woman was a welcome one.

"Good. Now I want you to imagine being two years old. You just ate broiled organic chicken and steamed spinach for lunch, both of which happen to be your least favorite foods on the planet. You're tired. You're hungry. All you want is a strawberry ice-cream cone. Your mother promises you just such a treat, but first you have to accompany her to the beauty salon, which is bright and fun and full of people who love you but always smells funny."

He opened one eye and peered at her. "Do I really need this much detail?"

She swatted him—a complete departure from a soft press of lips on his cheek but somehow just as unsettling. "Don't interrupt. I'm setting the scene. So far, you have yet to get a taste of strawberry anything, but your mom says that if you sit on the nice spin-

ning chair and don't squirm, the delicious will soon
be yours. Your beloved nanny, clearly distraught but
powerless to stop the unfolding events, distracts you
with a bottle of sparkly nail polish. Then, BAM!"

Amy's hand came crashing down onto the dash-
board.

Ryan couldn't help it. He jumped.

Her laughter, low and compelling, filled the car.
"Exactly. Out of nowhere, a complete stranger sta-
ples a sharp metal object through both your ears at
the same time. Lily felt utterly betrayed, poor thing.
And she never did get her ice cream."

"Let me guess—you were the one who had to
spend the afternoon soothing her?"

She shrugged, but he could tell the day had worn
on her. Now that she was up close and personal, he
could see dark circles under her eyes, the slight lines
of anxiety around her mouth. He had to sit on his
hand to refrain from wiping them away.

"I'd have given my soul for some strawberry ice
cream to bury our collective woes in. Still would."

This, at least, he could do something about. Moving toward her feet, he reached for the black bag that
rested under the dash. Experience had long since
taught him that the needs of the chauffeur were slated
well below that of his passengers—any of life's ne-
cessities had to be within arm's reach, or they didn't
exist until the sojourn was complete.

His knuckle grazed her ankle as he pulled back,
and he allowed himself a moment to enjoy the sight
of her legs, long and muscular and indicative of her
previous life as a dancer. Off-limits nannies shouldn't
be allowed to have legs like that. A man could only

get through so many lonely nights before he started to dream of sleek limbs wrapping around him and never letting go.

Thankfully for them both, she lifted those sleek limbs away from his grasp. Out of reach, out of mind. Or at least in theory, anyway.

"What are you doing down there?"

"Collecting on your soul." He rummaged around until he found the Pop-Tarts that rested at the bottom of his lunch bag. He tossed the silver package onto her lap. "They're not strawberry, but they should do the trick."

She let out a squeal and tore it open. He loved that she didn't try to turn down the gift of his dinner or protest against the kindness of the gesture. She was clearly a woman of unapologetic, voracious appetites.

Through a huge mouthful, she said, "You're a savior, Ryan. I don't think I've ever been so happy to see overprocessed sugars in my life."

"It'll probably ruin your appetite for five-hundred-dollar pâté."

"Fuck pâté. I was about to start eating my shoes."

He laughed softly and leaned back in the seat, enjoying the companionable silence as Amy devoured her snack, wishing he could extend the moment for hours. Life would be so easy if this were all he had to worry about. Making Amy happy. Enjoying having her near.

Unfortunately, the night wasn't his to squander. They both were jolted out of the moment by the sound of a knock at the driver's side window. Ryan looked over, startled to find Jake squinting into the over-tinted glass, but a feeble gesture at the back door made things more clear.

Apparently, Ryan needed to get out and open the door for him. These were the depths to which he had descended—playing doorman on top of everything else. With an apologetic shrug and an over-exaggerated bow to Amy, he swept outside and helped the able-bodied Jake into his seat.

"What are you doing up there?" Jake asked, sliding in with a frown.

Ryan didn't get a chance to hear her response, but he noticed Amy got physically out of the car and walked in through the back door, rather than climbing again. How ladylike. How unlike her.

"Ready to go?" Ryan buckled himself in and glanced at the rearview mirror, his foul mood returning as suddenly as it had dissipated. Amy had chosen the middle seat—so close to Jake she could have been sitting in his lap, and something about her expression had shifted. Gone was the easy smile, the ready laugh. She looked coy and smitten and girly and...

Fuck. She looked like a woman about to go on a date with Jake Montgomery. And head-over-heels excited about it too.

"Ready as I'll ever be," she said.

He let out a grunt. That made exactly one of them.

FIVE

If there was anything Ryan hated more than a picnic, he had yet to discover it.

Oh, sure—dining al fresco seemed like a good idea from afar. The rosy-hued romance of the setting sun. A blanket spread over the ground, encouraging everyone to lie down and roll around for a while. Wineglasses filled so generously you pretended not to notice the specks of dirt floating on top.

As it so often did, reality failed to live up to expectations—at least from the chauffeur's perspective. From where he leaned on the outside of the town car, pretending not to hear the low, rolling feminine laughter sweeping his way, Ryan felt only the repeated bite of twilight mosquitoes and the angry corrosion of his stomach lining.

Would it have killed the bastard to apprise him of the evening's events beforehand? It was one thing to drop the happy couple off at some swanky restaurant and hide out until the car was called back, nursing his resentment in silence and scowls. It was quite another to stand here with his thumb up his ass while they cooed sweet nothings into each other's ears a few yards away.

Except... He shifted and squinted, trying to get a better look at the lounging couple, neither of whom appeared to be doing any actual lounging. Amy

jumped to her feet, gesturing wildly at herself, then
Jake, then the car. And back at herself.

Adrenaline, that good old friend he went far too
many days without anymore, rushed through him. He
placed both hands on top of the car, stabilizing himself as he peered closer. Jake was an ass, but he wasn't
an *abusive* ass. At least not as far as he could tell. But
when Amy held up her hands as if warding Jake off,
Ryan slid over the hood and trotted up the hillside.

Adrenaline was also what prodded him to keep
going long after he realized she was laughing and
not in any danger at all. This wasn't the looming-
sense-of-danger kind of adrenaline, though. It was
more like the red-hot-jealousy kind, filling him with
an unreasonable urge to run Jake over with the car.
Jesus. Maybe he needed to rethink this hands-off
Amy plan. Maybe she wouldn't even want him anyway and he was just wasting his time.

"Amy. Jake." He nodded at both of them, his hands
shoved deep in his pockets to keep them from inad-
vertently finding their way around Jake's neck. "You
two need a hand?"

Jake didn't seem at all upset to see him standing
there, so low did Ryan rate on the importance scale
in his eyes. "Yes, actually. I was about to come get
you. You can pack up the picnic and load the car. Amy
and I are going to walk along the creek."

Amy pushed herself forward, arms crossed mu-
tinously over her chest. She had leaves in her hair,
which Ryan desperately hoped had been placed there
by virtue of gravity rather than friction, and a scowl
on her face. "And I told him we can pack our own
things. You aren't here to wait on us hand and foot."

"He doesn't mind," Jake said.

He *did* mind, but it didn't seem worth interrupting the argument for. Let them argue. Let them despise one another. Let this be the worst date in the history of bad dates.

"You know what your problem is, Jake? You've never had to clean up after yourself." She pointed at the basket, which spilled out a cornucopia of cheeses Ryan couldn't pronounce and probably would never eat. "Even the twins have to help me put their toys away when they're done with them. Pick it up and carry it to the car."

"But that's *why* I got us a chauffeur. So we could walk instead of washing dishes."

Amy turned to Ryan, sure he'd be on her side for this. Honestly—Jake expected everyone to do exactly what he wanted, just because he wanted it. He said stop, and the world held itself suspended to see what happened next. He said jump, and all women under the age of forty pulled out their trampolines and best bikinis before asking how high. "Ryan, please explain to my date how, in the real world, we pick up after ourselves. We vacuum our carpets and wash our socks and live to tell the tale."

"Don't look at me. I have a housekeeper. She comes once a week."

Amy's mouth fell open just as Jake barked with laughter. "See?" Jake said. "Even the help has help."

"I'm sure he does his own dishes."

"Nope," Ryan interjected easily. "*He* exists almost entirely on takeout and Pop-Tarts. There's never so much as a dirty fork in the place."

"Laundry?"

"Biweekly delivery service."

She caught the glint in his eye and bit her lip to keep from giggling and losing what remained of her moral high ground. Ryan was being obtuse on purpose—she'd seen several dirty forks in his sink, along with an impressive collection of cooking pots. "He washes his own car at least."

Ryan tilted his head in acknowledgment of her blow. "She has me there. My hands are work-worn from all the bubbles. I'll never model again."

"Fine." Jake looked back and forth between Amy and Ryan, his glance sharp. "The chauffeur can go for our romantic sunset walk. You and I will clean up."

"Excellent." She clapped her hands, much as she did when Lily and Evan managed to make it to the bathroom in time. Her triumph felt similar too. For all Jake was a gorgeous scrap of a man who knew his way around a good Prosecco, he had quite a bit of growing up to do. It was starting to seem as though there was yet one more Montgomery for her to rear. "You pack up the remaining food. I'll clean the plates off."

With a wide-eyed nudge at Ryan, she ushered him in the direction of the river. Even though she didn't mind having Ryan around—enjoyed his company much more than was good for her, in fact—Jake wasn't going to be the least bit pliable if he felt he needed to perform in front of the chauffeur. He was too used to putting on an act, playing for an audience.

And she would know. She'd watched his sex tapes—all twelve of them. The man knew how to work a camera angle as if he'd been born in the spotlight.

"Should we stop by the soup kitchen with all

our leftovers on the way home?" Jake asked as he wrapped up a huge wheel of Brie they'd barely had a chance to dent. "Maybe volunteer to serve dinner while we're there?"

"I'm surprised you even know what a soup kitchen is."

He looked up, a flash of dark emotion crossing his face so quickly she might have imagined it. "Oh, you know how it is. I saw it in a Dickens production once. Don't forget I used to date that Broadway actress."

"You assume I follow your personal life that closely?" Sex tape number nine. Brunette. Incredible vocal range. The internet was a dangerous playground, and she knew all the best hiding spots. "I *do* have a life outside the Montgomerys. I wasn't just sitting around all that time I was gone, pining for home."

"Ah, yes. How could I forget? Dancing."

She bit her lip and looked away, sure he could see the lie on her face. Technically, there *had* been dancing. And costumes. And a rapt audience. Some days, there had even been lines hours' long to see her perform. But not in the way everyone believed.

She mumbled an incoherent sound that could have been taken either as a confirmation or the onset of pneumonia.

It must have worked, because Jake gave up the pretense of industriousness and lifted a hand to her neck. As her hair was swirled up in a semi-fancy knot, all that separated the softness of his palm and her heat-flushed skin were a few wispy strands.

"In all that time, I never did date a dancer." His grip on her neck tightened, and he brought his face closer. No—*his lips*. He was bringing *his lips* closer. "I'm dying to know, Amy. Just how flexible are you?"

She shoved him backward, but he didn't lose the smile that lingered on his face and in his eyes. "Come on. Just a little hint. Are we talking splits here? One leg behind the head? *Both* legs behind the head?"

"Don't be gross."

He pretended to be hurt, his lips in a pout. "The female body is never gross. Don't let anyone tell you otherwise."

"All human bodies are gross." She wasn't falling for this schmooze. Not from Jake. If this were an ordinary first date with an ordinary man—say, with Ryan, whose head could be seen bobbing in the distance—she'd have played along for the sake of romance. Cooed a little. Flirted back.

Oh, yes. If Ryan wanted to schmooze her, she'd lie back and patiently await his ministrations.

"I respectfully disagree."

"You don't do anything respectfully." She reluctantly turned her attention back to Jake. "And the things that come out of a woman's body are just as disgusting as what comes out of a man's. Even more so if you count childbirth. Have you ever seen pictures of a mucus plug? Can you even imagine what something called a mucus plug looks like?"

Jake crossed his fingers as if staving off a vampire and backed away. Even in retreat he moved gracefully, the perfect breaks in his slacks folding over each foot like origami. "You wouldn't dare. Don't sully the majesty of the vagina with your cruel and mocking words."

She whipped out her phone and did a quick image

search. When she found the most grotesque picture she could find, she let out a triumphant laugh and texted it to him. A cheerful chime rose up into the darkening sky, indicating her success.

But Jake just pulled his expensive-looking phone from his pocket, dropped it to the dirt and crushed it under his heel.

"You're so dramatic sometimes." She pointed at the mess. "And now you have to pick that up too. You can't leave broken shards of glass and plastic for the birds. They'll build nests with them and accidentally stab their young."

Jake looked as though he wanted to say more, but something about the firm set of her mouth must have convinced him she was serious. She set about finishing her share of the cleanup, uncertain whether or not she should say more. This wasn't how the evening had unfolded itself in her head. She *liked* Jake. Heck— she probably loved him if you took into account all those years of childhood friendship and adolescent adoration and unfortunately recent Google stalking.

She'd thought that in coming out here tonight, they could chat about old times and slip back into the friendship that had once been the center of her world. Perhaps they could share a few inside jokes. Maybe they could even walk along the river while she outlined all the ways he might begin redeeming himself.

Not this. Not this slightly oily seduction routine she suspected had seen quite a bit of use in its day. Watching Jake grumble as he picked up his broken thousand-dollar phone was the most real he'd been all evening.

He straightened and stabbed a finger at their now-reassembled picnic. "Am I also supposed to carry that back for us, your majesty?"

"Well, if you don't think you're strong enough, I can always call the strapping young chauffeur back to do it for us."

"He's hardly strapping."

"Have you seen his arms? They're like cannons. Every time he's around I feel like I just won front-row tickets to the gun show." This sally, said only to provoke Jake, struck her as being rather true. She wouldn't go so far as to say she'd *ogled* Ryan's arms, but the man clearly had a bit of strength in him. It was probably all those lug nuts he yanked around.

"Do you want me to challenge him to a fistfight? Is that it?"

Amy tilted her head and gave the question serious consideration. In theory, she found the concept of two men fighting for fun to be rather grotesque. There was nothing entertaining about purposefully hurting another human being, and shattered teeth weren't her favorite male attribute.

But in practice? She had to admit the idea wasn't without merit. There was something about those hard bodies tossed into a cage together, sweating and heaving as they sought handholds in unlikely places, that burned slow and steady in her veins.

She could almost see it now. Jake would fight with his wits, parrying quickly, toying with his opponent. Ryan would barrel in, head down and fully swinging. It would be brutal and bloody and brilliant.

"If I said yes, would you promise to fight him over in that mudpit?" She pointed toward the river's edge. "Stripped to the waist? Because that would be awesome."

Jake just shook his head and reached for the picnic basket. "And you thought I was gross for asking how flexible you are."

RYAN TRAILED JAKE and Amy from a distance, giving them a chance to load up the town car before he rejoined them. He'd heard the sounds of their argument and wouldn't have interrupted on a dare. It seemed the longer they were alone, the more they descended into adolescence.

Although he was relieved to discover that fact—elated, really—he couldn't understand it. Amy had to be the nicest, most easygoing woman on the face of the planet. Picking a fight with her would take all of his concentration—and even then, it wasn't a sure thing. All she'd have to do was smile, and he'd be lost. A man couldn't argue with the sun.

"Well, you two?" There was a spring in his step that hadn't been there before, and he did nothing to stifle it. "Are we ready to move out?"

Both of them looked up as he approached, and both of them seemed to focus on his arms—Amy with a laugh and admiration in her eyes, Jake like a man who might want to put those arms on a spit and eat them for dinner. Ryan tried not to let either one of them unsettle him, though Amy was in a fair way to accomplishing it. Her admiration was a heady thing. He could show her a thing or two he wanted to do to her with these arms.

"I hope you enjoyed your walk," she said politely as she opened her door and slid in. Ryan made a motion to get Jake's door, but the man seemed to finally realize the futility of being formal around a woman like Amy.

With a skip and a whistle, Ryan made his way to the driver's seat. He almost wished he'd gone for the hat after all, as it was an ideal time to cock it at a jaunty angle and assert his victory. Unfortunately, Jake didn't seem to recognize Ryan's superiority. He just tapped on the front seat and asked him to take the long way home.

"The long way?" They were in the middle of nowhere, a Connecticut outpost he was pretty sure was private property that didn't belong to the Montgomerys, miles from any road with an actual speed limit posted. They were already *on* the long way.

Taking his bewilderment as an assent, Jake slapped the leather seat twice and leaned back to place a not-so-subtle arm along the back of Amy's seat. At least this time she'd chosen to sit all the way to the right. Ryan would take what satisfaction he could from that.

"You can stop sulking now," Amy commanded, her voice carrying easily up to the front as Ryan pulled onto the road. "I'm sorry I spoiled your picnic with good manners, but I had a lovely time."

"Do you realize I've picnicked with princesses on top of the Eiffel Tower?"

"How very Disney of you. Wasn't it windy up there?"

"You're missing the point." From Ryan's glance in the rearview mirror, he could see Jake's hand snaking closer to Amy's shoulder. He could also see that she didn't move away. "I can do better than this. You threw me off my regular technique. I wasn't expecting you to be so…"

"Right?" Amy almost felt bad for Jake. The poor man wasn't used to being wrong when it came to women, had no framework for what to do when the things he wanted didn't fall at his feet. Not at all like Ryan, whose scars spoke of a long, hard path where elbow grease and spit polish were simply a way of life.

Mmm. No man should overlook the inherent advantages of spit polish.

"The problem isn't that you're right." Jake leaned in and interrupted her reverie. The hand he'd not-very-cleverly placed over the back of her seat drooped low, his fingers grazing the bare skin of her shoulder. She shivered at the light touch, at the deft hand darting lower. "It's that you're irresistible. You were supposed to grow up to be a lot of things, Little Amy Sanders, but irresistible wasn't one of them."

He was going to kiss her. She knew it. She felt it all the way down to her toes, which weren't very romantic, as years of wearing pointe shoes had rendered her feet into grotesquely misshapen and wickedly strong beasts. Common sense warned her to pull away, and she knew the backseat of Ryan's car was neither the time nor the place for this to happen, but instinct took over and reminded her that it had been a long time since anyone showed an interest in kissing her. One peck wouldn't hurt things. A light graze, a press of lips, a taste of Jake's powers, maybe a little jealousy up there in the front seat...

All of a sudden, Jake was on top of her.

She screamed, that much she would remember later. She screamed and bit down on her own lip so hard she made it bleed and flailed against Jake's limbs as she struggled to get out from underneath him.

"What the——?" Jake struggled too, and for one panicked moment she thought he was going to hit her. But then the car came to a stop and she realized they were tilted at an angle, her window half-covered with the long wispy grass that banked the side of the road.

"Are you okay?" Ryan materialized as if out of nowhere, his face hovering anxiously over her own. She realized, through the fog of confusion, that he had crawled halfway into the backseat and was tugging anxiously on her seat belt. Next to her, Jake also struggled to right himself. "Amy? Are you hurt? What day of the week is it?"

"I'm fine." She waved Ryan off and got herself unbuckled. The taste of blood—metallic and sharp—rushed over her tongue, and she lifted the back of her hand to her mouth. It came away streaked with red. "Mostly fine. I hurt my lip."

Ryan didn't move, and a look of intense concern clouded his eyes, adding to the turbulent gray color that was always so difficult to read. Worry painted him in strong, handsome angles, and she found herself momentarily awed by the sight.

"What day of the week is it?" he repeated.

"Sunday." When Ryan's eyes flashed again, her floundering feeling only increased. "No, it's Friday. Sorry. I get all flustered when I'm on the spot like that. I've always been terrible at tests."

"Don't worry." Jake leaned in, joining them in a trio of too-close faces and breaking whatever spell Ryan had been weaving. "I'm also fine. But what the hell just happened?"

As it was clear a car accident had sent them flying into the ditch, there was no need to elaborate from there. Ryan and Jake got out of the car easily, as their half was tilted upward, and Jake remembered only at the last minute to extend a hand to help her across the backseat.

They surveyed the damage with varied levels of interest. Amy, whose car could have taken a sledge-hammer to the hood and been none the worse for wear, couldn't see anything to get worked up about, but Ryan and Jake took one look at the broken head-light and crumpled hood and shared a manly cringe.

"It's not that bad," Amy said, trying to lighten the mood. She tilted her head. "If I squint, I can't even see the dent."

"Dents," Ryan said quietly. "Plural."

"I hate to say it, Ryan, but you're done for." Jake shook his head and moved closer to her side. The *non-bloody* side, of course. Jake's reputation for profligacy was second only to his reputation for fastidiousness. Her lip was already beginning to feel fat and puffy in addition to split open. "Dad barely forgave me for a scratch on the door, and I'm his flesh and blood."

Amy waited for Jake to say something more, but he merely let out a low whistle and kicked the tire. What that was supposed to accomplish, she had no idea. But people were always doing it in the movies, so she kicked too.

"Sorry," she said when Ryan cast an enquiring look her way. "It seemed to sum the situation up quite nicely."

"Damn straight." Ryan gave the tire his own kick—his firmer and with an angry zing to it. That zing worried her. Surely a chauffeur who sat behind the wheel six days out of the week was allowed an accident or two? Wasn't that what insurance was for?

"Let's tell him I did it," she said quickly. "Let's tell him I saw something swooping toward the window and screamed. A bird. Or a flying squirrel. That sounds exactly like something I'd do."

"What *did* cause you to lose control?" Jake asked, looking askance at the pair of them. "I've seen your work before. You did an insane sliding parallel park in that art thief/con woman heist movie a few years ago. I don't see how a backwoods turn could do you in."

"Did you really do that?" Amy ran through the list of movies she knew Ryan had been a stunt driver for, but she couldn't remember that one. Action movies weren't really her thing, so she'd seen only a handful of them. She needed to start visiting the rental kiosk more often. "Could you do it again?"

"Of course I could." Ryan sounded insulted, but he was avoiding eye contact with both of them, and the tips of his ears had turned red. "And of course you're not taking the blame. It was an accident. It happens. Believe me—I know."

Accidents happened to *her*, sure. She'd been in so many fender benders that random parts of her car fell off in a strong windstorm. Accidents didn't happen to highly trained drivers who were traveling at twenty-five miles per hour. Something about the tense way Ryan held himself had her backing off, though. For all that he could be sweet and endearing, there was a rough underbelly to the man that made her hesitant to poke too hard.

"Well?" Jake looked a question at them. "Should we push the car back on the road and get going? No sense in delaying the inevitable. If there's one thing I know about dealing with my father, it's that confessing and facing his wrath is best. Like ripping off a cast with your bare hands."

"That's not how the metaphor goes," Amy said.

Jake raised a doubtful eyebrow. "How much more painful do you think it is to rip off a cast than a Band-Aid?"

She recalled a broken leg Monty had as a teenager, back when casts were those huge, lumpy plaster cases that eventually got covered in crudely hand-drawn penises. She also recalled the withered, pasty, god-awful-smelling limb they unearthed the requisite six weeks later.

"I guess I can see your point. But I still think it's a better idea for me to cop to it. Mr. Montgomery likes me."

"Don't you dare." Ryan practically barked the words out, and she accepted them as the command they were. She was also acutely aware of the press of Ryan's hand on her back, hot and strong and... nudging her toward the back of the car? Seriously? He wanted her to push a vehicle out of a ditch in this dress?

It turned out the answer was yes. At least she had the satisfaction of seeing Jake being forced to exert a little muscle next to her, his jacket off and shirt rolled up to reveal perfectly ropey forearms.

Would you look at that? It seemed Ryan wasn't the only man around here making plans to appear at the Montgomery Manor gun show. She hoped she got invited when the event finally took place.

She knew exactly who she'd end up rooting for.

SIX

ONE THING RYAN had quite a bit of experience with—people in positions of authority yelling in his face.

There was an art to taking a good ass-ripping without losing one's sense of dignity. He'd seen many a man hang his head in shame, accepting his fate without demur. No one respected those guys, least of all him. There was nothing to celebrate in cowardice.

But he'd also seen plenty of men fly off the handle and end up losing everything. No one really respected those guys either, which was something he'd learned the hard way.

"You're absolutely right," he said, refusing to look down from Mr. Montgomery's round, reddened face. "It was careless and irresponsible of me."

Mr. Montgomery rubbed the side of his nose and shuffled through some papers on his home office desk, searching through an unkempt stack that sat firmly under a domed crystal paperweight. Anyone meeting Mr. Montgomery for the first time would be surprised to discover he was the force behind the largest chain of luxury hotels in the world. He looked an awful lot like a poorly organized Colonel Sanders, his robust frame draped in the beige linen suits he favored, which wrinkled as the day wore on until he resembled nothing so much as an exhausted shar-pei. It took him at least ten minutes to locate anything in his mess of an office unless his personal assistant, Katie, was on hand to point him in the right direction.

When he'd first received the call asking him to interview for the position of chauffeur, Ryan had made the mistake of assuming slovenliness of exterior meant Mr. Montgomery was equally unkempt upstairs. Nothing could be further from the truth. The man saw everything, knew everyone, and controlled both with a force of will that was downright frightening.

"Do you care to elaborate on that statement?" Mr. Montgomery asked.

"No, sir. I don't."

There. That right there. The sharp look of intense focus—from eyes so piercingly blue they stabbed like a shard of ice—was just the tip of what the man was capable of.

"So, if I'm understanding you here—and please correct me if I get something wrong—you took one of my cars out. Without my permission. To escort my son on a date. With my children's nanny."

Ryan nodded at each halt in Mr. Montgomery's speech, feeling sick. It was a disaster no matter which way they looked at it. And Jake was right—waiting a day to tell him hadn't helped matters any.

"At which time you proceeded to run the car into a ditch and cause several thousand dollars' worth of damage."

"I'll pay it back."

Mr. Montgomery raised one of his hands—a large, meaty appendage decked only with his thin gold wedding band. Ryan took the gesture as a clear no, which was only to be expected. If erasing an accident were as easy as writing a check, he wouldn't be in this situation in the first place.

He waited for the next words—the ones that would show him the door—to fall on his ears. Getting fired was never a pleasant sensation, but he'd weathered worse than this before. So imagine his surprise when the door wasn't shown to him. It opened instead, showcasing Jake in the doorway wearing his customary smirk.

Ryan felt no lost love for the guy, but he had to admit to enjoying a surge of appreciation at the sight of that smirk. It took balls to show that face to a man like Mr. Montgomery, even if you did have a safety net in the shape of shared DNA.

"I hope I haven't missed the axe falling," Jake said, moving into the room as if on air. "I do so love to watch a grown man cry."

"You're just in time," Ryan said wryly. "But I'll save you both the trouble. *And* the entertainment. I appreciate the opportunities you gave me, Mr. Montgomery, but consider this my formal resignation. I'm sorry to have damaged your car."

He extended a hand, expecting to shake and be done with it. He had no idea where he'd go next—if maybe he could eke by on his tiny savings until good news arrived—but he'd be damned if he'd leave with his head hanging. At least this time no one could blame him for being under the influence of alcohol. He'd been under the influence of something else entirely.

Jake tossed himself into a chair, heedless of the fact that the other two men were standing. "I hate to follow a grand speech like that one, but I think we all know what really happened in that car."

"We do?" Ryan swallowed heavily. He hadn't meant to be so obvious.

"Yes, we do." Jake returned his stare with a level calm. "I'm sorry, Daddy Dearest. I made Ryan trade me places. I was trying to impress Amy with my driving skills and fishtailed on the gravel. It was a rookie mistake, and the shame of it has haunted me all night."

"That's not—" Ryan began, but a quick warning shake of Jake's head stopped him. More curious than anything else, he kept his mouth shut and waited to see what Jake said next.

"I'm a reckless, feckless scoundrel." Jake shrugged and inspected his fingernails. "I told you summoning me home was a bad idea. If you knew what was good for you, you'd reinstate my inheritance and send me packing. There's no telling what I'll be up to next. Or who I'll damage with my heedless ways."

Mr. Montgomery stared at his son for a full sixty seconds, an awkward minute in which Ryan struggled to understand what was going on. Was Jake Montgomery—a man who would gladly throw an entire bus full of people under their own vehicle—standing up and taking the blame for him?

Not only did it make no sense, it was completely unacceptable.

"No. That's not—"

"Ryan." Mr. Montgomery quelled him with a stare. "Let my son speak, if you please."

"It's just a car. I'm sorry for the damages, but no one was hurt." A look of real concern marred Jake's brow. "Well, not much. Amy's got a fat lip today, but she says she barely notices it."

Ryan tensed. If Amy had been any more hurt than that...

"You've seen her today?" Mr. Montgomery asked sharply.

"This morning. I wanted to make sure she was okay—see? I can clean up after my messes. I even gave her some special medicine." He winked. "Lips like those require some careful looking after."

Oh, hell no. It was a good thing the bastard was standing up for him right now, or they'd both be rolling on the floor. Insinuations like that—and in front of his own father, no less—kicked Ryan on a visceral level.

"Am I to understand you intend to keep seeing her?"

Jake placed a hand over his heart and sighed. "If she'll have me."

"She's not one of your toys, Jake. She's an *employee.* You do understand the dynamics of the situation, do you not?"

"She's your employee. Not mine." Jake stood and tugged his sleeves back into place around his wrists.

"And if I ask you to back off as a personal favor?"

Jake laughed, a sound that rang hollow and stopped as abruptly as it started. "You're going to have to offer me something a lot better than that. Amy is worth at least ten of you." As a parting shot, he added, "And don't fire Ryan. I put him in an impossible situation. The fault is one hundred percent mine."

And that was it as the door shut carefully behind

him. No explanations. No apologies. Just an assumption of blame that was in no way his own.

Ryan's head swam.

"Well." Mr. Montgomery cleared his throat. "What have you to say to that?"

The only thing he could say. "I'll pack my bags this afternoon."

It was the worst possible time for him to leave—and there was no way he could count on a letter of recommendation after this—but the other option was unacceptable. He wouldn't place himself in Jake's debt for a job he wasn't even sure he wanted in the first place. Ransom Creek was supposed to be a stepping-stone toward Hollywood, a way station on his journey back to the top. Nothing more.

"No. I don't accept your resignation."

Ryan stared so long that Mr. Montgomery actually cracked a smile and told him to relax. "Do you know how it is I've been able to keep my hotels afloat in the current economic climate?"

The response on Ryan's tongue—that the whole world knew he'd married Serena Clare for her family's money—obviously wasn't the right one in this situation, so he opted for the safe answer. "Good business acumen?"

Mr. Montgomery chuckled and steepled his fingers. "While my vanity thanks you, the truth is that I've made it my habit to invest in people, not businesses. Surely you've noticed that the majority of the staff here is unemployable in any traditional sense of the word?"

Alex and his military past. Ryan and his stunt career. Even Amy, who'd given up her spot on a touring ballet company to become a nanny. That wasn't even counting all the other staff members he hadn't allowed himself to get to know. They were all over-qualified for this life of servitude. Yet here they were.

"I've noticed."

"It's not out of the goodness of my heart, I can tell you that. I know it might behoove me to sugarcoat the situation and pander to your pride, but I have too much respect for you to stoop that far, so I'll give it to you straight. In my home and in my hotels, it's always been my goal to engender an environment of loyalty, to ensure that the people who rely on me for employment feel more than just a sense of financial obligation."

Fancy words for "You buy them."

"I care for them. As more than cogs in a machine. As *people*."

Ryan wasn't falling for it. "It was kind of you to give me a chance, but I don't think—"

"I don't pay you to think. I pay you to drive and to follow my orders, both of which you've done admirably up until yesterday." There was that smile again, kindly and cold and unsettling all at once. "It's not my intention to lose a good driver because of my son's irresponsibility. What I'd like to do instead is add to your duties."

"Sir?"

"Sit, please." He waited until Ryan arranged his limbs in a semblance of relaxation. "What do you know about Jake's relationship with Amy Sanders?"

Too much. Not enough.

He chose one. "Nothing."

Mr. Montgomery accepted the statement with a

nod. "I was afraid of that. As much as I'd hate to lose you, I'd hate to lose Amy even more." An almost cherubic expression passed his face. Was it possible her charm had actually pierced that fleshy, ironclad exterior? No wonder Ryan and Jake had already fallen at her feet. No mortal man stood a chance. "She's not just an employee to me. She and her mother, well, they're family. I won't sit back and watch my son trifle with her in an attempt to get at me."

"Sir?" Ryan echoed.

"She and Jake can have nothing to do with one another," Mr. Montgomery continued, as if Ryan hadn't spoken. "It's one hundred percent nonnegotiable, and I need an inside man to make sure of it. Are you following me?"

Not really. "I won't do anything that would hurt her, if that's what you're asking me for."

"Of course not." Mr. Montgomery didn't elaborate. "What I'd like for you to do is keep an eye on the pair of them."

"You want me to spy?" He had no room for incredulity, he knew. Spying was exactly what he'd been doing yesterday. Spying and careening into a ditch when it seemed Jake was about to land a kiss on Amy's lips. Surely that made him the worse of the two men sitting in the room right now.

"Think of it more as playing chaperone. Jake already likes you—I've never seen him stand up for anyone's job before. Use that to your advantage. Watch the pair of them. Keep the relationship from developing further by any means necessary. I'll gladly increase your salary. What do I pay you now?"

Ryan felt as though he was being pushed to the edge of a cliff. "I don't want your money."

One of Mr. Montgomery's bushy white eyebrows, as rounded as the rest of him, rose. "None of it? I find that hard to believe. I've been paying your salary for two years."

"I only mean I don't want any additional money. Not for this."

"I see," he said slowly, and Ryan got the impression that he really did see—much deeper than Ryan was comfortable with, much closer than anyone had peered in years.

"And what if I were to offer you more than that?"

More than money? There was only one thing in the world Ryan wanted more than cold, hard cash, and it didn't bear thinking of. Not even Mr. Montgomery's influence extended to Hollywood. Not even he could get Ryan behind the wheel of a stunt car again.

Could he?

Ryan repaid Mr. Montgomery's careful evasion with some of his own. "I'm not sure I understand you."

"I disagree. I think you understand my terms perfectly. Make my job easier, Ryan, and I'll see what I can do about yours. You'd be surprised how many of my hotels are located on the West Coast."

"I'm not for sale," Ryan said, his voice a growl.

But he could feel himself wavering, sensed the familiar slippage of temptation under his feet. This time, though, it wasn't the call of a whisky on the rocks that sent him reeling. It was the thrum of speed in his veins, of danger and excitement around every corner. He could practically taste the burned rubber in the air.

It tasted fantastic.

"Of course you're not for sale," Mr. Montgomery said. It was clear neither one of them believed that, but Ryan persisted, forcing himself to hold firm.

"What you're asking of me is wrong."

"I don't disagree." Mr. Montgomery nodded twice and then stopped, a bobblehead on broken springs. "But I've always found that the further I go in business, the more often I'm called upon to make difficult decisions. What seems like clear-cut black and white at the bottom of the ladder takes on indistinguishable shades of gray from way up high."

Ryan found himself picking up where Mr. Montgomery left off, his agreement clear in the up-and-down movements of his head before he realized what he was doing.

Oh, God. Was he really agreeing to this? If Mr. Montgomery was *this* against Jake's involvement with Amy, there was no reason for Ryan to interfere. The man had singlehandedly brought a decaying hotel empire back to a place of crowning triumph. He'd crushed a competitor using nothing but legal clauses and the sheer force of his will. He'd even gotten Ryan to somehow feel as though quitting was the last thing he wanted to do right now. He could definitely stop his son from dallying with the nanny.

But Ryan didn't want Mr. Montgomery to be in charge of that. He didn't want this shrewd, powerful man to hold Amy's heart in his hand and squeeze whenever he felt the urge.

If any man was going to hold her heart, dammit, it was going to be him.

"You see, Ryan?" Mr. Montgomery rose and extended his hand, bringing the conversation to a halt. Ryan had no choice but to shake it. "I invest in people. Did you know I had my assistant call a few of the studios in Hollywood before I hired you? I wanted character references."

He grimaced. "I can't imagine they were very good ones."

"Horrible. Any other man would have sent you packing."

The implication—that Mr. Montgomery wasn't *any other man*—hung in the air between them.

"I thought you hired me because I was cheap."

"I hired you because I liked what they had to say."

"And what was that?"

"That you're unpredictable. Reckless. You take uncalculated risks with other people's property." He paused. "That you were washed up and everyone knew it but you."

Jesus. That was worse than he expected. "Is this where I ask why those qualities appealed to you?"

"You could." Mr. Montgomery walked him to the door, a heavy hand on his shoulder. It was a possessive hand, a paternal hand. "But I think you already know the answer."

Except he didn't.

To own him? To redeem him? To toy with a man who had nowhere else to go?

It was probably option D. *All of the above.*

SEVEN

NOT GETTING INVOLVED in other people's lives was supposed to be simple.

The day Ryan wrecked the car that ended his career, he'd walked away from the twisted metal wreckage without so much as a single scratch. No blood, no bruises, no sign of anything broken unless you counted the damage to his ego and the soul-crushing realization that he'd singlehandedly destroyed his own dreams.

Lay low for a few months, his agent had advised when he'd begged—pleaded, prostrated himself— for a way back in. *Sober up. Find stable work that keeps you behind the wheel. It might take some time, but we can fix this.*

With those words tucked in his pocket to strengthen him, he'd been willing to take up Mr. Montgomery's offer to move to Connecticut and play chauffeur for a while. He'd stay away from the vices that had ruined him. He'd adopt the AA mantra at a literal level, taking life one day at a time. And even though he didn't *actively* avoid people, he didn't seek them out either. Having spent most of his life driving solo, he figured a few months of retreat wouldn't kill him.

But a few months had turned into a year, and one year had stretched endlessly into another. If he wanted to start moving again, something needed to happen—and soon.

Driven by motivations he refused to examine head-on, Ryan found his way down the access stairwell to the nursery, which was housed in a wing of rooms offset from the main structure. Since he'd grown up in a tiny apartment with a father who rarely concerned himself with his only son, it seemed beyond indulgent to keep the kids so far removed from everyone else they might as well have been away at boarding school.

But there was a lot about this place that oozed medieval pretention. This was hardly the worst offense.

Although Amy had exaggerated when she'd said you could hear them screaming from afar, it was easy to tell where the kids were playing. They made quite a bit of noise—most of it laughter.

He allowed himself to stand, listening for a few moments, basking in the simplicity of it, before he knocked.

"Come on in," Amy's voice called. "We're just fleeing from bears in here. Scientific name Ursus something. Ursavus? Who cares? They growl. *Grr.*"

Squeals of delight greeted Ryan as he pulled the door open. Visions of delight were there too—Amy rolling on the floor with a small girl in her arms, a little boy sinking his teeth into her leg, all of them set against a backdrop that looked like an indoor playground for the overprivileged, complete with a hand-painted mural of a fairytale castle on the wall.

"I'm sorry," he said tersely, feeling more out of place than he cared to admit. It wasn't just the kid-friendly atmosphere that did it—after the meeting he'd just had with Mr. Montgomery, it was difficult to look her in the eye without feeling like a complete shit. "I came at a bad time."

"Oh, no worries. The more the merrier."

Amy waved an arm, heralding Ryan into the nursery with a smile. His voice was gruff, his stance even more so—but all she could think was how happy she was to see him. Visitors to the nursery were rare enough as it was. Visitors who looked at her like *that*, as if he wanted to simultaneously hide his head under the playroom throw rug and throw her onto the rug for some play time of a different sort, were definitely rarer.

"I came to see how your face is doing." Neither the voice nor the stance softened as he remained in the doorway, not coming or going. Just staring.

"I've decided to go on living despite the pain."

"I'm so sorry about yesterday," he said, not cracking a smile. "I should have never…"

She shooed the twins toward their play kitchen, hoping their hunger would have them gnawing on the wooden food long enough to allow her a grown-up conversation.

"You should have never what? Accidentally run a car off the road? Don't worry too much about it. I only look slightly horrific." She moved closer and stuck her lower lip out in a pout to prove her point. The cut looked a lot worse than it was. She'd always been a bleeder.

Ryan reached up and ran his thumb lightly over her lip, his touch grazing the surface of her skin. There was nothing to the gesture, really—a concerned chauffeur looking after his damaged passenger, but she felt a shiver work through her all the same. His hands held the right amount of roughness to cause a tingle; the taste of him was a little bit motor oil, a little bit soap. A masculine taste. Like he'd rubbed up against cars and ran his hands along long, tapering fuel lines.

Against her better judgment, she allowed her mouth to fall open, encouraging his thumb to move in farther, where it plunged deep before he pulled himself sharply away.

"See?" she said, her breath caught in her throat. "No lasting harm done. These lips will someday kiss again."

Ryan's eyes flared with unmistakable interest, his gaze fixated on her mouth. It would have been the perfect moment for him to see for himself how injured she was, to pull her close and give her split lip a workout it wouldn't soon forget.

"Amy, I—" His voice wavered.

She leaned in close, mouth parted and eyes drifting slowly closed, sure the moment of reckoning was about to arrive…when his hand on her shoulder propelled her gently back.

"I was wondering what time you get a break today."

Oh. Right. Children.

Despite the mortification of *not* kissing a man when one's puckered lips were mere inches from his, she shook herself off and was able to answer with a semblance of dignity. "Don't be silly—I don't get breaks. I barely get time to pee."

When all he did was continue studying her in his inscrutable way, she added, "I'll be footloose and fancy free about seven when Sheryl shows up to take over, but you'll probably be long gone by then."

"I can stick around."

She cast a quick glance at her watch. "That's hours away—it's barely two now. I couldn't ask you to do that."

"You aren't asking me to. I'm volunteering."

"If it's about the accident, please don't worry." He was making a big deal out of nothing, if you asked her. Everyone made mistakes. She knew that better than anyone. "I'm fine. You wouldn't believe how easily I bleed. I'm a vampire's dream come true."

"It *is* about the accident, but not in the way you think."

"Oh, God. Did you get fired?"

He grimaced. "I almost wish I had."

Guilt took up its usual residence in the pit of her stomach. Here Ryan was, obviously having a crappy day in the aftermath of ruining one of Mr. Montgomery's cars, and she was practically attacking him with her bleeding, oozy face. No wonder he kept his distance.

"You could join the rest of the staff at lunchtime tomorrow instead," she suggested. That would be nice. The group setting took some of the pressure off, and even taciturn, broody chauffeurs had to eat, right? "I don't always have a chance to head down there at lunch, but Serena is having a photographer in to take some of those mommy-child-tastefully-naked-together pictures at noon, and I declined her offer to watch."

A smile lifted a corner of his mouth. "I have no idea what that sentence means."

"The less you know, the better." She was unable to suppress a smile of her own. "Apparently, she's had these Anne Geddes–style pictures taken every six months since the twins were born. I'm praying she gets over it by the time puberty hits. There are some memories a child never recovers from—and the ones with photographic evidence are ten times worse."

Ryan relaxed and ran a hand over his hair, filling Amy with an urge to follow his path through that soft, short stubble. It was such an intriguing mix of textures, like a five o'clock shadow made of puppies. "I guess one lunch won't kill me."

"One might even say the nourishment will help you go on living."

He chuckled softly, but she could tell that he was distracted. He cast a hurried look over his shoulder, as if longing for the door to approach him rather than the other way around.

"I'll see you at noon tomorrow, Chauffeur Lucas. In the kitchen. With the steak knife." Amy pushed him toward the door, helping him find the easy way out. As if her desperation wasn't enough to drive him away, he also had all these kids around to make him uncomfortable. There was something about a nursery that horrified men, as if they thought fertility might be contagious.

He dug his heels into the floor and stopped them both midstride, and she had to place both hands against his chest to keep from slamming right into him. *Unf.* She didn't move right away—Ryan was a very solid man with a very solid chest. It was as though all his strength was kept bound and contained there, a beast waiting to be unleashed.

She savored the feel of him under her fingertips for a moment—probably too long of a one, probably once again overstepping his boundaries—unable to help herself. There was a heck of a lot more to Ryan than a few stunt car wounds and badly damaged pride. There was a man in there. A hot, hidden, fascinating man. A man she was becoming more and more determined to uncover.

"You should probably put something on that lip," he said gruffly.

Once more, he lifted his hand to her face.

Once more, she sort of opened her mouth and drooled into it.

And then he was moving away and out the door before she realized she was trying, yet again, to kiss him.

RYAN FELT RIDICULOUS as he ran his hand along the stone-lined walkway connecting the garage to the rest of the house, the texture scraping his fingertips until they tingled. The passage itself was one he knew well, as he often had reason to move from one building to the other, but he'd never walked it before with the intention of paying a social visit.

It wasn't that he had anything against Alex and Holly and the rest. And he was looking forward to spending his lunch hour with more than just a package of Pop-Tarts and the darts he'd gotten in the habit of throwing at a wooden beam while he ate. Unfortunately, this was one of those situations in which time had carved an awkward pit and shoved him right into it. He'd held out for so long, refused all overtures of friendship so many times, that to turn around and suddenly start playing nice looked—and felt—weird.

But breaking bread with coworkers didn't mean

he'd given up on his plan to leave Ransom Creek. Accepting Holly's food wasn't the modern world equivalent of eating the pomegranate seeds and tying the bonds to Hades forever.

For Amy. He was doing this for Amy.

After the way she'd looked at him in the nursery, as if he was all man instead of some kind of monster who planned on using her relationship with Jake to further his own ends, he could at least have lunch when she asked. He'd have all the lunches in the world if he thought it might help him out of this mess.

The sounds of laughter met him long before he reached the swinging kitchen doors. Built like a restaurant and probably equipped better than one, the Montgomery Manor kitchens were similar to everything else in the house—over-the-top and unnecessarily extravagant. He'd only been there a few times, during his initial tour of the place and at last year's Christmas party—which hadn't been optional—but his impression had always been one of cavernous sinks and spotless, gleaming stainless steel.

"So I told him flat-out. Either you let me into the green room to see for myself, or I'm sneaking the entire goddamn paparazzi out back and waiting for you there."

The laughter increased in volume and pitch.

"Hey, Ryan." Holly looked up in the middle of setting a platter of food in the center of a long wooden table and nodded a greeting as he approached. "Good timing. We were just about to start."

A few other friendly greetings assailed his ears—Alex and Philip with a few of his gardening crew members. The tall, nervous-looking personal assistant, Katie, and her dad, Sarge, who oversaw the running of the household. Georgia, the energetic handywoman who came to the Manor a few times a week to fix the things no one else wanted to. He grunted a general greeting to the collective group, but his attention remained fixed on the man sitting physically *on* the table. Not content with having everyone rapt and adoring, Jake had actually pushed some of the plates away so he could hitch himself up on one corner, waving a fork over them as if he owned the place.

Which, technically, he did. Or would someday, once Mr. Montgomery died and his children took over in his stead.

"Ryan, you came!" Amy sprang to her feet and pulled out the chair closest to her. She looked fantastic and at ease, a loose braid slipping over one shoulder, an oversized yellow top layered over shorts, her entire demeanor in keeping with her long-standing competition against the sun. "I'm sorry. It's kind of a full house today."

"That's because you're here, sweetie." Holly gestured at the platter, which held stacked sandwiches and what looked like some kind of grainy salad, and winked at Ryan. "No one ever makes a special trip when it's just me and my quinoa."

Ryan felt his ears flush as he sat down and let loose a string of internal curses. He wasn't sure if the surge of violence was directed more at himself for being so transparent, or at Jake, who appeared to be here for the same reasons as him.

Clearly, proximity to Amy came at a price.

He took in the sight of her, smiling and puffy-lipped as she swiped a cherry tomato shaped like a flower and tossed in it her mouth, and realized how easy it would be to pay it. How quickly he might get into debt for the simple privilege of being near her.

"It's a help-yourself sort of meal." Holly passed him a plate. "I've got to get back upstairs with the pumpkin I emptied out."

"Oh, geez." Amy dropped her head to her hands. "She's doing the pumpkin one?"

"Pumpkins and my best stockpot. I don't know whether she's recording those two for posterity or planning on serving them for Thanksgiving dinner."

"She's putting the twins inside pumpkins?" Ryan took a sandwich but passed fearfully over the quinoa. "People actually do that?"

"This isn't even the worst one." Holly shook her head. "Last time I had to do them in cabbage leaves."

Georgia poked her head up, her brown hair, curly and wild, moving as if a separate entity. "The time before that, it was flowerpots. I had to find the right sizes to pose all three of them without exposing any naughty bits. It was a lot harder than you'd think."

They all laughed, and it was only then they realized Jake was in their midst, still elevated at his perch on the table, listening with a smile.

"Oh, sorry." Amy was the first to recover. "We're being super rude."

"Just blowing off some steam," Philip said.

"The cabbage ones were pretty cute," Holly offered.

Jake raised his hands in a gesture that was half apology, half politician. "Don't backtrack on my account. You guys should just be grateful you haven't seen the portraits she had taken of herself right before their wedding. Then you'd *really* have something to talk about."

Ten pairs of horrified eyes turned Jake's way, but Amy had to laugh. She wasn't sure if there actually were some kind of boudoir pictures hidden under Mr. Montgomery's mattress, or if Jake was trying to make them feel better about gossiping behind the family's back, but it worked. She reached under the table and squeezed his knee.

It was a show of solidarity. A little friendly pressure. Nothing more.

But when she turned to look at Ryan, she snatched her hand guiltily back. She'd never been the sort of woman who could successfully juggle two men at the same time, as the amount of lying involved far exceeded her skill set. Granted, Ryan wasn't exactly tripping over himself to be the first in line at her kissing booth, but there was no denying she'd grope his leg under the table in a hot second. And Jake? He was her friend, her childhood companion, the man who would probably buy out her kissing booth just because he could.

Was it better to be pursued by an old friend you didn't have any real interest in beyond flirtation, or to lust after an unattainable chauffeur? Did *better* even exist in that situation?

Jake winked as he rose from the table, impervious, as he always was, to everything but what he cared to acknowledge. "Don't worry, everyone. Your secrets are safe with me. I've outgrown my urge to run to Stepmama with tales."

"Aren't you going to stay and eat with us?" Georgia asked between bites. She had two enormous sandwiches heaped on her plate, and Amy was pretty sure a third had already been consumed. Georgia did a lot of manual labor in her handywoman trade, but Amy had never seen someone with the ability to consume so much at one time without swelling out in a food baby. It was unfair. Her own food baby made an appearance so often she'd nicknamed him Soren.

"No thanks," Jake said politely. "I only came down to see how things were going. Ryan, if I could have a word before I go?"

She looked up sharply at the sound of Ryan's name falling from Jake's lips, the power of command in the request so clear it might have come from Mr. Montgomery himself. Ryan must have felt it too, because he got up wordlessly and followed Jake out to the hallway, his body tense enough to send a tremor through the room.

It was impossible to eavesdrop without drawing the attention of everyone else at lunch, or Amy would have tried. She wasn't ashamed to admit it. She'd often thought how awesome it would be if the house had those air vents that joined rooms for maximum gossip acquisitions. As a kid, she'd also hoped for secret passages.

But Montgomery Manor was disappointingly modern. Real life had a way of completely ruining things.

The lunchtime chatter turned to ordinary topics, and Amy forced herself to relax and enjoy the company. Even Sarge, who spent most of his days shouting out orders in a hoarse voice—not unlike a dog who'd had its bark removed—used mealtime as an opportunity to unwind. Work hard, play hard. It was a motto Mr. Montgomery embraced not only in his business life, but at home as well.

Of course, that didn't mean she wasn't acutely aware of how long Ryan was closeted with Jake. Or that she didn't run through various scenarios in her head about their topic of conversation. Macho stuff like sports and carburetors? Nah. Jake had never been into that kind of stuff like normal boys were. The difficulties of maintaining a crease in your slacks? No way. Ryan seemed like the kind of guy who would rather eat his clothes than talk excessively about them.

When Ryan finally returned—alone—he had the grim look of a man who had been challenged to do just that. And as if maybe he was deciding between condiments.

"What was that all about?" Amy asked as he returned to his seat. She'd never been very good at subtlety. That was for women with tact and dainty limbs. "Important driver things?"

He turned to look at her, his eyes clouded. "Something like that."

"Is this where you're going to tell me to mind my own business? Because you totally can if you want. I was just telling Sarge the other day that I thought he'd look dashing with muttonchops, and he threatened to lock me in a closet if I didn't shut my trap."

"What did you say?" Sarge cupped one hand around his ear and leaned over the table.

"I said you'd look dashing in muttonchops," she repeated, louder this time. "The big, hairy ones all the way down to your chin. Civil War style. You know, like the ones from your youth."

Sarge had been at the Manor even before her mom—he was practically a fixture, like the cherub fountain in the garden. More than one rumor floated around that he was actually a ghost tied to the land and unable to leave or risk entering the ether. His daughter, Katie, had never confirmed or denied these claims. Though, to be fair, she almost never talked at all—not even when Amy tried her very hardest to draw her out.

Sarge raised a gnarled finger and pointed it at her in warning, but his lips wobbled at the sides. "That's enough out of you."

"See?" Amy said happily. "I'm a menace."

Ryan looked as though he believed it. "What time do you have to be back to the nursery?"

"Eager to get rid of me, Lucas?" Her playfulness didn't lighten his mood any, but she wasn't about to let that get her down. He was *here*, and that was enough. She'd accomplished the impossible and gotten Ryan out of the garage during the workday. Now if only she could get him to stay long enough to work her busybody magic. "I have until Holly returns with what remains of the pumpkins and her pride. That could be five minutes from now or, let's be honest, five hours. I probably need to stick around either way. I'm a slave to my duty."

Ryan pushed back from the table, and she thought for a moment he was going to leave, that she'd failed in her mission of Befriend the Hot Chauffeur. But he merely turned and lifted the plates from Katie's hand as she started clearing the table.

"I'll take those," he said kindly. Over his shoulder, he called back to Amy, "As long as you're stuck where you can be at Mrs. Montgomery's beck and call, we might as well do the dishes for Holly."

Katie's eyes flew to Amy's in an exaggerated gesture of surprise, a smile lurking in the dark brown irises for what had to be the first time. All Amy could do was offer a wide-eyed stare in return.

A sweet gesture to do dishes. From the last man on earth who volunteered anything. Who knew that would be the one thing on this planet that could render her speechless?

"I DON'T HAVE any more of an idea how to run this thing than you do." Ryan leaned down and examined the panel of complex buttons on the outside of the large stainless steel appliance. "Are you sure it's the dishwasher?"

"What else could it be?" Amy drew close and dipped her head so it was on an even level with his, her hair tickling the side of his neck.

Pineapples. Today she smelled of pineapples.

"I don't know." He pushed what looked like a power button and was greeted with the unmistakable screech of metal on metal. "A garbage disposal?"

"Oh, shitballs." Amy stabbed at the same button—and then, when the screeching increased, at all the buttons she could reach. "I think it might be the dumbwaiter."

A rattle and a clank sounded before the ominous lull of silence filled the kitchen. Amy giggled and turned around, as if showing her back to the machine would render it invisible—a child's game, another charming way her perspective of the world differed from everyone else's.

"If I'm not mistaken, we just sent the entire load of dirty lunch dishes to the dining room," she said, her delight easy to read.

"Oops."

"I think you should offer to wash Holly's car for the rest of her life when she gets back. Maybe she'll be so grateful she won't notice."

"I may have to." He pushed a few more buttons before finally giving up. "You wouldn't consider her the type of woman to hold a grudge, would you? Like the kind of grudge that might lead to untraceable poisons in my dinner?"

"Holly? Nah." Amy waved a hand and hoisted herself up on the kitchen counter—also stainless steel, but much easier to navigate in terms of technology. Also much more pleasant to look at, what with her long bare legs swinging to and fro, mesmerizing him like a hypnotist's pendulum. "She's old school. Think ground-up glass shards. Toadstools. That sort of thing."

"How comforting."

"Or a knife plunged in your back."

"I'm not sure that's better."

"Told you," she said happily. "In the kitchen. With a steak knife. I always win at *Clue*."

"I'm not falling for that one again," he said. "Every time you say you're good at something, it's a secret code that you're actually terrible at it. I saw your laser tag score."

She laughed and patted the counter. Ryan found himself leaping up next to her before he could think of a good reason not to. They remained there, thigh-to-thigh, awareness of her proximity crackling in the space between them, for what felt like hours. In reality, it was only a few seconds, but time had a way of losing meaning when a man struggled to pull out the words he didn't particularly enjoy harboring in the first place.

Hey, Amy—want to hear something weird? Your employer is so against the idea of you dating his son that I've been hired to keep you apart.

Hey, Amy—what would you say if I told you I'm planning on using your personal life as a stepping stool for my own career? Crazy, right?

"Did you know Holly from before?" he asked instead. It was cowardly of him, he knew, but yesterday's outrage had given way to a sense of acceptance he couldn't quite shake. Was it really the worst thing in the world to keep an eye on someone you cared about, whatever the motivations?

"As a kid, you mean?" She shook her head. "Oh, no. Holly came with Serena. The cook we had growing up was this huge, jolly man named Patrick who used to sneak us cookies under our plates. I think it was his life goal to fatten us up, like the witch in Hansel and Gretel, but without all those nasty plans to eat us afterwards. I liked Patrick. He quit when Mrs. Montgomery—the *first* Mrs. Montgomery, I mean—died."

"I'm sorry. Were you close to her?"

Amy closed her eyes and tried to conjure up an image of Mr. Montgomery's first wife, who she remembered as being a sharp, controlled woman who was beautiful to look at but scary to touch. "I didn't really know her, to be honest. She was always busy with work and her charity functions, and for some

reason, my mom was always careful to keep me out
of the way when she visited the nursery. I don't think
she liked me—or at least, she didn't like the *idea* of
me. Nannies aren't supposed to have families of their
own or love anyone but their charges. Otherwise it
spoils the illusion."

"So you're not allowed to have a life outside the
twins?"

"I *don't* have a life outside the twins," she said
with a laugh. "It's just me and potty training as far
as the eye can see."

"But that's not true." Ryan's natural intensity drew
the lines of his face taut. "You have a lot of things.
You have your friends and your family and your dancing career."

The smile on her face froze into position, the deer
in headlights making a rapid return. "I'm retired,"
she said tightly. "Twenty-six is ancient in the dance
industry—ballet years are worse than dog years and
cat years combined."

"I don't believe that. Not for a second. I chatted
with your mom a few times before you took her place
here—did I ever tell you that?"

"No. No, you didn't." Amy sat up straighter. For
some reason, the idea of Ryan and her mom hitting
it off filled her with a warm, effervescent sensation.
Her mother was a good woman to turn to in a pinch,
and Amy didn't doubt for a single second that she'd
done her best to make Ryan feel welcome. It was a
nice thought to linger on, as if her mom had paved
the way for their eventual friendship.

Or more. You know, if he ever decided he wanted

more. And if Amy didn't make a total fool out of herself in the meantime.

"She didn't tell you embarrassing stories about how I used to take naked baths with Jenna or anything, did she?" Amy asked.

"We weren't *that* close. Why? Did you take a lot of community baths when you were a kid?"

"I don't know, to be honest. You should ask her."

"When I see her again, I will."

Some of the warm fuzzies in Amy's gut multiplied. Not *if* he saw her mom again, *when*.

"You totally dig my mom, don't you?" When his ears began to change color, she laughed. God, he had cute ears. They were like mood rings. Pert, adorable, auditory mood rings. "It's okay. She's pretty much my favorite person on the face of the planet. I wish I had a chance to see more of her—I don't think I realized how much of my life would be taken up here."

"It requires a lot of people and a lot of time to run this household."

"It does." Amy nodded. "And my mom *really* doesn't like that I quit my job to be a part of it."

He waited, not expectantly, but as though he knew with absolute certainty she'd keep talking. And she wanted to, she really did, but it was harder to form the words than he realized. There were many things about her life that *no one* here at Montgomery Manor knew about.

"She says I'm giving up my life by choosing to spend it here instead of on the stage." Amy splayed her hand on the counter, staring at the spaces where her fingers didn't touch. "She thinks I'm lowering myself, and that it's her fault for not being well enough to take care of the twins herself. It's hard for her to see me taking the same path she did, I think. She wanted more for me."

"She used to talk about you." Ryan relaxed and leaned against the tiled backdrop. "About your dance troupe and how proud she was you were a part of it. She used to get this look in her eye, like you were superhuman or something. I was totally intimidated by the idea of you coming to work here. I had this vision of a seven-foot-tall ballerina who dazzled audiences and spoke four languages."

Amy swallowed heavily, unsure how to evade such a pack of bald-faced lies. It wasn't that she'd ever set out to purposefully mislead her friends and family about where she'd worked all those years—she really hadn't. After twelve years of private lessons, she was sent away at age eighteen to study classical ballet at Mr. Montgomery's expense, and it had been her intention to justify his faith in her a thousand times over. She knew, even back then, that she'd never be as smart as Jenna, as charming as Jake or as driven as Monty, but it hadn't seemed outrageous to imagine she could carve out a niche of her own in the world.

And she had, in a way. It was just that her niche wasn't shaped the way she'd led everyone to believe—not so much an elegant cutaway as a small, cramped hole.

It all started when an early performance in Paris, Texas, had been misinterpreted to mean something of an entirely different order—and country. Things had progressed steadily downhill from there, but she'd been powerless to stop it. Everyone had just been so freaking *proud* of her when they thought she was making it big. Disappointing them with the truth—that her most successful audition to date had been to play the role of Fairy Princess Number Three at a theme park in Iowa—had seemed needlessly cruel.

And the worst part was that she'd liked being a Fairy Princess a heck of a lot more than she'd ever liked the rigorous diet and exercise and constant struggle to keep up with all the other dancers with flawless, flat-chested builds and way more skills than her. She'd *liked* dressing up in the billowing pink gown every morning and waving a magic wand at little girls whose eyes lit up at the sight of her. She'd *liked* dancing the waltz every night with her pretend Prince Charming, a theater major and aspiring actor who, like her, had all too quickly realized that the world of prefabricated castles and regular paychecks was preferable to the constant rejection of the real world.

She almost told him.

She almost opened her mouth and told Ryan about the lie she'd perpetuated every Sunday when she called her mom to chat, every lie she continued telling now that she was home and content to remain here. *This* was her castle now. *This* was what she wanted. She might not get to wear her pink gown anymore, but the light she saw in Lily's and Evan's eyes whenever she approached gave her the same feeling of satisfaction.

But how did you admit to a man whose past was littered with empty whisky bottles and death-defying stunts that your biggest problem in life was falling in love with mediocrity and a tiara?

She couldn't do it. No matter how much she might want to.

"I only speak four languages if you count being able to ask where the bathroom is," she said, feeling like a cheat. "*Baño. Toilette. Loo.*"

"*Loo* is technically English."

"See? I only know three languages. I'm the least intimidating person on the face of the planet."

"I know," he said simply. "It's one of the things I like best about you."

She had to laugh—partly because it was such an absurd thing to say, but mostly because she felt suddenly giddy. He *liked* her. He frowned and made it a point not to kiss her and begrudgingly accompanied her to mealtimes, but he liked her all the same.

"Oh, yeah?" She bumped his hip playfully. "What are the other things?"

"Fishing for compliments?" He made a tsking noise as he flung her words from the other day back in her face. "Shame on you."

She gave in to the impulse to grab his hand, which rested in the narrow gap between their legs. Lifting it, she studied the rough palms and short nails, ran her finger along a light scar that cut from knuckle to wrist. He was warm to the touch, the texture of his skin coarse.

He watched alongside her, curious but not withdrawing, as if seeing the extremity for the first time. "I like a lot of things about you, Amy, but most of all, it's how you always put other people first that really blows me away."

She didn't look up or acknowledge the way that

compliment—innocuous and kind—made her want to cry. "How'd you get this one?"

"I'd like to say it was a piece of scrap metal from a '67 Chevy I jumped over a river, but I think it might actually be from where I dropped a screwdriver a few years back."

"You don't remember?"

His fingers grew tense. "I don't remember a lot about those days. It's the reason I don't do bars, remember?"

Oh, she remembered. She remembered each time she saw him frown, each time his gaze turned inward and distant. Unable to stop herself, she lifted his hand and kissed the scar, a featherlight touch of her lips on skin so rough and delicious she had an overwhelming urge to keep going—strong forearms to bulging biceps to sinewy neck, where a vein throbbed its warning at her.

"There," she said, and released her grip instead.

His hand stayed aloft, almost accusing her. How dare she initiate human touch? How dare she desire to press her lips on him?

"That's what I do for the twins," she explained, hoping to rob the moment of its awkwardness. "Kiss it and make it all better."

He continued staring at his hand before dropping it to his lap. "I think that stops working sometime around the age of four."

"Do you?" she asked, feeling sad—though whether for Ryan or herself, she couldn't quite say. "Not me. I like to think it never stops working."

"Amy, listen. I'm not—" He lifted his eyes and

stared into hers. She waited, breathless, for what came next. A kiss? A confession? A slap on the face?

He sighed instead, the doors closing on the moment with a crash. "I know it's not what you want to hear, but your mom is right. That's the compliment you deserve most. I'm sure the twins love having you around, but you can do better than this place. You *are* better than this place. Why did you come back?"

She answered as truthfully as she could, feeling it vital that he understand her motivations, if not the exact details behind them. She could handle other people thinking she'd lowered herself, that she'd settled by choosing a life as a nanny, but not Ryan. She couldn't bear the thought that he might look at her and see something *less*.

"My mom was reaching a point where she needed to retire. She's young, but she has fibromyalgia. Even though she hates admitting it, keeping up with the twins got to be a real struggle. And of course she loves them way too much to hand over the reins easily, so she probably would have kept working through the pain and fatigue until she collapsed. Which is why Mr. Montgomery called me up and asked if I wanted to take over. He set up a pension for her and I arrived the next day. We sort of ousted her, and she's having a hard time coming to terms with it."

Ryan frowned. "You came at his bidding?"

"I came at his request. It's not the same thing." And if you asked her, it wasn't that big of a deal either way. Even if she *had* been dancing her way across Europe with the world falling at her feet, she'd have come home the second Mr. Montgomery said the word. "Why does that make you so upset?"

"It doesn't. It's just…" He looked away and the back of his neck tensed, leaving her with the strong impression that he was angry. But if he was, the feeling either dissipated or he managed to hide it. He hopped down from the table before extending a hand to help her.

She slipped her palm into his, savoring the rough texture of his hand—how hot and dry it felt, almost feverish. He kept his grip for longer than was necessary, his gaze searching as they stood face-to-face. "I sometimes wonder about how much control he has over you. Over all of us. Promise me you'll be careful, okay?"

Careful of what?

She thought she said the words out loud, but she must not have, because Ryan didn't elaborate. He just shook his head and turned away as Holly came bursting into the kitchen, ending their tête-à-tête with several pieces of broken pumpkin under her arm.

EIGHT

"WELL, CAR MAN—what's the word?" Jake sat behind the wheel of the 1939 Buick Coupe at the far end of the garage, driving nowhere. Ryan had been in the middle of replacing the fuel pump on the coupe when he left the night before, assuming no one would enter the sacrosanct grounds of his workplace in the meantime.

He should have known better. There wasn't a thing on this planet Jake considered holy unless you counted his own reflection. Despite the early hour, the bastard looked bright and chipper and right at home in the burgundy leather driver's seat, a fedora and a pinstripe suit away from traveling through time.

As if to cement his suitability to a bygone era, Jake jumped out of the convertible without bothering to open the door and shoved his hands deep in the pockets of his perfectly creased slacks. Had he even gone to bed last night?

"Did you decide which car you can sneak out for my moonlit ride into New York next week?" Jake asked. "I'm ready to put the old girl's top down and see how she purrs."

Ryan's hands formed twin fists, and he had to remind himself that he was being goaded on purpose. It didn't take a genius to realize he was being used as a pawn in some sort of game of power between

Mr. Montgomery and his son. One man wanted him to help woo the nanny. The other wanted him to stop that very thing. He was caught in the middle with nowhere to turn.

Which was fine. Whatever. He could handle himself, would walk away with his head held high before he'd let either man do so much as scratch his surface.

But the fact that they seemed to be using Amy as well... Instead of loosening, his fists only grew tighter, feeling a powerful pull to implant themselves in Jake's face. Amy might see nothing but good intentions and dewy-eyed affection when she looked at those two men, but that was proof of the existence of her good nature. Not theirs.

"I don't recall agreeing to sneak you out anything." Ryan admirably restrained himself from planting his fists anywhere bones could break. "I told you—your dad was less worried about the damages I caused and more worried about the fact that I drove one of the cars without his permission. If you want to take Amy out again, you're going to have to get creative."

"Creativity has never been my strong suit. But then, neither has falling tamely in line with my father's plans."

"And why, if you don't mind my asking, is this my problem?"

"Because you owe me." Jake sidled up next to him, so close he could wrap an arm around Ryan's shoulders, but somehow all the more remote because he didn't. There was something about the way that man carried himself—close but so far above—that made Ryan itchy under the collar. Who was he kidding?

Everything about this man made him prickly. "And because you know my dad would hate it."

Ryan held himself perfectly still. "What does that have anything to do with this?"

"Let's just say I have a radar for antipathy directed at that man's door. It calls to me. Warms me to my very soul."

"That's a strange way to talk about the man who gave you life." Not to mention a man whose money provided Jake's entire overblown day-to-day existence.

"Am I wrong?"

He paused. No, Jake wasn't wrong. But he wasn't right, either.

Ryan chose his next words carefully, determined not to take a side. "I've known a lot of powerful men in my lifetime—Hollywood is practically teeming with them. In my experience, powerful and great rarely go hand in hand."

"Well, that's where you're wrong, my friend. My father is both powerful and great."

"You say that like it's a bad thing."

"On the contrary, I say that like a man who is neither. Ignore me, Ryan the Car Man, if you expect to leave this place alive. My words are tinged with jealousy. I can't be trusted."

Ryan believed it. And then didn't believe it, because it sounded an awful lot like one of those riddles he'd always hated as a kid. *A prisoner faces two guards: one who will lead him to death, the other who will lead him to freedom. One guard always lies and the other always tells the truth. The prisoner can ask only one guard one question to save his own life. What is that question?*

And *where can I get a fucking drink?* wasn't the right answer.

"Well, if you won't give me a car," Jake continued, walking slowly around the coupe and trailing his fingers on the pristine cream finish, "at least tell me what else there is to do around here."

"Work."

"Hilarious."

"Ride a bicycle."

"Even funnier."

"Play laser tag."

"Right. Because that's exactly what women love to do in their downtime."

Ryan didn't bother to correct him. Jake was clearly chafing under the restrictions of his current predicament, and Ryan was happy to let him continue doing so. Let him chafe so much he bled.

"What I'm looking for is a grand gesture. Something big. Something memorable."

"Something that will eventually get back to your dad's ears?"

Jake released a quick laugh—one that, if Ryan didn't know better, sounded genuine. "Naturally. If there's one thing you need to know about my family, it's that we rarely do anything without an ulterior motive. We've usually got three or four of them overlapping. But it *would* be nice to come up with a date that Amy might actually enjoy going on. Despite what you think, I do care about her."

There was a note of sincerity in that remark too—

which was what Ryan would later blame for the words that crossed his lips next.

"Her mom."

Jake's head snapped up, his eyes glittering cold and hard. "I beg your pardon?"

"Her mom." Ryan stepped closer, refusing to look down at the challenge the other man practically radiated. He'd committed to it now—to the unpleasant idea of helping plan this date, to helping Jake impress Amy so he could secretly keep an eye on things per Mr. Montgomery's request.

Fuck. This family was phenomenal at twisting his motivations around theirs, mixing the two until he no longer knew which ones belonged to him.

"You want a high-profile date, her mom is it." Ryan shook his head at his own folly. "Take the pair of them out to lunch or to a beach or something. I know Amy would love a chance to see more of her—and she practically raised you, right? Even your dead heart must feel something for the woman."

Jake's piercing gaze softened, something like admiration overtaking him. "It's perfect."

Of course it was—it was exactly what Ryan would do in Jake's stead. "I know. You can chat about old times together. Be your charming douche bag self."

Jake's laughter, this time, was a shout no one could question the veracity of. "You really hate me, don't you?"

"Even more than your father."

"Then why are you helping me?"

Ryan paused, wondering how best to answer that question. The truth—that the lure of Hollywood being dangled in front of him had him questioning every scruple he'd ever had—was one he didn't care to think too much about, but he couldn't come up with a believable lie.

"Oh, I see," Jake said a long pause later. "You *like* her."

Ryan looked away, his throat tight. His feelings for Amy were the least relevant factor here. Even if the sight of her made it difficult to breathe, even though he'd almost fallen into her kiss and never come up again, he could at least assuage his conscience on that score. He wanted her—he *ached* for her—but he wouldn't trifle with her just to scratch a particularly insistent itch. He wasn't an animal.

"Of course, there is still the tricky matter of transportation to contend with." Jake fixed his attention on his fingernails, acting as though he hadn't just peered directly into Ryan's soul. "I'm clearly grounded here, and I hate to ask the lady to lower herself to the role of chauffeur."

It was Ryan's turn to acknowledge a begrudging laugh. "No. Life doesn't get much lower than having to shuttle other people around, does it? I'd offer you my own ride, but it only has two wheels. But if you don't mind sitting in a vehicle that costs less than twenty thousand dollars, I can probably find a way to make alternate arrangements. There's a rental company downtown."

"You'll arrange things and do the driving?"

Ryan shrugged. Why the hell not?

To his surprise, Jake extended his hand. Even more to his surprise, he found himself shaking it.

"Thank you," Jake said. "I appreciate you doing this for me."

"I'm not doing it for you," Ryan said, but he could have saved himself the breath. They were both aware of that fact already.

"YOU'RE REALLY NOT going to give me *any* hints?" Amy was one squeal away from being a kid on top of a Ferris wheel, complete with cotton candy smeared in her hair. "Not even an eensy weensy one?"

"Did you talk like that before you were a nanny?" Ryan asked, his voice rougher than he intended. "In grown-up conversations, I mean?"

She stuck out her tongue. "Somebody's grumpy wumpy today."

You don't know the half of it. "I guess I didn't realize you loved surprises so much."

There was everything childlike about her expression, which professed a fondness for surprises that surpassed ordinary mortal belief—and nothing childlike about the way she turned and performed what could only be termed a *booty dance*. Arms in the air, striped shirt stretched taut against her breasts, ass out, she was a pole away from getting dollar bills stuffed in her panties.

They were both lucky Ryan was damn near broke.

"Are you kidding?" she asked when she was done. Her face suffused with color, brightening the freckles across her nose. "I live for surprises. Especially when they involve an afternoon off for no reason at all. Jenna said she flew in just to watch the twins for me today—had this whole story ready to go about how she wanted some alone big sister time. Wasn't that sweet of her?"

Yeah. Sweet. Or possibly the machinations of a brother who had all sorts of blackmail he kept stashed under his bed.

"I'm sure she's a real gem," Ryan said dryly.

"Oh, she really is." He wasn't sure whether Amy purposefully misunderstood his sarcasm or not, but there was no mistaking the warmth in her tone. "Haven't you ever met her? She's fantastic. Even though it would have been really easy for her to coast through life, she's wicked smart and even more beautiful. You'll fall in love with her on the spot—every man does."

"That shows what you know. I've always had a taste for highly unattractive women."

Amy released a peal of laughter and wound her arm through his. He jumped at the sudden brush of contact, willing himself to stop being such a dunce even as the blood grew heavy in his veins and settled in his groin. If he didn't stop losing his shit every time Amy touched him, things were only going to get complicated. His cock shifted. *And obvious.*

"Oh, Ryan. Of course you like attractive women. You're a car man. Car men are notorious for only going after the hot ones. It's all about the tits and ass for you guys."

"Is that a fact?" he asked in a strangled voice. Amy leaned closer as she spoke, her own tits pressing warm and tempting against his arm. He felt like he was twelve years old again and taking a girl to his first dance. Those slow dances had been an agonizing balance of copping as much of a feel as you could without springing into an awkward boner and scaring your date away. Most of the boys he knew had to wear a cup underneath their Sunday best.

Come to think of it, that wasn't such a bad idea…

"Oh, yes. I have theories on the subject. Entire dissertations. I've always been long-winded." Amy began leading the way to the garage through the stone passage. It was underhanded of him, and slightly Montgomery-like, but he'd managed to swing it so that both Jake and Amy's mom were waiting at her house for them to arrive and head to the beach as a collective group. Which gave him half an hour— possibly forty-five minutes—in which he had Amy all to himself.

He purposefully slowed their steps.

"Want to hear my theory?"

"I'd love nothing more," he said, and meant it.

"Well, it's like this." She paused and turned to face him. She did that, he noticed—stopped whenever she was having a conversation, determined to give her full attention to whoever happened to be her lucky partner at the time. "Car men—that's guys like you and Mr. Montgomery—are obsessed with things like speed and winning and flashy exteriors, right?"

He inclined his head in agreement. "That's true. Is this where you tell me that we also only like women who are fast and flashy? Because you're not breaking any ground with that one, I can tell you that right now."

"Oh, that's only the start of it. Because even though you're all about the flame paint jobs and the sweet rims—stop laughing. I'm quite hip with the kids these days. Sweet rims are all the rage."

"I'm sorry," he managed. "Please continue."

She cleared her throat and stared him down. "As I was *saying*, even though you're all about the sweet rims, you'd never be caught dead rattling along in a gorgeous car with a piece of crap engine inside. Would you?"

"Of course not."

"Exactly. That's because you guys always focus on the car's engine first. You get in there and play with your nuts for hours—honestly, Ryan, if you're going to keep laughing, I'm not telling you the rest of my theory—and if anything is the least bit off, that baby stays in the garage. The killer body only matters if everything under the hood is already in working order."

He stopped laughing as suddenly as he'd started. Amy was beginning to make sense. He *did* enjoy a killer body. And as he was rapidly coming to learn, he enjoyed the inner workings even more.

"So for *you*, a nice exterior to run your hands over is useless unless there's a flawless engine to match. Which means, of course, that anytime you see a car guy out with his curvaceous Porsche, chances are he's already looked under the hood and given it his seal of approval. No one is more attuned to the whole package than a car guy." Amy nodded once, pleased with herself. It was still a working theory, but she'd had ample time to lie in bed—*alone*—lately, trying to figure it out. "Well? I see I've rendered you speechless with the depth of my wisdom."

"You've rendered me something," Ryan said, his expression difficult to read.

She thought for a moment that he might keep going, open up for once, but he gave a small shake of his head and checked his watch. "But we should probably get going. I have an itinerary I'm supposed to stick to." He shoved his hands deep in his pockets and continued walking.

"And you're really not going to give me a clue where we're going?" She rushed to keep up. "Not even to tell me if I'm wearing the right thing?"

He stopped and looked at her. *Really* looked at her—his gaze running over every square inch, leaving no thread of fabric unturned. *Undressing her with his eyes* seemed the most accurate phrase.

"You'll do," he said, once she stood stripped and naked and, if she was being honest, panting a little. If he was capable of starting her engines—pun intended—without even laying a finger on her, what would happen if he really tried?

Oh, man. If Ryan wasn't about to whisk her away on a date with another man, she'd... She'd, what, exactly? Attack him in the empty passageway? Sneak into his apartment in the middle of the night and lie in his bed, waiting and naked, until he came home?

Obviously her seduction-planning skills needed a bit of a tune-up.

"How'd you get recruited into all this anyway?" Amy asked. They bypassed the garage and went out to the employee lot. Ryan led her to a car she didn't recognize—understated, white, bland, a lot like her, actually. "Is that what Jake was talking to you about the other day at lunch?"

"Sort of." That wasn't much of an answer, but it was all he gave her to work with.

"And why are you driving this heap around?" she

continued as they both got in and he started the car. "Planning on taking us into another ditch today?"

This time, she got a reaction. He swiveled to stare at her, and even though he wasn't looking out the windshield, he still somehow managed to get them turned around and heading safely down the winding drive—a testament to his superior driving skills.

"Too soon?" she continued cheerfully. "I thought it might be, but I wanted to make sure."

"You could have just asked."

"Oh, okay. Ryan, are you still feeling a wee bit sensitive about crashing Mr. Montgomery's car into a ditch?"

"Yes. Yes, I am. Thank you for asking."

Unthinking, she dropped a hand to his thigh and gave it a squeeze, lingering long past the point of mere friendliness. There was a lot of strength in that thigh, power in the flex of his muscles under her fingertips. She was something of an expert on a man's quads. Half the reason she'd stuck with dance as long as she had was her obsession with the mesmerizing movements of a male ballet dancer's be-tighted lower half.

He looked down where her hand met his leg and then back up at her. She let go, her face hot.

"Don't feel bad on my account," she said, shaky from the contact. "That minor accident was the most excitement on four wheels I've ever had."

"It wasn't that exciting."

"To *you*, maybe. But I don't even speed."

"Ever?" Ryan glanced at her, a mischievous smile replacing his reserve, wiping away at least half a dozen years from his face. And was it her imagination, or were they suddenly moving faster than they had a minute ago? "No lead foot late at night when you're feeling sleepy? No joyrides when you were a teenager?"

"Of course not." Amy sat up, feigning shock. "I've always been a perfect daughter. A model pupil."

"Who also participated in underage drinking behind laser tag dumpsters."

She set a hand on the door to steady herself. Okay, they were *definitely* going faster now. "If you must know, I also skipped chemistry once to smoke pot with the grunge kids. Except I don't think I did it right, because I didn't feel the least bit funny afterwards, and even got an A on my Spanish test. But you can't fault me for trying—a girl needs *some* adventure to look back on with regret and longing."

"You want adventure?"

"Right now?" She looked nervously around. One of the many benefits of living at Montgomery Manor was the relative isolation. Not only did the Montgomerys have enough private acreage to own the view in a three-hundred-and-sixty-degree rotation, but the previous Mr. Montgomery had struck some kind of deal with the state that designated the surrounding land a wildlife preserve—even though there wasn't much in the way of wildlife *to* preserve. No one could build; no one could develop; no one ever just happened to be driving by.

The roadways transformed in front of her eyes from deserted paths of concrete to racecar tracks.

"Better say the word soon." Ryan was smiling. Beaming. Loving this. "I'm about to come up on the main road. Once I make that turn, it's nothing but slow sailing and a life not worth regretting."

"Do it," she breathed.

He cupped a hand over his ear and leaned close. "What's that? I'm not sure I heard you correctly."

"Let's see what this baby can do."

She shrieked as Ryan did some kind of insane maneuver with the handbrake. One second they were flying over the roadway; the next, they were spinning in a perfectly controlled arc and crunching the tires to a rubber-burning halt. Her stomach rose up and settled again, making her feel as though she were on a roller coaster.

Before she had time to do much more than admire the fact that he'd somehow turned the car around in less time than it took her to breathe, they were speeding off again, the rev of the engine building up and letting go in time to his movements on the clutch.

Ryan paused only long enough to look over and gauge Amy's reaction to the sudden blur of trees all around them. "Drive it like you stole it," he joked when it appeared she wasn't going to ask him to stop.

As they whipped over the familiar roadways, he didn't push the speedometer nearly as hard as he could have—not even close to as fast as his foot itched to go—but it was enough to remind him of everything he'd lost. He'd forgotten how incredible it felt to do this sober, not so much punching a clock as it was fulfilling some deep-seated, unnamed need to soar.

They flew over a small wooden bridge that ran over the actual Ransom Creek for which the town had been named, landing smoothly before turning at a sharp sixty-degree angle. Amy gasped next to him, and, with another careful turn of the wheel, he brought the car to a skidding halt.

"Wait—that's it?" Amy pressed her feet against the floor, as if she could will the car moving again. "You can't stop now. We barely got going."

He turned to study her, his heartbeat fast but steady, adrenaline bringing clarity to his thoughts. Racing always had that effect on him—stripped him of everyday nerves and worries, smoothed out his troubles so he could see them clearly, lying out flat like the road ahead of him.

And for the first time in a long time, he *could* see his troubles clearly. He also didn't particularly like what he found, obvious to the point of obscenity. His problem wasn't this place or the people in it.

The problem was *him*.

There was no doubt in his mind anymore. He had to get this life back. He *had* to. Driving was like oxygen to him, and he hadn't realized until this exact moment that he wasn't suffering from a blow to the pride or a loss of income or even loneliness here in Ransom Creek.

He was suffocating, clear and simple.

"A taste is all you get," he said, more for his own benefit than Amy's. "I normally do this kind of thing on a closed circuit and with safety gear on. I'm not taking any chances with you on board."

"Aww," she cooed. "That's so sweet and condescending."

Her laughter reeled him back in, ripping him from the past, dissolving the rosy glow of the future, plunging him back in the here and now. Before he knew what was happening, he leaned across the gap and captured her laughter with his lips. He couldn't help it—dizzy from the realization that he'd never be a normal man with normal desires, knowing that he'd do whatever it took to find a way out of here—he had to know what the kind of easy joy she had to offer tasted like.

Candy and grapes. She tastes like candy and smells like grapes. It was a combination he never knew was intoxicating, a rush of sensations that overpowered him and threatened to topple everything.

Unable to stop himself, he deepened the kiss, the high of the car ride wiping him of his inhibitions and reservations in one fell swoop. Capturing her bottom lip between his teeth, he forced his way in enough to stroke his tongue against hers, enjoying the soft, sweet texture as her mouth opened to let him in.

Her laughter turned to a sigh. Her sigh turned to a moan. And he found himself falling further and further into each progression until he realized his hands had somehow found their way around her.

He jumped back, mouth open, breath coming fast, his heartbeat jumpstarted in ways that no amount of stunt driving could ever manage.

Wrong. This is wrong, no matter how incredibly right it feels. What kind of a man dreamed of leaving one second and grounded himself in a woman the next? He was escorting Amy on a date with another man, for chrissakes. He'd been hired by their shared employer to spy on her in exchange for his golden ticket home. There were so many blurred lines here he got cross-eyed just thinking about them.

"Sorry," he muttered, staring at his lap to avoid the flushed look of surprise on her still-parted mouth. She was dazed and soft and in danger of getting kissed again. "We should probably get going. Jake is waiting for us."

"Jake?" Amy echoed. "Oh. Yeah. Jake."

Ryan braved a peek at her. She had a hand pressed to her lips, her eyes sparkling with some sentiment he couldn't unravel. But it didn't look like loathing—not that Amy could ever loathe anyone.

She offered him a weak smile. "We don't want to be late. For all his lazy airs, he *is* kind of a stickler for punctuality."

Ryan's head pounded as he pulled the car back onto the road, this time taking all the turns at a twenty-mile-an-hour pace that he controlled as carefully as he did his emotions.

"Is that what you see in him?" he asked, knowing as he did that the question was quite possibly the stupidest one to ever cross his lips.

"His punctuality?" Amy frowned and then quickly turned to the window. "Yes, Ryan. The most attractive thing about any man is his ability to be in the right place at the right time. The best love stories can be boiled down to nothing more than a case of impeccable timing."

He didn't ask the question that burned in his throat and in his mind: Did that mean he was too early?

Or am I much too late?

NINE

THE DAY WOULD have been vastly improved if someone had thought to bring candy.

Amy was a big believer that candy made any situation better. Oh, she knew there were some people who drowned their sorrows in alcohol, like Ryan. He might not like to talk much about his past, but you could tell, just by looking at him, that every day was a struggle not to give in to the strong pull of taking-the-edge-off.

A great many other excesses could be seen beckoning to the people she knew and loved. Her mom couldn't go a day without her rhododendrons. Jake was a big fan of mirrors and any reflective surface that caught the light. Evan and Lily needed each other in a way that made her feel the ache of only childhood in ways she never had before.

But her? She mostly wanted a huge chocolate bar. Maybe with nuts in it. Something fancy like macadamia nuts or pecans, though—not walnuts. Never walnuts. Walnuts were like a squirrel exhibit at the zoo. You know they're technically animals, and someone must care about them, but who really chooses squirrels over something cool like elephants or lemurs or penguins?

"Amy! Are you even listening to me?"

She sat up, startled out of her daydream and salivating more than was seemly for a public place. "Of course I am. That's fascinating. Absolutely fascinating."

Her mother clucked and settled more firmly into her beach chair. "You have no idea what I just said, do you?"

"Don't be silly," she murmured. She followed suit, wiggling her shorts-clad bottom into the sand to find a more comfortable position. Huge sunglasses hid most of the glare from the overhead sun and she fought a sleepy yawn. Even though the day was winding down and the spring air growing chilly, the Silver Sands Beach had a way of capturing the light and holding it close, reluctant to let it go without a fight. "You were telling me about that thing. The one you did. That one time. In that one place."

Her mom reached over and swatted her arm. "I was saying you should go over and play volleyball with the two young men who keep looking over here. I think they need a third."

That got her attention. She flipped her sunglasses up and peered around, disappointment settling alongside the growing hunger pangs in her stomach. Neither Jake nor Ryan was looking at her. They barely even remembered she was here.

"Are you kidding? They don't want me to play. They're having a showdown to prove who's worth more as a man. Give a guy some big white balls to play with, and all of a sudden he's twelve and showing off in the locker-room showers again."

Her mom also lifted off her sunglasses and leaned closer, an unmistakable purse to her lips. "Is that what they're doing?"

"Showing off?" *Um, yes.* A thousand times over, yes. Not only had Ryan jumped away from that kiss in the car as though she was some kind of sexual leper, but he'd pretty much taken over her date with Jake, leaving her with no chance of winning *anyone's* affections today.

It all started when Jake had settled into the front seat of the car while she and her mom wedged into the back. His snide comment of "This is the best you could do?" to Ryan became a heated discussion on how difficult it was to rent a luxury car in a town like theirs, and things had only escalated from there. It was now officially a pissing match—and both men were pointing straight into the wind and letting it all go.

Amy looked over to find that her mom's pursed lips were trained on her own head now. "Sweetie, they're not showing off over *you*, are they?"

"Please." Amy released a long scoffing noise that became a cough and then a throat gurgle and then possibly fluid down the wrong tube. "That's absurd."

"Amy Winifred Sanders."

"I didn't do anything! I could melt into the sand right now and neither one of them would notice or care."

She could be standing there naked and both men would probably throw her a towel and tell her to stop interrupting their game. She'd never felt less desirable in her entire life. How Ryan could kiss her like that only to blink, apologize and start talking about the weather was beyond her scope of imagination. She'd been ready to combust on the spot. Hell—she *still* was. Every time she started thinking about the way he'd just grabbed her and thrust his tongue into her mouth, taking control of her the same way he did a car, she felt her pulse pick up and her insides liquefy.

She tried fanning herself with her hand, but it only made things worse.

"Men only show off when they're fighting for a female's attention. It's the way of the entire animal kingdom." Her mom leaned closer, as if reading the hot-blooded desire Amy was trying so desperately to conceal. "This is not okay, young lady. You promise me right now there is nothing going on between you and Jake Montgomery."

Jake? *He* was who her mom was concerned about? "Don't worry. I wouldn't touch him with a ten-foot pole. He's been around the block so many times he's worn a path into the sidewalk."

"Then why are you so red?"

"It was bright out today. I'm probably sunburnt."

"This isn't a joking matter. You know I love that boy to death, but he is not the man for you. I'm pulling a maternal veto on this one." The ice in her mom's voice could have frozen the entire Atlantic, had she directed the words along the lapping blue waters instead of at Amy. "Promise me you won't have anything to do with him."

"It's not what you think—"

"Promise."

Amy didn't respond right away, even though she had nothing to lose from reassuring her mother. She might be enjoying spending time with Jake, glad to have him back in her life and showing an interest, but she wasn't about to start crying into her morning cereal over a man.

At least, not *that* one.

She lifted a hand to shield her eyes as she took in the pair of men standing a short distance away. Sometime in the past five minutes, they'd divested themselves of their shirts and decided to play a game that looked less like beach volleyball and more like let's see who can spike the ball harder into the other guy's face.

She bit her lower lip as she watched. It was an undeniable fact that beach sports made the most out of a pair of hard heads and harder bodies. Sure, she'd seen more than her share of the summer Olympics before, tuned in to the swimming and beach volleyball for a bit of eye candy before guiltily showing support for the ping-pong team, but she'd never personally known her oglees before.

Jake was tall and chiseled like a fine sandstone column. Beautiful in a godlike sort of way. Ryan was... *unf.* Ryan was one of those guys who didn't have a single inch of fat on him but still wasn't over-the-top muscular, both lean and bulky at the same time.

Strong. He looks strong.

"What about Ryan?" Her mom's gaze followed Amy's. "I always thought he was cute."

Yes, Mother. Cute. As if that word could possibly contain the overwhelming sensation that she'd like to lick the sand from his shoulders and never stop until she'd explored every last inch of his body.

"Ryan is...complicated."

"Complicated is good. Complicated keeps the mystery going."

Amy stared at her mother as if she were from a strange land—a land where parents urged their children to fall for men with enormous chips on their shoulders and confusingly hot-cold signals. A land where men went without shirts and drove fast cars and made swoony feelings congregate in unladylike places before unceremoniously tossing a girl aside.

"Besides," her mom continued, "you know John wouldn't have hired him if he wasn't a good person. John has always had a sense about these things."

To date, her mother was the only person in the world who dared call Mr. Montgomery by his first name. Even Serena had the disturbing habit of referring to him either by his title or as Big Man. To be fair, she called Evan her Little Man, so it might have been a family thing instead of an anatomical one.

God, she hoped so.

Amy got to her feet and brushed off the seat of her shorts. Her mom's hand stopped on her arm. "Where are you going?"

"To go stop their competition sometime before the sun goes down. If we don't eat soon, I'm going to have to start fishing for our dinner."

Her mom didn't let go. "Remember what I said, Amy. Jake is trouble. He's a good boy at heart, and we all know he's got a way with the ladies, but you have to remember that more than all that, he's..."

"Complicated?" Amy supplied.

Her mom swatted her on the bottom. "Don't you dare. Smartass."

"Hey, there. My mom and I were wondering if we should start gathering some of the dead, washed-up crabs on the beach to eat, or if maybe you have alternate dinner plans."

Ryan stopped in the middle of serving the ball and turned to face Amy. His arms fell to his sides at the sight of her, sleepy and glowing, a woman who'd been lolling in the sun for hours. Her loose-fitting shirt slipped off one shoulder; her hair was tousled, her skin radiant.

He blinked, hoping that maybe the way she affected him—like a sledgehammer to the gut—was a trick of the light, a side effect of the furious workout Jake had been subjecting him to since they set foot on the volleyball court. But when he opened his eyes again, there was no mistaking it.

He wanted to touch her skin, to feel her come to life beneath him. More than all the other things he longed for right now—a fast car, a fresh start, an ice cold beer—what he really wanted was *her*.

Shit. Something had to be done about that. If the kiss in the car was any indication, it obviously wasn't working anymore to try staying friendly but detached—and playing beach games with Jake while pretending he didn't feel each movement of Amy's eyes on his back wasn't fooling anyone. Least of all him.

"Hello?" She waved her hand, catching him staring. "Food? Crabs?"

"As delicious as rotting seafood sounds, I'm going to have to pass." He pushed his feelings aside, ignoring the overwhelming sensation that they were about to take over. *Work. Focus on work.* He did still technically have a job to do here. Chauffeur, spy, peon. He glanced over at Jake. "Amy and her mom are starving. Should I bring the car around?"

"Oh, no—you don't have to leave your game."

Amy placed a hand on his arm to still him. As overheated as he was from the one-on-one volleyball match he'd somehow gotten pulled into, her smooth palms felt delicious and cool. And incredible. *Incredible* definitely made an appearance on the list. "It looked like things were about to get interesting over here."

"Things have been interesting since the second we arrived." Jake leaned on the net, watching the pair of them through the hair that had fallen in his eyes. "Well, Ryan? What do you think? Are you ready to forfeit the game?"

That depended on which game they were talking about. "I could always go grab some takeout and bring it here, if you prefer. Sir."

"Stop acting like a deferential ass. No one here is treating you like a second-class citizen. I'll play you for it."

He narrowed his eyes, searching Jake's face for clues and coming up empty. Was this another one of those ulterior motive situations? Why was it so fucking hard to tell with the Montgomery men? And why did he keep trying?

"Play to twenty-one?" Jake asked. "Loser has to take Amy's mom and go fetch dinner. Or are you afraid of a little challenge?"

That settled it. Ryan didn't care what Jake's end goal was. Beating that bastard at anything was a temptation no man could withstand. "Oh, you're on, Montgomery. I'm going to enjoy slaughtering you a lot more than I should."

"Um, hello?" Amy waved her hand. "How come no one is asking me to throw my hat in the ring? I have arms and legs too. I can play volleyball and op-press womankind with my machismo just as well as both of you."

Guilt worked through him, ending in a warm flush. "I'm sorry. We've been neglecting you, haven't we?"

"Oh, I'm having a great time." And she really was. No work. Her mom nearby. Two men who might or might not have been fighting over her. A not-so-secret wish for the blond one to win. "But as much as I've enjoyed watching you leap around the sand without your shirts on, I think it's time I show you how this game is played."

"Are you going to take your shirt off too?" Jake asked hopefully.

She stuck her tongue out at him. "Very funny. All I need is for one of you gentlemen to step down and let me take your place, and this wager can get started."

Jake and Ryan exchanged looks of equal wariness, and she had to suppress a bubble of irritation from escaping her. They couldn't *stand* the idea of unlock-ing horns long enough to let her have a turn. She re-ally was the least common denominator here. "Oh, come on, you guys. You're being ridiculous. Let me play for you, Jake. I can totally win."

"I fight my own battles, sweetheart. You know that."

She turned to Ryan. "Well, Ryan? What do you think? I'm telling you—I'm really good at volleyball."

"You always say that. Remember the pinball fi-asco?"

"That machine was fixed!" she protested. "I think those soccer kids hacked the game or something. Is it possible to hack pinball?"

Jake looked back and forth between the two of them. "Soccer kids?"

"We played laser tag last month," Amy explained. "Ryan promised to help me win against a bunch of punk kids who hang out there every week. You remember the place on Hiawatha, right—the one with the arcade attached? It's still standing. Hasn't changed in over a decade."

Jake glanced at Ryan with a quirk in his brow. "Laser tag, huh?"

Ryan shrugged. "I tried to tell you."

She put her hands on her hips. "This is your last chance to restore my belief in the existence of decent men in this world. Either have enough faith in me to let me take your place, or singlehandedly crush the forward progression of the feminist movement. It's your choice."

Jake responded by looking off into the distance, gifting her with a glimpse of his perfect profile and a burning desire to throw the volleyball at his head. Ryan, on the other hand, relaxed into a reluctant smile and tossed her the ball. "I can't afford to have something like that on my conscience." He gave a slight bow. "I'd be honored if you'd take my place in the duel and show this cocky bastard how it's done."

She cried out in excitement and kissed him on the cheek—scratchy and warm, tasting of salty air and athletic sweat. *Oh, man.* Now she really wanted to lick the sand from his shoulders.

"I knew I could count on you to stand up for me," she said, keeping her tongue in place only with considerable restraint.

The beach and all its contents faded into the background as Ryan stood motionless, locking her in his gaze, trapping her with the gentle, almost painful plea she saw there. His finger came up and flicked her on the cheek. "Of course. No matter what else happens, I'll always have your back."

And that, right there, was the problem. She didn't want Ryan to have her back. She wanted him to take all of her.

She smacked the ball with her open palm and nodded once, firm and sharp. "Don't you worry, my friend. I've got this one."

Loser had to go take her mom and forage for supplies? Done. Jake was as good as demolished. She was going to win some alone time with Ryan if it killed her.

RYAN WATCHED AMY block one of Jake's hits for the third time in a row, and let loose a catcall. "Sorry," he said as an aside to Amy's mom, Linda, who sat next to him watching the game. "I can't seem to help myself. I've never been so happy to see a man lose in my life."

"The game's not over yet." Her eyes moved back and forth as she watched the ball move over the net. "I wouldn't start counting your chickens."

But Ryan felt fairly sure he could count all he wanted. Not only could Amy jump much higher than seemed possible for someone with mere human genes, but she kept up an almost constant stream of triumphant, cocky smack talk that had Jake missing easy hits and falling further behind.

And she was graceful—crazy graceful, sending perfect arcs of sand where she dived, her form im-

peccable as she leaped up and spiked. Sometimes, he
was even able to wrest his attention from her legs,
which flexed underneath her tiny jean shorts in a
mesmerizing dance of muscles and skin, to actually
watch the game.

But not often.

"Oh, nice one, sweetie!" Linda called. She looked
over and grinned, her smile so much like her daughter's it was obvious where Amy got her sunny disposition. "You're right. The outcome of this one is
pretty clear."

"I know," he said. "And now I feel bad. I let Amy
take my place, but I didn't think she could play, let
alone win. I thought for sure I was handing in a forfeit."

Linda's hand snaked over the top of the beach chair
and pressed his warmly. "Yes, but you still let her
have a chance. That was sweet."

Ryan coughed and looked away. Not many people accused him of being sweet, and he wasn't quite
sure what the appropriate response was. *No, I'm not?
Thank you? If you only knew my real motivations in
being here today?*

"Yeah, well. I'm already the fourth wheel. Stepping down to let her play was the least I could do."

They watched as Jake made a spectacular dive
that, unfortunately for him, resulted in a face full of
sand and another lost point.

"Ooh, that one is going to hurt tomorrow. Sand
burn."

Ryan just laughed.

"And you're hardly the fourth wheel. Unless that
young man over there recently acquired an ability

to think about anyone but himself, I'm guessing this entire day was your idea. Not his."

Ryan was startled by her blunt approach, though he probably shouldn't have been. The Sanders women also shared a way of catching a man off guard no matter how many walls he might try to build around him. Casting her a sidelong look, he evaded the obvious with a slowly drawled "What do you mean?"

"I mean thank you," she said simply. "I've enjoyed today very much, and so has Amy. It's good for her to get out and have fun like this. She's too cooped up, too involved in those kids' lives. I sometimes think…"

"She does seem to have a thing for the Montgomerys, doesn't she?" Ryan picked up where Linda left off. He saw Jake slap Amy a high five and glowered. "All of them."

"They're a difficult family to shake," Linda agreed. "And I should know. I stopped in Ransom Creek one day when I was eighteen, bound for New York to make my fortune. I think I was hungry or thirsty or maybe I needed to stretch my legs. I'm not quite sure. All I remember is that I met John in line at the grocery store and haven't left since."

That sounded ominous. And typical of this place.

"Can I ask you a favor?" Linda continued.

"Sure." He took a long pull from the bottle of water at his feet while he waited for her to gather her thoughts. Unlike her daughter, Linda had a way of moving slowly and methodically, as if each action was thought out ahead of time. He wondered how much of that was her condition and how much was simply her.

"You're a good kid. You wouldn't want anything to happen to her."

He didn't like where this conversation was going. He glanced over to where Amy was getting ready to serve the ball, her head held high, her determination clear. "Of course I don't. I can't imagine anyone wishing her harm."

A noncommittal sound escaped Linda's lips as she also directed her gaze at the roped-off volleyball court. "It'd mean a lot to me if you could make sure nothing happens between her and Jake. Romance-wise, I mean."

He shot up out of his chair. That was it. That was the absolute end of his patience with this topic of conversation. In the back of his mind somewhere, he knew he was taking his frustrations out on the wrong person, but the irritation in his voice was unmistakable. "If you're all so worried about whether or not she dates the guy, why don't you talk to her about it like adults? At what point did it become the job of the chauffeur to sneak around and meddle in other people's personal lives?"

His irritation didn't take. Linda's eyes grew a little rounder, but she was unmoved as she asked, "Did John ask you to step in?"

"*Ask* isn't the right word."

She had the audacity to smile. "I should have known he'd take care of things. I don't know why I ever questioned it." She placed her hand on Ryan's arm. "Don't take it the wrong way, hon. I just thought you might have a few reasons of your own for wanting to steer her away from that boy."

He had a hold on enough of his anger to recognize her meaning. *Jesus.* He'd thought he'd been doing a fairly good job of hiding his feelings, but if this woman could see right through him after a few hours at the beach, he was obviously deluding himself. He had it bad.

Since there didn't seem any way to deny what was so patently obvious, he just sighed and reconciled himself to playing the part of the fool. The dancing puppet fool.

"Regardless of where I fit into things," he said tightly, "I still don't see why you're all so determined to keep the two of them apart, but refuse to actually *do* anything about it."

Linda watched the pair in silence. Ryan looked too, taking in the sight of Amy and Jake arguing over whether or not the ball had hit the line on his side. They were in each other's faces, angry and voluble, about two insults away from throwing down and duking it out like a pair of bickering children in the sand.

"Don't you?" Linda asked, smiling softly at them. She patted Ryan's arm again. "I'd have thought it was fairly obvious by now."

"I STILL CAN'T believe you won." Ryan shook his head as he led Amy along the water's edge. The sky and the sea spread out before them like both sides of paradise, the constant roaring in his ears only partially due to the surf drawing back out into the ocean. "I thought for sure I was going to end up on dinner duty."

In fact, he'd been halfway counting on it. What might have been a dream come true in another lifetime—a romantic walk on the beach with Amy by his side—had taken on nightmarish proportions as he struggled to keep his hands in his pockets and his heart in his chest.

"And I still can't believe you doubted me. It's one thing to go up against a guy like Alex with laser guns. But Jake is easy to beat at just about everything. All you have to do is make him lose his cool. While he's in control of himself, no one stands a chance. But the moment it slips?"

"I'll have to remember that."

She laughed and pinched his arm. "Don't you dare. He's been nice today."

He grunted his negative response.

"Why so hostile? He likes you. I can tell."

Right. *Like* wasn't what Jake Montgomery felt for him. Curiosity, maybe. Competition, sure. But anything even resembling friendship? Please. Ryan didn't have friends. Especially not rich, overprivileged playboy ones.

"He needs me. It's not the same thing." Unable to help himself or the feeling of tight jealousy that solidified his core, he asked, "What do you see in that guy, anyway? Besides the obvious?"

"Why is everyone suddenly so judgmental about my relationship with a man I've known my whole life?" She kicked at the sand and promptly spit out a mouthful of collateral damage. "First my mom, now you…"

He looked over, trying to gauge her mood, getting nothing but exasperation from the downward curl of her lips. "What exactly did your mom say to you?"

"Oh, not much. She only tried to extract a blood oath that I wouldn't throw myself at him, like I'm lining up to be some notch on his bedpost—which she knows I'd never do. I don't think it's fair everyone assumes that just because I'm a girl and he's a guy, there has to be more to us than friendship. Maybe Jake needs someone to believe in him, to show him that the bevvies of women falling at his feet is a sad place to plant his sense of self-worth. Maybe I'm trying to be *nice*."

"You're just friends?"

Amy watched as Ryan's brow wrinkled and un-wrinkled again, unsure how to proceed from here in her one-sided courtship. The sun was low on the horizon, hanging heavily in the sky, and the splash of the waves tickled at their feet. With any other man, it would have been a perfect time to enjoy a *From Here to Eternity* moment. With any other man, though, the moment would have already made the first move.

She stopped and watched the waves, wriggling her toes deeper and deeper in the sand until they grew numb, before she felt brave enough to meet his eyes and force the words that needed to be said. He was watching her with his usual guarded expression, but for the first time, she didn't let that deter her. "I'm not interested in him, Ryan. Not like that. I have feelings for someone else."

The implication behind her statement—that *he* was that someone—sat heavily between them, a pile of waste neither one of them wanted to deal with. Even though Amy itched to say something more, she forced her tongue to lie still, biting on the tip until it bled. If Ryan didn't want her, he could at least have the balls to say so.

She could tell when he finally found what he wanted to say by the lump that moved down his throat, and tears pricked at her eyes at the sight of it. She almost wished she could yank her confession back, but it was too late for that. Her heart was already on the line.

"I shouldn't have kissed you in the car. I'm sorry about that."

He sounded so sad she couldn't help but reassure him. "It's okay. I liked it. I liked it a lot, actually."

He actually groaned—the kind of groan that signaled physical pain, as if he couldn't bear to think about it again. The best freaking kiss of her life, and he was acting like she'd stuck a shiv in his gut. "I still shouldn't have done it. Not that it wasn't nice, of course. It was nice."

Yeah. She licked her lips, as if she could recapture the sensation of his mouth on hers again. *Nice.*

"It's just that I'm leaving."

The chill in her toes worked up through her spine, causing her to break out in goose bumps. "You're what?"

"I'm leaving Ransom Creek. Have I ever told you that?" He looked away, casting his glance out over the ocean like a lure. "I never intended to be here for so long—it's always been my plan to get back to stunt work as soon as I can find a way to clear my record. A DUI is pretty hard to get around when you're a professional driver, but I'm trying."

"Oh," she said, unsure what else to offer.

"It's not so bad." This time, he really did cast over the ocean, picking up a rock and tossing it so that it skimmed over the waves. Once, twice, three times before plunging into the murky depths. "It looks like all the trying is about to pay off. *That's* why I shouldn't have kissed you. Not because I didn't want to, but because I probably won't be around long enough to do it again."

His meaning sank in almost immediately. Ryan wasn't planning on becoming a permanent fixture in Ransom Creek, and was therefore unwilling to become one in her life. It made sense, explained why he kept himself so distant from the rest of the staff, gave her a way to preserve a solid sense of confidence in herself.

And there was no mistaking that it was a considerate thing for a man to do for a change. He was like the anti-one-night-stand.

But that didn't make it hurt any less.

She caught his eye and gentled her wobbling mouth into a smile. "How about I make a deal with you?"

"What?" He turned a startled look her way. "What kind of a deal?"

She had to laugh despite the fact that he'd just leveled her with his confession, leaving her flailing for a foothold. "It's not a bad deal, I promise. I know I seem like the clingy, needy type, but I'm a lot stronger than most people give me credit for. Kissing and running away isn't going to kill me."

He grunted in reply.

"So I'll give you that one in the car free of charge," she continued. If noncommittal man sounds were all she was going to get out of him right now, she'd take them. "But the next time you kiss me, I won't be so easy to push aside. Next time, I'm going to assume you mean it."

A tiny smile ghosted over his mouth. "That seems fair."

"Of course it is." *More* than fair, if you asked her.

"I'm exceptional at negotiating fair deal contracts with difficult people. One more bite of peas and you can have a cookie. Go down for a nap quietly and I'll do the duck waddle race again."

"Why do I feel like there's an insult somewhere in there?"

She linked arms with him in a show of solidarity, as if to prove to them both that they could do this. Acquaintances, coworkers, friends. How hard could it possibly be?

But she made the mistake of looking into his eyes and balked at the emotion she saw reflected there— emotion that seemed to want to throw her to the beach and ravish her in front of the seagulls. And the flex of his arm against hers proved he could do it, if only he'd give himself the chance.

"It's not an insult." She forced a smile. "Just an observation."

She also observed her mom and Jake moving up the beach, several large bags of food in hand. She couldn't decide whether she was more grateful or disappointed to see them heading their way.

Not that it mattered. Gratefulness and disappointment wouldn't do anything to move the man walking next to her. So they wouldn't move her either.

TEN

"I HEARD YOU drove bitch on a date with Jake and Amy yesterday. That must've been one fun ride."

It was a good thing the date between Jake and Amy had been less of a romantic interlude for two and more of a family outing, or those two sentences would have had Ryan throwing a punch that wasn't deserved—and probably receiving one that was. As it was, he could only muster up enough emotion to grimace at Alex, dressed head to toe in black, as he marched across the pavement to join him.

The last thing he needed right now was to be reminded of yesterday's torments. Ryan had actually looked Amy in the eye and said *thanks but no thanks.* He'd kissed her and torn himself away, had the audacity to tell her to her face that what she had to offer wasn't nearly as good as the promise of his career again.

Grimacing was all he had left.

He and Alex stood outside Montluxe, the historic Hartford building that served as the prototype for the highest-end chain of Montgomery hotels, as well as the office home base. Quite a few days of the week found Ryan sitting by the marble posts and potted palms out front, waiting for his next command—or, if the stay was a lengthy one—chatting underground with the valet parking staff. They sometimes even let him park a few of the cars if things got busy.

"What's this?" Ryan cast an exaggerated look around in hopes of deflecting some of the attention from himself. "They let you off your chain today? Living it up in the big city?"

"Very funny." Alex nodded up to the top floor of the hotel—lucky thirteen. Unlike the rest of their facilities, the Montluxe line was all about exclusivity. No site was taller than thirteen floors and there was rarely a room to spare without a six-month's advance reservation. Prestige paid well. "There's a VIP meeting today. No expense spared. All I'm supposed to do is stand here and look pretty—which is a hell of a lot more than I can say for you. What's with the long face?"

"I drove bitch for Jake and Amy yesterday."

Alex barked out a laugh. "Touché. What happened?"

Ryan had no idea how to respond to that. Yesterday had to have been one of the best days he'd had in a long time—and also one of the worst. The highs of that wind-whipping drive over the Montgomery roads had been demolished by the lows of breaking a woman's heart. The joy in getting that much closer to what he wanted was sullied by the realization that he'd never kiss Amy like that again.

And to top it all off, guilt gnawed endlessly at his stomach, smelling of a rat.

"Nothing happened. I drove to the beach. There was sand and food and volleyball. The usual."

"You have an odd definition of usual."

His glance was sharp. "What's that supposed to mean?"

"Nothing, man. I'm trying to pass the time. You're in serious need of a day off. When was the last time you did something fun?"

"I just spent almost a whole day at the beach."

"Okay, fine. When was the last time you did someone fun?"

Ryan refused to answer that question on the grounds that it was irrelevant and depressing. Nodding up at the hotel, he asked, "Who's the VIP, anyway? Someone I'd know?"

"Probably. It's a big-shot Hollywood type. I didn't catch the name. Small dude. Pointy shoes. No hair—not even eyebrows."

Already strung on edge, Ryan's nerves took a severe turn for the frayed. "Are you serious? Is his name Len?"

"Maybe? I think they might be in negotiations for a movie location or something." Alex shrugged. "Like I said, it's not my business to know. I'm only here to smile and wave—or, you know, frown and look menacing. Which is basically the same thing to me."

If only Ryan's job were that simple. Standing around looking pissed off seemed to be his default mode lately—and the idea that Len Brigand, one of the most influential producers in Hollywood, was sitting upstairs with Mr. Montgomery right now only set him off even more. So Mr. Montgomery hadn't been bluffing. He really did have the right connections to hold up his end of the bargain.

And Ryan had officially held up his end in return. He couldn't stop hearing Amy's words from yesterday, filling him with hope before leaving him flat. *I'm not interested in him, Ryan. Not like that. I have feelings for someone else.*

That was pretty much all the proof he needed, wasn't it? His obligation to Mr. Montgomery was filled. There was no reason he couldn't ride up those elevators right this second and demand his payment. Intentionally or not, he'd officially pushed Jake out of the picture.

But at what cost?

"You know that guy or something? You look like he's about to come out that door and steal your soul."

That was a strangely apt way to put it. Ryan leaned on the top of the car, wincing as the hot metal singed his arms. "Can I ask you something?"

"You can ask, but that doesn't mean I can answer." Alex's tone left no room for doubt. He wasn't bragging or showing off—not wearing the cocky fool's cap that fit Jake so well. Just being honest. Not even torture would extract all of Alex's secrets.

Ryan tried anyway. "What kind of influence does Mr. Montgomery have on you to keep you working for him?"

The flash that took Alex from friend to foe and back again was so brief Ryan might have missed it, had he not been paying attention. But he *was*, and he knew a deep and sudden fear for his safety and the safety of everyone in a one-mile radius. It was a feeling he remembered having on a movie set once where he'd had to work around a male lion. The animal's handler had warned them that for some people, there was an evolutionary reaction to a lion's roar—that the simple sound of his rage would trigger a flight or fight response and mimic the physical sensations of extreme danger.

Ryan had been one of the unlucky few. Every time that damn animal had roared—which, after three days of shooting, had been difficult to count—he'd felt the urge to point his car in the opposite direction and hit the gas.

Alex's silence felt a lot like that.

"So you've drunk the Kool-Aid, huh?" Alex eventually said.

"What?"

"You gonna be another conspiracy theorist? Been talking to Katie?"

"Mr. Montgomery's assistant?" Ryan frowned. "What does she have to do with anything?"

Some of the sensation of danger ebbed away, and Ryan could only assume Alex was taking back his roar.

"You have no idea what I'm talking about, do you?" Alex sighed and ran a hand over his shorn head. "I don't want you bothering Katie with this, but she's got a working theory—mind, she's got paranoid theories on everything from sex slavery to the dairy industry, so she's hardly a reliable source—but she seems to think that Mr. Montgomery only hires people to work in his home if he can blackmail them into complete subservience."

No surprise there. Mr. Montgomery had admitted as much that day in his office.

"Well, of anyone, she'd know, wouldn't she?" Ryan asked. "She has access to all the personnel files—and her dad's been working for Mr. Montgomery longer than anyone."

Alex's level stare did much to set Ryan's adrenaline going again. "I'm not saying there isn't *some* truth to the idea. But I'm not saying there is, either."

Which, in Ryan's experience, pretty much guaranteed the second one. "At least tell me this. If it was possible for you to leave tomorrow and go back to the life you used to have, would you do it?"

Alex held his stare. "Yes. I would. Without question or a single backward glance. Would you?"

Ryan opened his mouth to offer a vehement *yes*. All he wanted in this world was to recapture the feeling he'd had in the rental car with Amy—the sensation that all of life's weights meant nothing, that not even gravity could hold him down. That goal was everything he'd held out for and held on to for longer than he cared to recognize.

But a large part of him balked at the thought of leaving like this. Leaving like this would mean he'd been nothing more than Mr. Montgomery's tool all along. Leaving like this would mean letting Amy go on thinking the best of these people—the best of *him*—when it was the last thing any of them deserved.

He closed his mouth again, unable to reply.

Alex laughed, a deep, rumbling sound with no humor in it. "He's finally got you snared, huh? I wasn't sure he could do it. I should have known better than to doubt that man."

Ryan's body grew cold. It wasn't possible. Yes, Mr. Montgomery had the capability to manipulate his career, but there was no way he could manipulate his feelings. He couldn't control Ryan's desires.

Alex seemed to disagree. "I'll give Katie this much—Mr. Montgomery's machinations run deeper than most of us give him credit for. You think that Hollywood man upstairs is here to free you? Think again, my friend. Mr. Montgomery has you exactly where he wants you. And *free* doesn't exist anywhere in the vicinity."

Ryan could only stare at him, but Alex quirked a smile and made the motion of a zipper over his lips.

"And that's the *last* I'm saying on the subject."

AMY PULLED OPEN the nursery door to find Ryan pacing in the hallway, looking as though he might enjoy punching a few holes in the walls. She wasn't sure *why* physical damage appealed so strongly to the injured male psyche—or what had caused him to appear at the nursery door in such a mood—but she knew the only way to counteract it was with tiny adorable humans.

"Ryan!" she called cheerfully as she ushered him inside. "Just the man I wanted to see. I'm about to take the twins outside for a walk, and I could use a helping hand. I don't suppose you were hanging around out there on the off chance that I'd need your services?"

She fully expected the horrified look that flashed over his face at her query—a terror directed almost entirely at the two small beings currently trying to shove a plastic spatula into a childproof covered electrical outlet. But she didn't expect it to dissipate as quickly as it came.

"Sure." He shrugged. "That sounds like fun."

Amy placed a hand over her heart in mock horror. "I swear, if you're about to tell me you adore children, there's a good chance I'm going to draw your name in my diary with heart doodles tonight. It's right up there with my robust men and tiny dogs fetish."

She regretted the words the moment they crossed her lips. *Chill, Amy. You already offered. He already declined. Let's not make a fool of ourselves here.*

"I don't dislike kids." He shuffled from one foot to the other, sharing her discomfort. "But I don't have much experience with them. There weren't a lot of free-range children running around the movie sets. At least not the kinds of movies I worked on."

"It's not so hard. You just have to imagine living in a world where you want everything you see and you're denied at least nine-tenths of it. Then you can imagine what it's like being two years old."

Ryan swallowed so heavily his Adam's apple bobbed. "You're right. That's not very hard at all."

Ignoring the rush of heat that worked through her at his words, she went to the closet and gathered up an armload of sweaters. Chances were they'd all be running so hard over the fields trying to keep one another alive they wouldn't need outerwear, but Serena had a big fear of the elements. After her CPR certification, Amy'd had to take a test on bizarre apocalyptic-like scenarios, like what you should do if you got trapped in a lightning storm. Apparently, you bent over and let it strike your butt. All that extra fat helped defray the electrical impulses from entering your brain.

"You're the official sweater holder." She handed him the stack and informed the twins that it was time for their walk. To put on a good show, she always strapped them into a stroller and set out along the formal garden path out behind the house, but the containment never lasted very long. The lines of brightly colored flowers so painstakingly planted and maintained by Philip and his crew suffered for her negligence, but no one had called her out on it. Not yet, anyway.

"Aren't they going to run away?" Ryan asked anxiously once they were out of sight of the house and strolling under a white marble gazebo that seemed to add a funereal air to the otherwise gorgeous hillside. He hated to undermine Amy's authority in this domain, but he wasn't sure even she could be forgiven for letting one of the Montgomery children fall down a well. "I think there are like eight creeks around here."

A flash of Amy's mischievous smile caught him by surprise. Without a word, she stuck a finger in either side of her mouth and let out a whistle so loud several birds in the trees took flight.

Both children fell to the ground and started rolling, their giggles filling the silence left by the end of Amy's piercing shriek.

"What are they doing?"

She laughed and fell to the ground. "Stop, drop and roll. Not the most creative of all my devices, but it does the trick. Get down. You have to do it with them or they'll think I just made it up."

He dropped carefully to a squat, eyeing the muddied ground askance. "You *did* just make it up."

She shared none of his concerns, landing on her side and rolling in the direction of the twins. Her tank top lifted where it met the band of her jeans, showcasing the soft, undulating surface of a body that demanded he obey its every desire. She stopped on the second roll, propping herself up with one elbow. "Do I question your superiority in all things mechanical?"

"Fine." He grumbled, but he did it good-naturedly. He rolled around a few times, unable to help himself from following closely in Amy's wake, her hair leaving a tempting trail of sunny gold for him to follow.

Ryan would swear later that it was an accident. There was no way he would have intentionally rolled on top of Amy in the middle of an open field with impressionable children within arm's reach. He never would have dared to pin her body underneath his, flush with laughter and exercise and fun—all those things that weren't sex but could easily become it. He definitely would have stopped himself before he dropped his lips to hers for a brief, fleeting kiss.

The touch of their mouths was barely more than a whisper. Could practically be ruled an accident. Might have never happened at all.

Except it had.

Amy lay perfectly still, blinking up at him with neither pleasure nor hatred in her eyes. It wasn't indifference either. It looked like…relief.

"Oh, thank God. I'm so glad you caved first."

Ryan didn't have a chance to think about what that comment meant before Amy's arms wound around his neck and pulled his head close. When their lips made contact for a second time, her mouth was open and willing, her tongue waiting. *This* kiss was no accident, and there was no way to pretend it hadn't happened. The press of her mouth seared him. It shook him. It made him forget every goddamn thing in the world except how much he wanted this woman to be his.

He groaned and gave himself over to the sensation of Amy pinned underneath him, lazy as he explored her mouth with his tongue, then urgent when he moved down to nip at the corner of her mouth and tug at her lower lip with his teeth. The silken pull of her mouth was intoxicating, filling him with a crazed kind of longing that made him want to howl. He moaned instead, and the way she writhed under him at the sound of it acted on his body almost immediately.

He was hard and straining for more, throwing every piece of caution and common sense to the wind, and he didn't even care. For the moment, they were two people alone in the world. There was no Jake. No Montgomery Manor. No twins.

"Wait." He pulled back and looked around, startled. "Where are the kids?"

"Oh, shit!" Amy sat up and tugged at her shirt, which had twisted around her midsection, revealing soft slopes and the perfect indentation of her belly button. "We lost them. I must be the worst nanny on the face of the planet."

It turned out their worries were unfounded. The twins had found a patch of daisies and planted themselves in the middle, ripping the tops off and giggling at the empty stems left behind. Their apparent safety didn't stop Amy from scrambling to her feet and hurrying over, kissing them both with a fervor that would have been more in place had they been found dangling over a cliff's edge.

Ryan joined them more slowly, taking his time with each forward movement of his legs, his erection still very much a presence. Issues of careless childrearing aside, that had been a...*kiss*. The kind that changed a man. The kind that changed everything.

"I'm sorry," he said softly as he approached. "That wasn't my intention in seeking you out today."

She tossed him an innocent look, complete with batted eyelashes. "You mean you didn't lure me outside using your powers of kindness to children with the sole aim of seducing me?"

He opened his mouth and closed it again. Seduction had been the last thing on his mind. What he really came out here to do was come clean. About her mom's request, about Mr. Montgomery's deal, about all the maneuvers being made behind her back.

It was what he should have done from the start.

"Don't look so frightened." She lifted a hand to cup the side of his face. Her fingers were light where they fluttered against his jaw. "I know you're not planning on staying in Ransom Creek on a permanent basis. I don't intend to get in the way of that."

"Amy, there's something I need to tell you."

Her hand dropped as if scalded by the touch, by the fire in his veins and the brimstone on his skin. "That sounds an awful lot like you're going to reject me again. Would it help if we pretended it never happened? We can blame the boobs, if that helps."

His gaze flew to her chest, startled. "What?"

"In times of trouble, I find they provide an excellent excuse. You were rolling. All of a sudden they were right there under you, and your body took over. It was clearly the boobs' fault."

He wanted to protest, to tell her that kissing her fulfilled a longing he suspected had only a small something to do with her body, but this seemed safer. She was giving him an out, a—*ahem*—soft place to land.

"I think you might be underestimating the rest of your charms," he said, though he took a moment longer before returning his gaze about a foot north. Her shirt was askew and her breathing still heavy, leaving his unsated needs even more unsated than they already were. "What else do you blame them for, if you don't mind my asking?"

"Oh, just about everything. Poor decision-making when it comes to men. An inability to shop for bras at discount stores. My questionable success as a ballerina."

He stopped at that last one. "Really?"

Her smile grew strained and her eyes shuttered. It was one of the few times he'd ever caught a glimpse of her other side—the side that hid things, the side that hurt. He wondered how deep it went, how far in she'd let him come.

"Well, I told you I just use the boobs as an excuse. I could have gotten breast reduction surgery, like some of the other girls, but the truth is that I was never all that good." Her smile stretched even tighter. "But don't tell anyone I admitted that out loud. When I'm an old woman, I plan to look back at my dancing days through rose-colored glasses and have twenty-seven grandchildren dandling on my knee, all of them begging me to tell them more about my famous past."

He knew it was backtracking, but the resolve he'd mustered up on the way to the nursery fled at the sight of that tight smile. He was beginning to see why everyone was so hesitant to place the unpleasant conversations of the world on her doorstep. There was something about being around Amy that brought out an inherent protective urge in people. He'd do anything to keep her from getting hurt.

"Twenty-seven grandkids seems a bit like overkill," he said. "Aren't we supposed to be collectively reducing the world's population?"

Her sunny expression returned. "I happen to be exceptionally fond of children who aren't my own." She swooped down and blew slobbery kisses on both of the twins' cheeks. "How do you know I won't adopt all of them?"

"You won't." Ryan wasn't the type of man to cast the women he found attractive into a maternal role, but there was no doubt in his mind that Amy would someday find herself rolling around in the grass for tiny humans she created herself. At least, she would if there was any justice in this world. "Actually, that's kind of what I wanted to talk to you about today."

Amy's eyes flew open. "You want to talk to me about adoption?"

"Well, no."

She ignored him with a gurgle of mirth. "Is this where you tell me that you're secretly Mr. Montgomery's love child, and that you were adopted out at a young age? Is that why he trusts you to take care of his beloved cars?"

Ryan's heart almost stopped.

There were precious few moments in a man's life when clarity came easily. He'd done enough soul-searching in the darkness of night to know that introspection couldn't untangle the threads of the past, that poor decisions made and consequences accepted were a muddled blur that rarely moved into focus.

This was not one of those times. The truth struck him with such sudden, blinding intensity that he almost reeled with the force of it. Mr. Montgomery being determined to keep Jake and Amy apart at any cost. Linda Sanders asking him to step in to do the same. The almost sibling-rivalry-like arguments that broke out whenever the two of them were in the same room together.

He gripped Amy's shoulders and turned her to face him. He searched for clues, for signs that he could be wrong—or right—but all he saw was the breathtaking, heart-wrenching smile of a woman he desperately wanted to kiss again.

"What is it?" she asked, losing some of her smile. "Why are you looking at me like that?"

"*Does* Mr. Montgomery have any secret love children?"

Instead of causing her to pale or swoon or cry out in anger, Amy laughed. "Oh, geez. Not you too, Ryan. I swear, if I had a dollar for every time someone asked me if he and my mom had a little something going on behind closed doors…well, I'm not very good at math, but I wouldn't be driving my Rabbit, that's for sure."

Relief beckoned from behind a locked gate. "So you *do* know who your father is?"

"Well…no." Amy was starting to get a little frightened by the way Ryan was looking at her. Gone was the playful kissing face she wanted to smoosh between her hands. Nowhere in sight was the aloof chauffeur she'd come to recognize. He looked almost like a stranger. Almost as if he wanted to cry. "I mean, I couldn't give you a name and an address to go hunt him down, but I know *of* him. My mom fell in love at eighteen. She fell out of love at nineteen. I happened somewhere in the middle."

"Oh." Ryan's shoulders sagged. "That's a relief. For a second, I thought..."

"Yes?" she asked, even though she already knew the answer. "What did you think? Explain it to me."

"I'm sure you can guess. Your mom working all those years as part of the family. You being raised alongside the Montgomery kids. How much Mr. Montgomery looks after you."

"He looks after everyone." He wasn't what anyone would term a *warm* man, but Amy knew where her loyalties would always lie. Mr. Montgomery had earned them, and she intended to repay in full. "That's just how he is. It's called being compassionate."

"I wonder."

She didn't much care for the suspicious deepening in Ryan's eyes. "*What* do you wonder?"

"It's just...are you absolutely sure that story of your mom's isn't some kind of cover-up? You said it yourself—your mom wanted a blood oath that you wouldn't date Jake. Doesn't that make you even a little suspicious?"

"Well, it does *now*." She eyed him askance. "Why do I get the feeling you're not telling me everything?"

"Because I'm not."

Amy paused only long enough to pick another bunch of daisies and dump them unceremoniously on the twins' laps. Thank goodness flower beheading held so much toddler appeal.

"Out with it," she commanded. "You're starting to scare me."

"What I have to say isn't nice. Or pretty."

"Contrary to how it appears, a lot of things about my life aren't nice or pretty. I won't wilt."

He sighed, looking very much as though he didn't believe her. "The other day, at the beach, your mom asked me to, uh, keep an eye on you and Jake."

"She did, huh?" Why was that not surprising? God forbid the woman just let things sit. God forbid she let Amy decide on her own life path.

"She did." Ryan nodded and then frowned. "And she's not the only one. The day after the car accident, when Mr. Montgomery called me into his office, he made me...well, let's just call it a deal I couldn't refuse."

"A *what?*"

Ryan passed a hand over his eyes. "A deal. He told me I could keep my job, but only on one condition. I was assigned to be your watchdog. It was very important to him that the two of you didn't, you know, take things to the next level. The irreversible level. The unthinkable level between two people who might possibly share a common genetic code."

"I..." Amy stopped. And blinked. If they weren't standing in a field of daisies under the bright sun, with no one around but a pair of toddlers who were definitely going to need a bath this afternoon, she'd have suspected this was some kind of elaborate prank. Alex and Holly and maybe Katie and a few of the grounds crew members would pop out with a video camera and a YouTube channel set up specifically for her. "Are you telling me he asked you to stop me from dating Jake because he's actually my half brother? And you *agreed?*"

Oh, no. No, no, no. She'd seen *Star Wars.* She knew the earthshaking revelation of the kiss Luke and Leia had shared, remembered the nausea of surprise and too much artificial butter flavoring on her popcorn. Oh, God. She was going to throw up.

"Ryan? Why aren't you saying anything? I'm freaking out over here." She flapped her hands as if to prove it. This was one step past deer-in-the-headlights. She'd gone straight for deer-about-to-pass-out-on-the-side-of-the-road. "And please take that worm out of Evan's mouth. No, Evan. Icky. Blech. Poison. Oh, but did you know they don't have any eyes? And they have five hearts. One, two, three, four, five. Like your fingers! Don't look at me like that, Ryan. I'm not being hysterical. I'm being educational."

He blinked at her. "He can eat the worm. It won't kill him."

She released a laugh-sob and shook her head. "He might choke. I'm not going to pass out or start screaming or anything. Please just grab it from him and set it free somewhere safe. Then we can talk."

Watching Ryan try to extract the worm from Evan was ordinary and endearing enough to bring her some measure of calm. He squatted down to the boy's level and explained how the creature had a life waiting for it deep in the cool, damp earth—much like he'd talk to any rational human being, patient and kind. So of course Evan promptly shoved the worm into his mouth and refused to open it up again, his cheeks puffed out and his eyes watering as the worm presumably made a home of his tongue.

"Evan Hanover Montgomery, if you don't let Mr.

Worm out of your mouth right this instant, you have to take two naps today." She paused. "No. Five. Five naps. One for each of his hearts."

Lily cast stricken eyes her way. That wasn't a punishment either one of them took very lightly. When it was clear Amy meant business, she took a commanding little step and put her hand out to her brother's mouth. "Pwease."

Without dropping eye contact with her, Evan opened his mouth to allow the worm—saliva and dirt included—to fall from his lips and into his sister's waiting palm. At which time she promptly presented it to Ryan, triumphant.

"Take it," Amy whispered when he hesitated.

"I miss my cars" was all he said as he accepted the wriggling creature and deposited it under a rock a few steps away. He returned to stand over them all, hands on hips, clearly done with his stint in the manny role. But once again, he surprised her. "Okay, you two. Listen up. Amy and I are going to sit right here. Your job is to find us as many rocks as you can and put them in a pile. Do not—I repeat, *do not*—put them in your mouth. Rocks. Pile. No eating. Go."

It did the trick. They set straight to work.

Ryan settled onto the ground next to Amy, trying to gauge her mood. She sat cross-legged and stiff-backed, her posture impeccable. It was difficult to tell if her erect position was the result of her years of dance training or outraged tension. If he had to guess, he'd say it was the second one.

"How bad is it?" he asked once he gathered up the nerve to speak.

"Well, it's not *good*. I haven't slept with him or

anything, if that's what you're asking. Still incest-free since nineteen eighty-eight." She groaned and dropped her head in her hands. "I can't believe I said that sentence out loud."

"You have to believe me, Amy—if I'd have thought for one second this was what Mr. Montgomery meant when he asked me to intervene, I would've told you right away. He didn't tell me *why* he didn't want you together. Only that it was important. I assumed it was because he thought you were too far beneath his son."

"You should have told me right away anyway."

"I know." He reached over and grabbed her hand, his stomach tight when her fingers wove naturally—and trustingly—through his own. "I'm sorry. I thought maybe I could just…you know. Be there. Support you. Make sure you stayed safe."

She looked over, her brows drawn tightly together in concern. "Does this mean you're going to be fired? Because you told me?"

It was hard to imagine feeling any more like a horrible human being than he already did, but with that innocently worded concern, he went from basement level to deep, dark hole. "No—God, no. Don't worry about me."

"But you said—"

He squeezed her fingers. "My job isn't the issue here, I promise." His future was. But Ryan refused to think about the Len Brigands of the world right now. More important than his stupid career path was the fact that Amy's hand was shaking in his. "Is it really possible you're his daughter?"

"I suppose so." All the fight seemed to have left

her. "Even though I always got the glossed-over, romantic version of events, my mom has never really gone into detail. There's no reason why the love of her life couldn't have been Mr. Montgomery. She does call him John."

"And you never questioned your parentage?"

"Of course I questioned it. I ranted. I accused. There was a whole week when I was fourteen when I went on a protest fast. I refused to eat until my mom told me my dad's name."

"How'd that work out for you?"

"She called my bluff and slipped celery sticks with peanut butter under my door at night. I didn't stand a chance."

He slid an arm around her shoulder and squeezed. She felt soft and angry and warm and relieved and so very much *alive*.

"I'm so sorry to be the one to have to tell you. You're obviously going to have to talk to Mr. Montgomery. If you want to do it right now, I'd be happy to keep an eye on the twins."

"Are you kidding? I'm not talking to him about this." She cast him a frantic look before her attention diverted to her charges. "Evan, share the rocks with Lily, please. There are more than enough to go around. That one is granite. *Gra. Nite.*"

Ryan peered at the small gray stone in Evan's chubby hand. "No, it's not. I think that might be limestone."

"Oh, so now you're a rock expert? Look, Evan— our geologist friend says its limestone. *Lime. Stone.*"

"You know they're two years old, right? Can they even say their full names yet?"

"If I don't teach them something new every day, Serena imagines we've done nothing but watch *Dora the Explorer* and eat syrup-smothered pancakes in bed. There are quizzes and everything."

"I hope you're well paid." Ryan shook his head and forced her back on to their earlier discussion. No wonder so many people got divorced when their kids were young. It was impossible to hold a rational conversation for any length of time. "But I don't understand. Now that we know what they're hiding, why don't you just come right out and ask Mr. Montgomery if he's your dad?"

She stared at him for a full thirty seconds, unblinking, making him feel as though he shared a mental level with the two children currently trying to ingest rocks. "If he *is* my dad, he obviously doesn't want me to know or he would have said something weeks ago. Months ago. Years ago."

He waited for the rest—the outpouring of angst or yelling or vows to begin fasting anew. It never came.

"That's it?" he asked. "You'll live your whole life under a cloud of doubt, non-heiress to a billion-dollar fortune, working for someone who refuses to acknowledge you as his own? That's the ending you want for this story?"

"It's the *only* ending for this story."

"But that's not how stories work," he protested, certain he was hearing things wrong. "The bad guy doesn't get to walk away without being held accountable for his actions. He doesn't get to keep being rich and powerful without consequences."

"He's not a bad guy." Amy's voice was strangled.

"He's not a good one either." That was an under-statement. "Think about it. This man has been hiding the truth of your birth for twenty-six years, probably forced your mom to agree to keep it a secret in ex-change for his support. For chrissakes—rather than admit his culpability, he set me to spy on you so you wouldn't go out with your half brother."

"That doesn't make him evil."

"No? And what if I hadn't told you about all this? What if you snuck out to meet Jake without either me or Mr. Montgomery knowing?"

Her lips wobbled dangerously. Driven by a need to comfort her, to make this situation and his role in it somehow okay, he placed a hand on her shoulder. "I think maybe it's time for you to have a chat with Daddy Warbucks."

She reacted as though struck before falling into a peal of laughter. It felt false to his ears, fragile and forced, but she rose to her feet and began gathering the twins' gear as if nothing had happened.

"I'm glad you find this so funny."

"I'm sorry." She wouldn't look him in the eyes. "But the second a man starts throwing *Annie* refer-ences at me, I'm a goner. You a big fan? Sun coming out tomorrow and all that?"

"It's not that odd. I did work in show business for most of my adult life."

"You worked on action movies."

"*Annie* is ubiquitous."

Amy clapped her hands. "And that, children, is our last vocab word of the day. *Ubiquitous. U. Biq. Ui. Tous.* It means that Mr. Ryan secretly loves musicals and doesn't want to admit it."

"Amy," he warned, but she did a spectacular job of ignoring him as they made their way back to the house.

In fact, she did a spectacular job of ignoring him for the rest of the afternoon.

ELEVEN

AMY SNUCK OUT of the nursery at nine o'clock that night, shoes in hand and socks on her feet.

Every floor in Montgomery Manor was made of either hard wood or harder tile. She wasn't sure what the family had against carpeting, but it was virtually impossible to pass through a room or hallway undetected. Heels clicked. Toes clacked. Children slid and fell.

Luckily, one of her few usable skills in this world was her ability to move lightly across the floor, sweeping her limbs so that they made almost no impression on the horizontal surface below.

"You're quiet, I'll give you that. But you're not invisible."

Amy whirled in the direction of the gravelly voice, spinning on the frictionless hardwood to find a male figure hidden in the shadows at the end of the hall. Any feeling of alarm she felt subsided when she realized who it was.

"Holy hell, Ryan. You scared the crap out of me."

"I can't imagine why. You were obviously expecting *someone* to be waiting out here for you, what with all these cloak and dagger antics."

She felt heat suffuse her cheeks and was grateful for the low lights of the hallway. The house was never completely dark—too many people lived inside these walls for that—but the Montgomerys liked to conserve electricity as much as the next ecologically minded billionaires. "I was afraid of running into Jake. Or you." Or Mr. Montgomery. Or anyone, really. All she'd wanted out of this night was to slide between the sheets and into oblivion, erasing the past eight hours in the blissful reaches of sleep. "I figured a little stealth couldn't hurt."

"A little stealth is always a good idea."

"Too much can be bad, though," she warned. "You're lucky I didn't scream and bring Alex running down here to protect the children."

"Who do you think let me in? I had no idea the house went on lockdown after eight."

"Standard procedure. Always has been." It had been a trial to get around as a teenager. No one came in or out of the house after dark except by the front door and with approval from the head of security first—not even a rope ladder or the occasional grappling hook made of sheets and twisted coat hangers was sufficient to scale these walls. "There are lots of crazies out there."

"There are quite a few crazies in here too." Ryan moved out of the shadows and gestured at her feet. Her socks had kittens on them, so she could only assume he was talking about her. "Did you go talk to him?"

Right. When the very thought of forming the words that would clarify her birth made her choke. She'd gone over it in her head a thousand times, and there was no good possible outcome.

Yes, Amy. You're my daughter but I never loved

you as much as I loved my real kids. Sorry. Do you want a raise instead?

Don't be ridiculous, Amy. You're not part of this family and you never will be. You're just an employee. Do you want a raise instead?

"When would I have had time?" she asked evasively. "It's not like I can lock the twins up while I run errands."

"There are at least twenty people in this house at all times. And you could have asked Sheryl to come in early."

"I'll do it tomorrow."

"You'll do it right now."

"You aren't the boss of me."

"Amy." He moved even closer this time, and she was struck by how dangerous this meeting might be in an alternate universe. It was so easy to feel safe and cocooned inside Montgomery Manor, with Alex standing guard and rules designed to keep everything running in tiptop shape. But Ryan was a strong man, a powerful man, and he could easily take her down before anyone came running.

Her breath came faster—not because of the danger of the moment, but because of how wonderful that particular image reverberated through her body, settling in a slow, steady burn between her thighs. She wished she could enjoy the sensation the way it deserved to be enjoyed, but she clamped her legs tighter in an effort to quell the mounting pressure. Was it too soon after Incestgate to start throwing herself at Ryan again? Was there a dedicated mourning period for that sort of thing?

"Can't we just pretend none of this ever happened?

I can solemnly promise never to go on another date with Jake." The very thought had taken on such a nauseating quality that she was pretty sure she couldn't ever look at a redheaded man the same way again. "That way you fulfill your obligations to Mr. Montgomery so you can keep your job and I uphold all the laws of polite society. No one has to be any the wiser. Pretty please?"

Ryan was tempted to capitulate. No neater solution to his dilemma existed. Amy was effectively cured of any and all infatuation with Jake. Mr. Montgomery would never have to know how it came about. And even though he should have been ashamed to admit it, he kind of liked knowing this family secret. It gave him power over them all—Mr. Montgomery, Jake, even Amy. Ryan was human enough to relish the thrill accompanying that feeling.

But he felt a surge of anger on her behalf, so powerful it almost overwhelmed him. From the day he'd run the town car into a ditch—and possibly even before, as far back as the day he'd been hired— Mr. Montgomery had been using him. He'd known Ryan's weakness, the one thing he'd sell his soul for, and leveraged it against his own flesh and blood. He'd manipulated Ryan into doing his dirty work so he could escape having to come clean about the real relationship between Jake and Amy.

And it had almost worked.

If there was one thing Ryan believed now, it was that Amy had a right to know if Mr. Montgomery was her father. She deserved a real place in this family, not just a chance to slave away in the nursery for kids who might or might not be her siblings. She deserved a part of their fortunes, a share in their love. She was a good person. She was the best person he knew.

"I know it's technically none of my business, and I know you have a history with this family that goes way back, but you can't just wish your problems away." That was one step short of drinking them away. "If nothing else, you at least deserve to know the truth."

"Can't we go back to piling up rocks instead?"

"What if I promise to go with you and wait in the hallway?" He grabbed her hand and gave it a light squeeze. Remembering the way she'd tried to wipe away the scars of his past with a kiss, he brought her hand to his lips and repeated the gesture. He lingered over the soft skin, the slightly salty taste, the pulse that beat erratically under his lips.

"Okay," she said in a soft exhale, staring at her hand. "You're right."

"Really?" Maybe this kiss-the-boo-boo-better thing did have some power.

"Yes." She caught her lower lip with her teeth. "But you have to come inside with me. I don't think I want to do this alone."

He clutched her hand even tighter, the gesture echoing the sudden constraint in the region of his chest. She was so trusting of everyone—she made it so easy for all of them to take advantage of her.

Afraid she might change her mind if they lingered, Ryan wasted no time in leading her toward the end of the hall, where a serviceable stairway led to all the main floors. It wasn't exactly a servant's entrance, but it wasn't *not* one, either. "He's in his office working late. I checked."

"That was very thorough of you," she said shakily. "Why do I suddenly feel like a prisoner you're leading to her death?"

"It's my natural strength and aura of command."

"No. That's not it."

"Thanks a lot." He paused only to open the stairwell door and usher her through. "Maybe it's my inherent love of justice?"

"Nope." She laughed, and some of the nervous shaking seemed to subside. "Try again."

"Hmm." He tapped his chin, playing along. "Could be my total disregard for my prisoner's health and well-being. You'll get to that office door whether I have to hoist you over my shoulder and carry you the whole way."

Amy pointed up the stairwell, which bore similarities to the kind of emergency stairs you'd find in a hospital, industrial but clean. "It's two flights up. I don't think you could make it."

Ryan growled his wounded pride. He wasn't a bodybuilder, but he took advantage of the Montgomery gym membership at the local Fit n' Bounce. They even knew him by name there—and that he liked the blue sports drink the best, that the red one made him break out in hives.

He grabbed Amy's forearm more firmly and twisted it, not hurting her, but in the kind of hold that would have her lifted over his head—or pinned beneath him—in a matter of seconds. The motion drew her naturally nearer to him, so close he could have counted each freckle on her nose. Although lines of anxiety around the eyes made her appear older than her twenty-six years, she was dazzling and full of energy and so beautiful it took his breath away.

"Do you dare to question my virility?" he asked, his voice a low rumble.

"That depends. Do *you* dare to question my ability to high-kick right between your legs?"

Despite his better judgment, he twisted more firmly, now so close he couldn't count any freckles at all. There was just him and her. Two.

"I'm not scared of you," he said.

Her head turned just enough so that her lips brushed his outer ear, her breath warm and almost painful against his sensitive skin. "That's good to hear, Ryan. Because you scare the crap out of me."

He thought about how close he'd been to letting her go without confessing his role in all this, about how he still hadn't told her what he might get out of this deal, and gulped. He was kind of scared of himself, too.

AMY WALKED THROUGH the door of Mr. Montgomery's office as if she were approaching the gallows with a sack over her head.

"Well, this is a pleasant surprise." Mr. Montgomery, always a stickler for things like gallantry, got up and pulled out a chair for her, making it appear as though her late-night visit was a cause for joy—and not an interruption to the bright lights, haphazard whirl of papers and half-eaten turkey sandwich on his desk that showed him hard at work. He nodded once to Ryan, who stood pressed against the wood-paneled wall, as though his presence meant nothing.

That didn't mean it actually *meant nothing*. Mr. Montgomery was one of those men you absolutely wanted by your side when the zombie apocalypse hit. He'd see all the undead heading your way, blink once, and then whisk you to one of his eight contingency hiding places for just such a situation. Nothing fazed him simply because he'd already imagined every possible outcome to what the Fates had in store.

Why wouldn't his chauffeur accompany his nanny-and-possibly-daughter to a scene of paternal confrontation? Stranger things existed in his imagination and were therefore already taken care of.

"I hope everything is all right with the twins," he said calmly. "Are they having trouble sleeping?"

She wished the light conversation felt half as ordinary as it sounded. "Oh, no. Nothing like that. Although I do think you ought to get Evan's hearing checked. I mentioned it to Seren—I mean, Mrs. Montgomery, the other day, but she thought it might be sinus trouble, which runs in her family." Speaking of running, her words were blurring together in a pathetic jumble. "Not that I mean to be a tattletale or anything, because obviously she knows her own children best…"

Behind her, Ryan cleared his throat. She wasn't sure if it was meant as a reprimand or a friendly reminder to keep her shit together, but she appreciated his support either way. She hadn't been kidding when she said she couldn't do this alone—she was worse at confrontations than she was at lying. Swallowing what she meant to say next, which could have been anything from the contents of the twins' latest diapers to a dialogue on Serena's parental habits, Amy forced herself to look Mr. Montgomery in the eye.

His kindly eye. His kindly, if slightly shaped wide

at the center and narrow at the end, like it had been pinched off in haste, eye. Much like her own, now that she thought about it. She'd always hated that shape, which made it difficult to put eyeliner on evenly, but it looked really good on the men of the family.

Oh, God. She couldn't do it. She couldn't bear the thought that his kindly eye might actually be cruel. She wouldn't be able to handle it if he was anyone but the man she'd always known and respected.

"I want a raise." She leaped out of her chair in surprise at her own demand, perilously near to jumping on the desk and bellowing her triumphant yawp.

Behind her, Ryan's throat clearing gave way to an even less discreet cough, and Mr. Montgomery's eyes widened enough that, for the moment, they looked perfectly round.

"Oh, geez. I'm sorry. I didn't mean for it to come out like that. It's just…"

"It's just that you've been on the job for a few months and you know how much work goes into it now, yes?" Mr. Montgomery asked in that gentle way he had. "You realize how sorely underpaid you are and have come to demand restitution?"

"Well, yes, actually." She had no idea how her mother had done this for so many years—and with double the children at her heels. "I do find myself working longer hours than we agreed."

Mr. Montgomery raised his hand, silencing her without the need to say a word. She let her mouth hang open, knowing as she did that she looked like a fainting goat. She felt like one too. One more surprise packed into this day, and she was likely to fall over and give up on the spot.

"Amy, what's the first thing I taught you about success? Do you remember? At the lemonade stand you and Jenna ran one year during Public Day?"

She closed her mouth, remembering. The Montgomery Public Days were an annual community event that had become something of a tradition. Every August, the family opened their home and their pocketbooks to throw an all-day party of carnival rides, fried foods and tours of the grounds. Her mother had thought it seemed crass to sell lemonade on a day that was supposed to be free, but Mr. Montgomery only lauded their entrepreneurial spirit. They'd made almost a hundred dollars.

"There's no such thing as free lunch?"

"No," he said slowly. "That wasn't it."

"Really? I could have sworn it was the free lunch one." She snapped her fingers. "Oh! I *know* it was. Because I'd just gotten done eating lunch, and then I got worried that you were going to make me pay for it, and then I started thinking about all the lunches I'd had at your house and figured I'd have to be your slave forever, like Rumpelstiltskin."

Ryan sucked in a sharp breath, too loud to go undetected but impossible to take back. He'd been trying to be invisible—supportive but not in the way—but Amy's words hit him hard. There was no denying the truth of what she said. She might as well have been a princess toiling away in the Montgomery dungeons, spinning straw to gold, the wicked half sister no one wanted to claim. That was basically how they treated her.

He couldn't be a party to that. He wouldn't.

"I've always found the no free lunch saying to

be pretty accurate," he said, joining the conversation despite his intention to remain the strong, silent type of supporter. Amy was clearly losing her nerve, and he wasn't about to let Mr. Montgomery turn the conversation around without a fight. "In Hollywood, nothing you put in your mouth comes without strings attached."

Ryan moved to stand beside Amy, ignoring the cold, appraising look Mr. Montgomery turned on him. It was the kind of cold, appraising look that probably reduced lesser men to stone, but Ryan found he didn't feel an urge to crumble. He felt protective and angry and out of control instead. And since his normal method of coping with that particular cocktail of emotions—a cocktail—was out of the question, he settled for staring down the man responsible for the bulk of them.

It worked pretty well, actually.

"Is that a fact?" Mr. Montgomery asked.

"It's a world where favors matter. Where deals are struck and bargains made—often without a care for who gets hurt along the way."

"I know something of Hollywood, I think." Mr. Montgomery tipped his head to the side, his meaning clear. *I know the people you need to get back in. I know the secret knock for the big boys' club.*

"True," Ryan said quietly. "But you don't know *me.*"

Nothing flickered on Mr. Montgomery's face—not fear, not approval, not anything approaching human emotion. At least, not until he turned to Amy. "The point I'm trying to make is that you don't need to keep pushing. That's the secret to success. Know when the answer is yes or close enough to it and step back. Of course the raise is yours, no question. You know you only ever need to ask me for something and it's done."

He extended his hand, unwavering and fleshy, stopping it in front of Ryan. Was he supposed to shake it, or was she? Since being the first—or the only— person in this room to shake his hand would reinforce the idea that Amy was half a person, toiling in the dungeons, Ryan kept his hands firmly planted in his armpits. He was done making deals.

Eyebrows raised and lowered again before Mr. Montgomery turned to Amy and pulled her into a bearlike hug. This man, who looked as kindly as Santa and would scare the crap out of Satan, actually initiated contact and held Amy so tightly he might have swallowed her whole. And Ryan—whether for good or for bad or because that was the way Mr. Montgomery wanted it—overheard him say, "You're a good kid, Amy. Thank you for taking such great care of mine."

And that was it. As assuredly as they had been welcomed into the office, they were just as forcefully removed from it, but from what Ryan could see, absolutely nothing had changed. It was a shift in the air, an unspoken command. Hell—for all he knew it was some kind of poisonous gas Mr. Montgomery expelled through tiny hidden vents.

But as Ryan followed Amy out the door, Mr. Montgomery stilled him with a hand.

"Thanks to *you*, as well," he said.

Ryan paused, waiting for the sarcasm to sink in, but he was struck with the extraordinary sensation that the man meant it. "For what?"

"For taking such good care of Amy. Keep it up—I think you'll like what I've got in the works. I knew I was right when I penned you as the man for the job." His smile had equal chances of being sincere or sinister. Ryan was one coin flip away from trying to figure it out when Mr. Montgomery decided for him. "But then, I usually am."

TWELVE

"THAT WAS THE worst Jerry Springer confrontation I've ever seen." Ryan waited until they were back on the nursery floor before he spoke. It wasn't that he assumed Mr. Montgomery's office was bugged or anything, but a man didn't speed away from the scene of a crime without at least *trying* to lose his tail.

"Should I have thrown a few chairs? Brought out a surprise guest who's actually his ex-wife? Demanded a paternity test? Would that have made you feel better?"

That last one would have, but he didn't say so. "I *am* a little impressed at the raise bit. I wonder if I should try."

"Ugh. Don't remind me." She stopped her fast pace down the hallway and slumped against the wall, sliding until she came to a seated position. Since it didn't look as though she planned on getting up anytime soon, Ryan did the same on the opposite wall, allowing them to face one another, legs close enough to touch but all the more significant because they didn't. "I told you I panic in test-like situations. I didn't know what else to say."

"Not even, *Hey, just curious here, but are you my dad?*"

She ignored him, her careful avoidance charged

with meaning. "It's not like I can even spend that money now. I'll feel dirty."

Ryan raised a brow—his crooked one, the one with the scar. "You'll feel dirty spending money you earned doing a hard job that someone appreciates?"

"Yes. And don't look so smug. Guilt and I have always enjoyed a complicated relationship. If you try to split us up, you'll only end up pushing us closer together."

"I've always found a clean break to be best."

"But he'll be so sorry afterward for what he did. He'll woo me back with his soothing words and gifts of chocolate, promising to be better next time."

"Are we still talking about the metaphorical guilt? Because he sounds like a dick."

She laughed and allowed one of her feet to fall casually to the side, brushing his. He tingled from the contact, small but meaningful. "You heard what he said in there—about me feeling free to ask if I ever need anything. I know you're not vying for the role of president of the John Montgomery fan club, but even you have to admit that was a sweet thing to offer. He's been like that for as long as I can remember, generous and supportive and always there when I need him, no questions asked."

"A father figure."

Amy nodded and averted her head. Her hair fell along the curve of her cheek, hiding her expression, but he didn't need to see to understand. He understood just fine. Shifting so that not just their feet but their entire legs brushed together, he waited until she turned back toward him, hazel eyes glittering, before speaking. "You're afraid, aren't you?"

"Yes. Of a lot of things. Like men who drive too fast and feel too much. I never pretended to be a brave person."

"You're afraid," he repeated. He grabbed her hand and stared at the delicate web of skin and bones, so strong and so fragile at the same time. "That's why you didn't ask. You're not scared that he *will* admit to being your dad—but that he'll admit he isn't."

"So what if I am?" She struggled to take her hand back. "Is that really so terrible? To want a man I admire and who's always taken care of me to be my father?"

He let her hand go, but at the expense of her legs. Dropping his hands to her shins, he scooted forward, bringing the pair of them even closer. He ran his hands up and down her legs, a pattern he hoped was soothing but suspected was more to comfort himself than her. Now that the touch barrier had been broken between them, he couldn't seem to get enough. "Of course it's not terrible. Of course you deserve that."

"And is it really so terrible to want him to *want* to tell me?" She sniffled. The sound of it—of her sadness—almost had him marching back up to Mr. Montgomery's door and pounding until she got the answers she sought. But the panicked look in her eyes—as though she were a cornered animal—held him in place. "I shouldn't have to stand there, feeling like I'm fourteen again, starving myself for answers. What's wrong with me that he'd go to such lengths to hide it? How can he be so nice and take such good care of me and *hate* me that much?"

"Amy—" Ryan's voice caught in his throat. "I can't answer that for you."

"Yes, you can." She blinked at him. "If anyone can, it's you."

A flood of panic surged through him, jumpstarting his pulse and making him feel, once again, as though he were trapped in a room with a lion. This one, he feared, was much more dangerous.

"You and Mr. Montgomery treat me exactly the same," she said, and there was such a dearth of malice in her tone, it damn well near slayed him. "So tell me. How can you sit there, being so nice and taking such good care of me, and *still* act like kissing me is the worst thing that's ever happened to you? Why is it that you don't want me either?"

Her cry moved through him as a resonant frequency, tuned to him and him alone. Forgetting where they were and who they were and how the hell he was supposed to function in the aftermath, he grabbed her around the waist and pulled her the rest of the way into his lap. She opened her mouth to let loose what he could only assume was a protest. Mindful that they were mere feet away from dozing children and their watchful nurse, he did what any sane man would do to keep the volume to a minimum: he kissed her.

This time, he didn't let surprise dictate his actions, didn't let the spontaneity of the moment hold him back. He gripped the back of her hair with absolute intention and brought his mouth to hers.

Amy whirled under the assault of Ryan's lips moving over hers, unable to do much more than cling and let him in. As her interactions with this man had proven, she was one of those women who would stand at the front porch after a date with her head tilted upward, waiting patiently for her kiss. No matter how great a date had gone, she could never bring herself to initiate that first foray into a man's mouth. Which meant the only time she ever got past longing was when a man either read her cues or decided to screw gentlemanly behavior sideways and take what he wanted.

Thank God Ryan was proving to be one of the latter. He shackled her with his hands, the firm press of his mouth ceaseless in its demands. She couldn't move, couldn't see, could barely breathe. Giving herself over to the fact that this was actually *happening*, that she wasn't misreading every cue in her stupid life, she ran her hands over the planes of his chest and settled more firmly against him.

But the motion—her sudden lack of passivity— seemed to jolt him to a greater sense of awareness, and he pulled back.

"I want you." His eyes searched hers, hands still gripping her with so much promise. "I want you so much that I've reached a point where you're all I can think about, where you're the only bright spot in my otherwise dreary existence. Believe me when I say that the only reason I've held back is because I don't want you to get hurt."

Because you're leaving. Because you think I'm weak. Because you think I can't handle a few tangled limbs and sweaty tumbles in the sheets before saying goodbye.

Amy wasn't sure where she'd gotten this reputation for frailty, but she was tired of it. Okay, so she wasn't the strongest or most impressive person living under the Montgomery Manor roof, and there was a good chance she *would* cry when Ryan eventually left—

whether that was two days or two months from now.
But that didn't mean she couldn't make her own decisions. There was no need to protect her from her
own goddamned life.

"It's never been an issue of not wanting you.
Never." Ryan reached up and traced her lips, his
movements slow and agonizing. "Please tell me you
understand how hard this is for me."

"I understand that you're full of shit." She smiled
against the press of his fingertips. "I think you should
ask me how I feel about the idea of hot, messy animal
sex before you go writing it off for the both of us."

He dropped his hands as if she'd spouted fire from
her mouth. "And how do you feel about hot, messy
animal sex?" he asked, his voice hoarse.

"I don't know. What do you think?"

Aware that it was cheating and unfair and underhanded, she thrust herself closer, breasts grazing his
chest, her nipples tightening into twin peaks of sensation through her loose-fitting T-shirt. "It's the boobs
again," she teased. "These wily girls refuse to take
no for an answer. Help me. I can't stop them. They're
taking over."

Ryan's only response was an overloud groan and
the very obvious shift of his gaze downward. From
his vantage point, he had a clear view down the front
of the plunging neckline—and he didn't seem to be
against enjoying it. She gave her shoulders a shimmy,
bringing a little jiggle action into the deal.

He licked his lips. "They *are* awfully persuasive."

"Maybe you should touch one. Just to see. You can
always change your mind afterwards."

"Jesus, Amy." His hand grazed the line where the

vee of her shirt skimmed her shoulders. Not quite boob territory, but close enough to cover her entire body with goose bumps. "Your body isn't the problem here."

"I'm not going to get clingy and needy afterwards, if that's what you're afraid of," she promised. "Give me a chance." She just needed one freaking man in her life to give her a chance.

"I'm not afraid that *you'll* get needy." Ryan's gaze lifted from her cleavage to reach into her eyes instead. *Oh, man.* Her boobs had been hoarding all the good stuff for themselves.

"Then what are you afraid of?" she managed.

"That *I* will."

She didn't have a reply to that—unless you counted the roaring of blood in her head, dizzying her and making her feel as though she were flying. Fortunately, there was no need for words. Ryan grabbed her again, ravaging her lips and her body and her synapses, and oh, God, why was she bothering with thinking anymore?

Thought was easily dispensed with for the next seven minutes. Seven minutes of heaven, not locked in a closet together at some adolescent party, but tangled in a hallway with low lights and no one near. It was practically the same thing, though she was pretty sure none of her teenage encounters included quite so much expert tongue. Ryan kissed like he drove—fast and hard and on the edge, a man who knew how to handle himself the second he slipped behind the wheel.

And in this case, she was happy to let him take the driver's seat. She started out ensconced in his lap but was soon pressed underneath him, pinned by the delicious weight of his body, unable to do anything more than writhe under hands that never seemed to stop exploring. Up and down her bare legs, slipping underneath the hem of her shorts only to pull away right before he got to the good parts. Under her shirt, over her bra, pinching at her nipples but never coming into direct contact with them.

In other words, he was doing everything within his power to rile her up, make her hot—but without ever forgetting where they were. A hallway. His place of employment. Another man's house. If anyone were to walk by, the two of them could separate and be decent.

Disheveled as all get-out, but decent.

"My room is down that way," she gasped when he freed her mouth for a moment, taking his time to drop kisses along her neck and the slope of her shoulder. She could feel the impression of his lips burning long after he pulled away. She would probably feel them forever. "Three doors. Possibly four. I'm having a hard time seeing right now."

He stopped kissing long enough to look up, flushed with desire, lips parted. "Are you allowed to do that?"

She laughed. "Have boys stay over if I want them to? Yes. This isn't a convent. It's my home."

"I know, but…"

Oh, he was not backing out now. Not when his erection was grinding against the juncture of her legs, the current epicenter of all her rational—and irrational—thoughts. She scooted out from underneath him and got to shaky legs. Giving in to the indulgence of a backward glance to find him staring openmouthed at her, she lifted her shirt off and tossed it to the hall-way floor.

"What are you doing?" he asked, his voice gruff.

She kept moving, an extra sway in her hips as she unbuttoned her shorts and shimmied them off her hips. "Leaving you a trail of bread crumbs in case you get lost along the way."

"Amy…"

She reached behind her and flicked open her serviceable white cotton bra. The only way to dress up that kind of bland plant material was to dangle it enticingly from one fingertip, which she did as she reached her door. It wasn't locked—unless someone wanted to steal her ancient ten-pound laptop or her collection of Old World maps, there wasn't much to take—so she pushed it open and slipped in.

One. Two. Three. Four. She flicked on the lights, assuming Ryan was right behind her. Five. Six. Seven. Was he seriously not going to follow her in here? No need to be squeamish. The nursery was far enough down the hall that no sound pierced the walls. Eight. Nine. Nine and a half. She slipped out of her panties—more of the same boring white cotton, though at least they had bits of scalloped lace at the edges—and tossed them out the open door.

Nine and two-thirds. Nine and three-quarters. What the heck came after that?

"Goddammit." Ryan stormed through the door and tossed all her clothes onto the floor. "Are you trying to kill me?"

He stopped, suspended in a swirl of desire that hit him from all sides, holding him momentarily aloft. In his haste to somehow find the ability to both walk and gather up Amy's clothes, he'd forgotten that he held *all* her underclothes. Nothing stood between him and her completely naked body except distance and air— both of which mattered for absolutely zero.

Amy's form had been molded by a creator both reverent and filthy-minded. There was a touch of innocence about the way her breasts hung heavy and full, an enticing lift at each tip where soft pink nipples reached for his touch. Her waist came in at just the right spot, a soft swell of stomach flared out past her hips to legs so long they seemed unreal. She was sweetly seductive, made him want to lower her to a bed of rose petals with Barry White crooning in the background.

But when she moved, not so much seducing him as shifting her weight from one leg to the other, it was as though he saw an entirely different woman. Her movements were a ripple of silk over water, of strength just under the surface of downy soft skin. This woman was *a dancer*. She could use her body to tell stories, to weave magic spells, to draw him in and trap him forever, endlessly striving for air.

"Would you please say something?" she asked, a nervous hitch to her breath. "In case you haven't noticed, I'm kind of naked here. Nudity has a way of making a girl feel slightly vulnerable—and it's already been kind of a vulnerable day for me."

"Fuck me, Amy." He couldn't tell if it was a comment or a command, but he could no more stop the words than he could prevent himself from slamming the door behind him.

Her smile spread, slowly and so bright he should

probably look away. But that smile was worth risking blindness for.

"Is that a good *fuck me*, or a bad one?"

"It's about to be a fantastic one." Somehow, he made it across the three or four feet that separated them, losing his shirt and shoes in the process. He should have taken his time to undress, said something sweet about the way the sight of her filled him with more than just lust, but the second he lifted a hand to the curve where waist flared to hip, instinct took over.

And his instincts? They weren't sweet ones.

The first time he got behind the wheel of a car, Ryan liked to take his time, get to know the placement of the pedals, the layout of the mechanics, the feel of the steering wheel under his hands. He could spend hours admiring a well-fitted seat. And he never ran before he walked, never pushed the pedal to the floor until he was sure he and the car had reached an understanding.

Being with Amy—touching her, feeling her come to life underneath him—was a completely different experience. Everything he knew about handling a car, and about handling a woman, was lost in the overwhelming desperation he felt in her presence. He wanted to be off and flying, heedless of the consequences. He never wanted to slow down again.

And Amy wasn't helping matters any. Everywhere he touched on her body was a curve, every graze of his fingertips on her skin set her sighing aloud. He captured those sighs one by one, his mouth greedily battling hers as they inched closer to the bed. When he felt her legs hit the edge of the mattress, he hitched her up and spun, settling himself in a seated position, holding her naked form to his.

"If you need me to slow down, you have to say so. I can tell you right now, I don't intend to bother coming up for air." He buried his head in the crook of her neck, nipping and sucking his way downward, not stopping until he had the firm tip of her breast in his mouth. Her skin felt like silk under his tongue, and he suckled deeply, forced to hold her firm as her back arched and she tugged his head closer.

Her fingers laced behind his head and held him tight. "Slow down?" She moaned and ground her hips against him as he took her other nipple into his mouth. "Why would I want to do that?"

Because I'll hurt you. Because I can't stop on my own. Because I'll take what I want and leave you in the lurch. He tightened his hold on her hips. "Just promise me you'll say something if I go too fast."

"Of course I promise, Ryan. But I trust you." She tugged on his head again, this time bringing him up to meet her in a searing kiss. The kiss itself was enough to ignite him—her tongue delving deep into his waiting mouth, the way she trapped his lower lip in her teeth on the way out again—but she chose that moment to begin grinding her hips against his. The slow, languid rotation of her body against his seemed calculated to get a rise out of him—literally—though there was no need for her to go to such lengths. In fact, if she didn't stop soon...

Dammit. This wasn't going to work. He felt too much, had fallen too far. If she remained in his lap for another minute, there was no way he could leave this room without being heartily ashamed of himself.

With his arms wrapped firmly around her waist, he lifted and swung her to take his place on the bed. She moaned and kicked, narrowly missing his nose. "Oh, shit. I'm sorry." She struggled to sit up, but he placed a hand flat on her stomach, pinning her to the bed—which, he noticed, was all done up in white. Fluffy white. Virginal white. The kind of white that told tales afterward.

"Don't worry about it. I've got fast reflexes."

She moaned again, this time settling more firmly into the pillowy comforter. "I hope they're really fast then. If you're about to do what I think you're going to do, you should know I kick a lot."

He paused, lifting and appraising her legs with renewed interest. They were such an intriguing mixture of long, lean muscle and soft flesh. Of course, they weren't nearly as intriguing in that moment as the damp, curly apex he sought.

"I thought dancers were supposed to have command over their bodies." He lifted her leg so he could kiss along the inside of her right knee. No immediate damage occurred, so he moved higher, teeth and tongue burning a furious path up to the middle of her thigh. God, he could smell her, taste her, drown in her.

"I can do this. Does this count?"

As the *this* in question was the spread of her legs wide enough to open the vibrant slash of her pussy, he rather thought it did. "Fuck, yes," he breathed, continuing his northward path. He'd just reached her inner thigh—a piece of delicious, glorious perfection—when there was some definite twitching in her muscles.

"Is it that you're ticklish?" he asked, only mildly

alarmed. He never backed down from a challenge. Especially not one that tasted like her—musky and decadent, a luxury he could no longer do without.

"Not ticklish." The sound was half pant. "I just have this tendency to forget myself. Which means flailing. And loud noises. Sometimes, I can't even remember my own name afterward."

He liked the sound of all those things. Unwilling to waste another moment with talking, he pressed a kiss as high up as could technically be counted as leg before finally reaching the treasure he sought.

Amy tried not to flail, she really did. There was something so ungainly about a woman—a supposed ballerina—who writhed and flopped around a bed just because some guy was able to find her... Oh, dear God. Her clit. Yep. It was right there. It was throbbing. And aching. And somehow tugging at her nipples until she thought they might burst from her chest and start singing show tunes.

She groaned and spread her legs wider in an attempt to keep them under control. She had no idea what it was Ryan was doing to her body right now, but she was pretty sure she was going to manacle her legs around his head and rip it off in her excitement.

"I refuse to be responsible for your accidental dismemberment. Just so you know." She clutched at her comforter, hands twisting the material into sweaty heaps at her sides. She should have had him sign a waiver—this was not going to end well.

But it did. It ended *very* well.

As if he knew his life depended on it, Ryan held her legs apart and firmly in place as his tongue flicked some kind of crazy, otherworldly maneuver on her ladyparts. One second she was a bundle of nerves strung up high and poised to fall, and the next she was cascading down into a pool of fizzy liquid pleasure. Muscles spasmed, her hands shook and God only knew what kind of sex noises came out of her mouth in the interim, but she finally hit the bottom and folded out like an accordion nearing its whinging, polka end.

He sat back and flexed his hands, making and unmaking fists, his forearms pumping with a delicious twist each time.

"What are you doing with your hands?" She struggled up on one elbow, unable to find any of her other bones. This messy animal sex stuff definitely had its benefits.

"I'm stretching. Keeping you pinned in place for that was a hell of a workout."

Her laughter came out in a whoosh as she flopped back to the bed. "If post-orgasmic stretching is something you enjoy, I think you should do lunges next. Fully naked lunges."

His own laughter was a strangled choke. "That is by far the strangest request I've ever gotten in the bedroom."

"Is it?" She liked that. She wasn't the best at anything—not really, not when you compared her to other ballet dancers or women who were able to mewl and give a decorous twitch as they came—but she liked knowing *something* distinguished her from the herd. Especially since oral skills like that meant Ryan must have a very grateful, sated herd hidden away somewhere. "Does that mean you're going to do them?"

He glanced down at his crotch, where she assumed—hoped?—he continued to show a lively and rock hard interest in her, and shook his head. "I'm not so sure I could in this condition."

She scooted further up onto the bed, not stopping until her head rested against the puffy white head-board. She squirmed and settled herself comfortably, content to command at her leisure. "I think you can. Ten lunges or I roll over and go to sleep."

"You wouldn't dare."

"It's eleven lunges now. Big, manly ones."

She wasn't sure she knew what a *manly* lunge was—or that she even cared to see one performed in the nude—but she was too far in it now to quit. Besides, there was a playful sparkle in Ryan's eye she wanted to explore further.

It was clear Ryan wasn't a man given to *play*—not without being forced first. He'd always be the guy standing on the fringes, cementing his outsider status with a frown. He'd laugh only when the joke slapped him on the face, participate in a group activity with the right amount of persuasion and wheedling.

But *this* Ryan? She was beginning to wonder. So far from requiring forced participation, he was jumping in—hands and tongue first. Maybe the bedroom was more his playing field. One-on-one games. Sex games.

She'd never really played sex games before—but, oh, how she wanted to. Even though she was sure her legs were suffering from some kind of postcoital spasm that would render her immobile for the rest of her life, she felt the warming call of desire pooling once again in her belly.

"Be careful what you wish for," he warned, the

playfulness traveling all the way to his lips, which lifted in a heart-stopping smile. He dropped his hands to the top of his jeans and undid the button, pushing just far enough to hint at the powers contained within. His stomach continued flat and hard all the way down, leading into a curly thatch of golden hair that peeked over the top of his straining fly.

"Twelve lunges," she said, mesmerized by the hitch of his thumb on his waistband and the coil of fingers over the top of his groin. He could have been an underwear model or a standing advertisement for cologne. She normally hated cologne on men—thought it made them smell a bit too much like desperation—but she'd have bought gallons of whatever Ryan was peddling in that moment.

He took another step forward, his pants falling an inch lower on his hips. The thick protrusion of his cock swelled, trying to be released into the wild, and she could feel herself willing its forward progression. *Escape, my friend. Be free. Don't let the confines of all that fabric keep you down.*

Ryan dropped trou. Well—it wasn't quite that sudden, more like a semi-striptease than a frat boy prank, but the end result was the same. Naked man. Gorgeous, turgid cock with a spring and a bounce in its step as it enjoyed its newfound liberty. And then he promptly turned on his heel and performed a perfect lunge.

Well, perfect when considered from a purely athletic standpoint, what with his hands on his hips and the careful dip of his knee. From an aesthetic standpoint...

She squealed and clapped her hands over her eyes,

though with wide enough slits between her fingers that she could see every mesmerizing clench of his milky white buttocks. "I take it back. I take it all back."

"You don't like my lunge?" He cast a playful look over his shoulder and whirled so that he was pointing rather, um, pointedly at her. "What about now? Like this? Do you want me to go deeper?"

He went deeper. A lot deeper. So much deeper she was pretty sure his balls grazed the floor.

"I'll never wash that spot again," she vowed, and collapsed against her bed in a fit of giggles. Her room, though the size of most two-bedroom apartments in town, wasn't nearly big enough to contain the force of that man as he worked his way across the hardwood floor, pausing only to look at her and make sure his spectacle was appreciated.

And, oh, how she appreciated it. She didn't have the willpower to glance away or the heart to tell him she'd never be able to look at a man stretching the same way again. She also didn't dare say what she was thinking—that his willingness to play into her demands had sealed this deal something fierce. Drawing out this spirited, boyish version of Ryan was now her primary mission in life, for however long he was willing to let her try.

Ryan Lucas was finally coming out of his shell, and she was going to do her damnedest to make sure he wouldn't fit back inside it again.

"There." He rose to his feet, supremely proud of himself and not the least bit softer for it. If anything, the exercise had only sharpened the glint of desire in his eyes, made him hungrier for release. "Twelve of the sexiest lunges this world has ever seen. Just as the lady requested."

"How do you know those were the sexiest I've ever seen?" she asked.

"I saw it in your eyes. That was admiration."

"On the contrary. That was horror."

Closer still, leaning over the edge of the bed, one hand working carefully toward her. Dammit. Her legs still weren't working properly, or she'd have been able to move out of the way before his fingers clasped firmly around her ankle.

"If that was horror, why aren't you screaming?" He tugged, pulling her to the end of the bed, pillows and blankets and his hard body smothering her all at once.

She gasped, drawing in a gulp of air in the brief moment he allowed before his lips crashed down over hers to claim his reward. There wasn't much on earth he could ask of her right then that she would have denied. Her body, her heart, her soul—they were all his for the taking, though the only one he seemed to have an interest in was the first one.

And that was fine with her. She'd take what she could get. With a yank and a firm grip that had her arms above her head, she was trapped underneath him, helpless against the power he wielded. He commanded her every movement, her every breath, even the mounting ache between her legs, begging for his entry.

"Condoms in the bedside table," she managed, using her body's undulations to show her approval. "There's also lube, but I have a strong suspicion we won't be needing that."

He smiled against her lips and snaked a hand between their bodies, not stopping until he reached her entrance. She could feel the slide of fingers against slick folds, her body so hot and wet for his touch she was probably embarrassing herself down there.

"Well, well. You *did* enjoy those lunges," he said, eliciting a gasp with the flick of a finger against her clit.

"What I'd really enjoy right now is your cock inside me, you braggart." She'd been striving for a coy tone, but she was pretty sure she'd just cackled.

After a brief second—or two, or three, or possibly twenty—in which his tongue moved roughly into her open, waiting, wanton mouth, he pulled away to grab a condom. "Wow. You have a lot of stuff in here."

"Don't snoop. Grab the goods and get out."

"Strawberry, lemon, chocolate...*pizza* flavored body paint?"

"It seemed like a good idea at the time. I was hungry."

"And I'm pretty sure these are office binder clips. Let me guess, you used these for—"

"Ryan," she said sternly, unwilling to let him finish. Nothing about that drawer painted her in a sane light, but everything had an explanation. Of sorts. "In case you forgot, there's throbbing going on over here. Painful, empty throbbing."

He laughed and pulled out a long purple dildo that had been molded in the semi-crescent shape of an alien's wang—a gag gift, she *swore*—and let it dangle from his fingertips. "I'm not sure I want to know what this *is*."

"If you don't stop judging my personal inventory, I'll be happy to demonstrate by shoving it up your a—"

That was as far as she got, as he somehow managed, amid all the treasure hunting and mocking judgment, to slide a condom over his length. With a growl
that was both playful and possessive, he opened her
legs and pushed himself between them. She felt the
delicious clench of her muscles tightening against the
invasion and brought her legs to her chest to increase the sensation.

"That's more like it," she cooed. God, she loved
being conquered by a cock like this, so full she felt
each minute shift of their bodies pull deeply at her
core.

"You're telling me." Ryan paused to brush the hair
out of her face. Her breath stopped as she waited to
see what came next—if he was going to say something heart-meltingly romantic about her eyes or
something with a harder edge, turning this into nothing more than skin and sex.

But he surprised her. "Okay, Amy. How many
lunges do you want this time?"

She was still laughing when she came. Laughing
and gasping and gripping his shoulders so tightly she
probably left marks behind, but neither one of them
seemed to notice. All she seemed to care about was
that her desire to draw the sensation of fullness out
for hours was surpassed only by the insistent tug of
an orgasm that would allow no such thing. There was
too much of him—hands, mouth, cock—to allow her
to lie back and enjoy a passive assault on her senses.

And even though she was pretty sure there were
more than twelve lunges that time, she did both of
them a favor and didn't keep track.

"You never told me you were hilarious in bed," she

murmured, their passion spent. She tried to pull away, but he shifted so that he remained inside her, his arms refusing to loosen their grip. She felt a tightness in her throat and let herself melt against the solid comfort of his chest. "You also never said you were a snuggler."

"I'm not."

"I'm no expert, but this feels an awful lot like snuggling."

He held her tighter and tucked his head into the crook of her neck, where his breath blew a ripple of goose bumps along her skin. "You talk too much."

"I'm just trying to figure you out."

"I'm not that complicated." His fingers slipped through hers. "I'm not hilarious and I don't snuggle."

"But?" she prodded.

"But I'll be damned if I'm letting you go one second before I have to."

THIRTEEN

"I BROUGHT YOU LUNCH."

Ryan looked up from the Maserati he was working on and grinned. In addition to a brown paper bag dangling through the open doorway of the garage, a leg—long and lean and muscular—made an entrance worthy of a showgirl.

"Be careful what part you lead with," he said, restraining himself from running his hands and lips and teeth all over that leg. If his fingers weren't covered in the glistening sheen and pungent odor of motor oil, it would have been a much closer call. "I don't want to lose my job because I was found making out with the nanny in the backseat of Mr. Montgomery's favorite Italian sports car."

Amy's head replaced the food and leg. Other than a slight look of exhaustion—which was no wonder, given the lateness of their activities the night before—she looked fantastic. No regrets, no awkwardness. Just her. "I told you already. No one is going to care if we're seeing each other. It's not a perfect family situation, I'll give you that, but we aren't living in a dictatorship."

Yeah, well. Forgive him if he didn't take her word for it. She probably saw the potential for world peace and rainbows reflected in Kim Jong Un's eyes.

"Is that what we're doing?" he asked carefully. "Seeing each other?"

She wasn't nearly as careful. With a laugh and a toss of the brown paper bag at him, she hoisted herself up on the workbench, heedless of the piston rings she knocked over and almost rolled to the floor. "Well, I've seen a lot more of you than I ever thought possible, that's for sure. Feeling sore at all today? Your thighs sure got a workout last night."

"I'm stronger than I look."

"So am I. Which is why if *seeing each other* is too much for you to handle, we can call it something else. Slapping fancies. The dance of the love monkey. Whatever."

"And you're sure you don't mind?" He knew he was only making things worse, prodding at a tiny cut as if determined to turn it into a gaping wound, but he couldn't help it. While his body appreciated Amy's generosity, his conscience was having a hard time making it fit. His conscience was having a hard time with everything these days. "Because last night was incredible, and—"

"Ryan, if you know what's good for you, you'll stop there." She brought a finger to his lips. "Let's just go with *incredible* for now."

He hid his flustered reaction by rummaging through the bag. Peanut butter and jelly sandwich with the crust cut off. Fish crackers. A juice box. "Did you steal this from a schoolkid or something?"

"I'm a nanny, not a chef. Peanut butter and goldfish are all I know. It'd be cheating if I had Holly do it."

"It's perfect." He gave up the monumental task of keeping himself away from her and drew close enough to steal a kiss. She stole it right back, robbing him of sanity and a sense of his surroundings. "Thank you for thinking of me. Did you eat already?"

"Actually, that's kind of what I wanted to talk to you about."

He washed his hands in a small stone sink and hoisted himself onto the worktable next to her. Taking a big bite of the sandwich—gooey and sweet—he waited for her to elaborate. Her shifty eyes and the way she was running her finger repeatedly around a piston ring were clear signs that this wasn't just a friendly chat.

"Don't look so worried," he chided. "If it makes things easier, I'll never mention lunch again. I relinquish all my postcoital rights to dictate your diet and exercise."

"No, that's not…" A slow smile worked across her face, and she pointed at him. "Oh, I get it—you're being hilarious again. Why do I get the sudden feeling I unleashed a beast last night?"

He took another bite of his sandwich and didn't say what he was thinking. *Because you did.*

"The thing is, I'm heading into town to have lunch with Jenna." Amy didn't know why it was so hard to just say it, but the words weren't as light on her tongue as she would have liked.

"That sounds like fun."

"Jake is going too."

She could feel Ryan's body stiffen next to hers, and she placed her hand on his thigh to reassure him. Damn. He was so rigid he could snap a belt around that muscle.

"O-kay," he said slowly. "What does that mean? Are you going to talk to them about…the situation?"

"It means I'm having lunch with some friends. That's all."

"Or possibly having lunch with some family."

"Friends."

"Or family."

"Or friends." She shrugged, but it was a feeble gesture, and they both knew it. "I've been doing some thinking, and it doesn't really matter which one they are anymore, does it?"

He set his sandwich down on the table—being careful to keep it on the plastic—and turned to study her. Darn it. It was impossible to be light and flippant when he looked at her like that. When Ryan was soft and flirty and hilarious, it was easy to forget that there was also this hard edge waiting for a chance to slice through. Not that she didn't like the hard edge. She liked it a lot. But it was cutting a little too close for comfort right now.

"You have to talk to Mr. Montgomery about this. Or your mom. Or maybe even swab the inside of Jenna's cheek when she's not looking so you can run a test. You can't leave this question lingering in the air."

"Why does it matter so much to you?" She reached for his hands and held them in her own. His rough palms felt good against hers, so unequivocally male. "I appreciate that your sensibilities are offended on my behalf, but it doesn't really have anything to do with you, does it?"

A growl escaped his throat as his fingers tightened on hers. "Goddammit. You make it too easy for people to take advantage of you."

She scooted closer and put a hand on his leg again. He felt less like steel this time and more like a man who enjoyed the sensation of a feminine hand moving higher. "Are *you* taking advantage of me?"

He drew in a ragged breath. "I'm trying really hard not to."

She smiled and kept going, her hand squeezing as it continued its northward journey. She stopped just short of manhandling him. "Well, that makes one of us."

He released a choking sound that could have been laughter. Either that, or it was the internal struggle of a man whose balls were within her immediate reach. "Take it from someone who spent most of his life pretending his problems didn't exist—you don't want to wait until the day everything goes up in flames. It's much harder to recover from that than you realize."

Ryan didn't talk about himself nearly enough to render that statement casual, and she felt the weight of his confession perched on her heart.

"And I promise you I don't intend to let things get that far," she said, hoping it was enough. "I know I can always go to my mom and ask her, point-blank, if Mr. Montgomery is my dad. She'd tell me. But I need to try this on my terms first. I appreciate that you're looking out for me—I really do—but I'm not so sure I'm ready to face what happens *after*. Once I know, that's it. There's no taking it back. My life here will never be the same. And you've already said you aren't necessarily going to be here to help me deal with it."

The look of anguish that crossed his face was enough to send her whole body quivering. It was an unfair amount of pressure to put on a man—holding his commitment issues accountable for her inability to move past deer-in-the-headlights mode—but it was the truth. If this was going to be the Amy Sanders show, then she was doing it her way. Slow and steady. Confrontation-free.

"Ryan, I look at you and I see what happens when a person is ripped away from the place he loves. Don't try to argue. I wasn't kidding when I said I'm on to you, that I've been watching you for a while now. It always seems to me that no matter where you are in this big house—what you're doing or who you're with—you always have an expression of such…despair. Like this is the last place on earth you want to be, and you're just waiting for the day someone invites you back to your own life." Hoping to ease some of his torment, she pressed her lips against his, soft and peanut buttery. "I know that feeling well. *Too* well. I don't think I could leave here again."

"The Montgomerys could hardly keep you from the whole town." He brushed the hair from her face, his hand lingering on the back of her neck. "Besides—even if they did, you aren't alone. I made the mistake of pinning all my hopes and dreams on one path, but you're full of options. You have your mom, your friends, your ballet."

"Don't be too hasty there, Lucas. Yours isn't the only career that circled the drain." Since that was yet another topic of conversation she'd happily bury and never face again, she distracted them both by swinging one leg over his lap. "Now kiss me, quick. I have five minutes until I need to leave for lunch."

He gripped her thighs and pulled her flush against him. Metal parts skittered off the tabletop and clattered to the ground, taking Ryan's sandwich with them, but he didn't seem to care. He ran a hand up, slipping between the warm cotton of her shirt and her skin, which felt soft and feminine under his rough palms.

"Five minutes isn't nearly long enough for me to do the things I want to," he said.

She arched into him and accepted his hot, needy kiss. Five minutes wasn't enough time for her either, but she'd take what she could get from this man. She had a feeling it might be good practice.

With Ryan, she knew she'd always be left straining for more.

"Do I HAVE something on my face?" Jenna lifted a napkin and dabbed daintily at the corners of her mouth. "Come on, Amy. You know I count on you to tell me when I have misplaced buttons and gnarly chin hairs. No one else will."

Amy laughed and forced herself to stop staring at the wide-eyed beauty across the table. "Ridiculous. You're flawless from head to toe. You've never had a wayward hair in your life."

Or moved with anything other than grace or made inappropriate bodily noises or said the wrong thing. With almost five feet ten inches to command, Jenna should have been a study of great, hulking movements and awkward angles. But poise was so deeply ingrained in her DNA that she never so much as stubbed a toe. And even if she *did* have something on her face, it would probably start a new trend. Mustard face patches. Coffee splotches as the new tie-dye.

Jenna patted her hair, the signature auburn tresses worn sleek and long, and said simply, "Thank you."

No fanfare. No false modesty. Jenna knew her worth and simply accepted it. Amy loved that about her.

On impulse, she grabbed Jenna's hand and squeezed—and also took a moment to examine her thumbnail. It was overly wide, just like hers, though Jenna's cuticles were so perfect they could have been carved of glass. She turned the hand over and glanced at Jenna's palm. Were life lines an inherited trait?

"You're being weird," Jake said, watching her.

Um. Yes. Yes, she was. She dropped Jenna's hand and forced her own two to clasp together in her lap. "I'm just so sad Jenna has to leave already," she said by way of explanation. "Can't you stay a few more days?"

"You still have me," Jake said. Like Jenna, he was all poise and hair across the table. They'd taken her to the only restaurant in Ransom Creek with cloth napkins, a French-style bistro whose menu items she'd been expected to not only pronounce, but understand—the result of all those years touring Europe, naturally. Damn those fake postcards she'd sent with pictures of the Louvre on them. She was pretty sure she was eating some sort of animal testicle right now. "Don't I count?"

"Nope," she said cheerfully, and speared another sperm sac with her fork. "You only want to hang out with me because you're stuck in Ransom Creek and are bored out of your mind."

Jenna sat back and looked carefully at her brother. Amy knew, based on the few private snatches of conversation they'd managed, that Jenna shared some of her concerns about the current state of Jake's life—spiraling, spinning out of control. Unfortunately, she was far too busy to do something about it. Amy couldn't name what it was Jenna did for the hotels, but it had something to do with a lot of foreign travel and mysterious meetings with mustachioed men in suits. At least, that was how she'd always pictured it in her head. It was all very glamorous in there.

"Be nice," Jake chided. "I'm suffering from the pains of rejection over here. I'm still having a hard time figuring out how the chauffeur got the better of me."

Amy's eyes flew open. "You know?" What else did he have insider information on? How deep in Montgomery Manor mysteries did he go? She grabbed Jake's hand and examined his thumb, flustered when she discovered another fine example of an overly wide nail. *Dammit.* Lots of people had similar-looking fingernails. They were fingernails, for crying out loud. There were only so many variations on a theme.

Jake gently withdrew his hand. "I might not be the most astute member of my family, but even I have the ability to smell out a romance when it's taking place right under my nose. Besides—no man suggests taking a woman out on a date with her mother unless he's in it for the long haul. He's clearly smitten."

The long haul part threw her, which was the only reason she could think of for how many seconds it took the rest of that statement to sink in. She sat up, alarmed. "Wait—going to the beach with Mom was Ryan's idea?"

"Of course it was. You didn't think I came up with that self-sacrificing gesture on my own, did you?"

"And he let you take credit for it?"

Jake waved a hand. "The mysteries of love. Don't ask me to explain them—I couldn't even tell you where to start."

"But…you…" She was confused and overwhelmed and so touched by Ryan's gesture that she was having a hard time finding the words. *Of course* it was Ryan who'd come up with the day at the beach. That was playful Ryan, sweet Ryan, the Ryan who would make sure she enjoyed herself even if it was at his own expense. Now that she'd started getting to know this man—both biblically and personally—she was discovering he was composed almost entirely of gestures like these.

It made her so happy. And so very devastatingly sad.

"*But I* nothing, Amy." He reached across the table and pinched her chin. It was a gesture she remembered well from childhood, from all those times she needed comforting and he'd been there to supply it. "I still don't think it was very nice of you to grow up so thoroughly without warning me first, but the truth is that you're too good for me. You're too good for all of us."

"That's not news. The rest of us have known that forever." Jenna rolled her eyes and continued picking delicately at her lunch—lettuce with a side of lettuce. "She's the heart you and Monty and I don't have. She always has been."

Amy gulped and stared at her hands, wide thumbnail and all. That, right there, was what Ryan would never understand about her relationship with the Montgomerys, why it was so hard for her to upset the balance of things now that she'd finally found her place again. When she looked at these people, all she saw was love. Acceptance. A home. It didn't matter if they shared the same blood as her—they would always be her family.

Right?

Oh, dear. Now she was crying.

"Well, shit." Jake looked back and forth between the two women, bewildered. "What'd we say?"

"She's clearly losing it," Jenna said calmly. "Sweetie, I think maybe you need to get out more—find some time to do your own thing. Dad says you haven't used the studio even once since you've been back."

"Oh." She sniffled, wiping at her eyes with the back of her hand, stalling for time. "I didn't know it was still there. I was sure it'd be a supply closet by now."

Jenna wiped daintily at her mouth. "Serena tried to put her exercise equipment in there, but Dad wouldn't have it. It was always his hope you'd find a way back to us, and he wanted everything waiting just as you left it."

"I'd like to see you dance sometime," Jake said, sounding as though he meant it. And not in a creepy way either, which only made things worse. Sincerity from these two was the worst possible sentiment right now. "I always meant to sit in on one of your shows."

"I tried once," Jenna said, also intent. "In Germany, I believe it was."

She waited a long moment, painful in the way it dragged on, until Amy was able to gather enough courage to meet her gaze. It was a mistake. She felt as though she was looking at a softer, feminine, much more attractive version of Mr. Montgomery—calculating but not cold, shrewd but not unkind. Jenna was clearly her father's daughter.

But am I?

"It was when I was there for the opening of the hotel in Zurich," Jenna added.

Calculating and shrewd, all right. Amy sank in her chair.

"Zurich?" she said weakly.

"I suppose I should have told you I was coming, but I wanted it to be a surprise. It was my own fault."

"She wasn't there?" Jake asked.

"Out sick for that performance, I believe." Jenna smiled and returned her attention to her lettuce. "Isn't that right, Amy?"

Amy—never adept at lying—did the only thing she could think of. With a bright smile, she shoveled in as much food as could reasonably fit and chewed. And chewed. And chewed. It was amazing what a full two minutes of wrapping her mouth around testicles could do to change an unpleasant topic of conversation.

She thought about Ryan and swallowed. That was definitely a trick she'd have to remember for later.

FOURTEEN

RYAN'S PULSE PICKED UP at the sound of wheels screeching.

Under normal circumstances, the rubbery squeal of a sharp turn had a way of filling him with excitement rather than dread. Screeching meant speed, and speed meant momentum. When a man had been mired in stagnation as long as him, anything that fostered forward movement was a thing to welcome with both feet on the pedal.

But that was his old life. Here, at Montgomery Manor, where birds chirped and people went quietly about their business, screeching wheels were practically harbingers of doom.

A female gasp and another screech had him rounding the corner of the basement-level hallway at a clipped pace. Darkness enveloped him almost instantly, save for the blinding flash of light as a car went up in flames.

He watched for a moment, emotions of regret and longing swirling through him, before speaking. "Did you know it's virtually impossible to make a car explode like that in real life?"

Amy screamed and fell off the edge of the couch, where she'd been curled in a ball, clutching a throw pillow embroidered with tropical birds. The rec room wasn't a place he normally sought—the wall-to-wall media center set aside for employee use reminded him uncomfortably of the past—but he'd sought her out everywhere else and had come up empty.

Now that he was here, it didn't seem like such a bad place, but that was probably Amy's doing. Her presence rendered the black painted walls somehow warm, the vintage movie posters more kitschy than pretentious. But then, she could probably make the desolation of the moon feel like home.

Ryan laughed as she rolled over onto her stomach and glared up at him. "You jerk. You scared the crap out of me. How long have you been standing there watching?"

"Not long." And long enough. He reached for the remote control that had been abandoned on the couch and pushed Mute. Watching *The Devil's Run* was hard enough on its own. Listening to it was torture. He'd done a lot of really bad action flicks early on in his career, complete with cheesy one-liners, scantily clad women and cars exploding for no reason other than a director with a love of pyrotechnics.

Though the pyrotechnics were pretty cool. A few of the burn scars on his forearms could be attributed to a little preshow experimentation with the squibs.

He reached out a hand. "You should have told me you wanted to see one of my movies. I have a lot better ones than this."

"I dunno—I'm digging the outdated special effects. You must have been really young when you got started."

"Young and stupid and careless," he agreed, hoisting her up. "It's why I got so much work. I did the movies no one else would."

He took a moment to wrap an arm around her waist and savor the fact that he was actually doing this. Holding her. Leaning in. Stealing a kiss, though calling it *stolen* was a bit of a stretch at this point. Her lips were willing, her tongue enthusiastic, her body pliable. It seemed wrong to take so much joy in the physical pleasures of her proximity when so much between them remained unfinished, but he didn't know what else to do.

He'd talked to his agent that afternoon, hoping for some kind of non-Montgomery-inspired miracle on the job front, but she'd had nothing for him other than another stricture to "Sit tight and keep up the clean profile." It had taken all his restraint not to tell her where she could shove her clean profile, then hang up the phone.

He didn't want to touch Mr. Montgomery's offer. He wanted to shove it deep in a drawer and pretend it never existed. But it was looking more and more as if a deal with that devil was his only option. He'd have to cash in on Amy's messed-up family life. Admit that Mr. Montgomery owned him—owned them all.

He groaned, a sound that was as much a plea for help as it was a visceral response to Amy's tongue sliding across his own. There was no happily ever after in his story, and he was weak to drag her into it. She deserved the setting sun, the kiss on the beach, the credits rolling to a theater full of happy sighs.

Not a bunch of assholes who would take what she had to offer and give nothing in return.

Amy took Ryan's groan as a sign he was about to start beating himself up again, so she dropped to the couch, tugging on his hand so he had no choice but to sink into the cushions next to her. This was clearly one of those times he needed to be coaxed into a good mood, and it just so happened she was in need of a good coaxing herself.

"Want to watch the rest of the movie with me?" she asked brightly. "You can give me a personal play-by-play, fill me in on all the insider gossip. Ooh, or point out the hot starlets who slept with you to get ahead."

"Nobody under the age of eighty calls them starlets," Ryan grumbled, but he made room for her as she settled herself lengthwise on the cushions and placed her head in his lap. No man could remain grumpy for long when a woman's mouth was less than a ruler's length away from his crotch. "And you're deluded if you think anyone uses the stunt crew to boost their careers. We were one very small step up from craft services."

"Ooh, craft services sound promising. Is that like découpage for movie stars?"

He ran an abstracted hand through her hair, playing with the strands and sending jolts of awareness down her neck, making her entire body feel like a limb returning to life after a deep, prickly sleep. "Not quite. They're the people who provide on-set meals."

"Even better. In case you haven't noticed, I have a soft spot for people who carry snacks. Now turn the sound back on. You're interrupting my Ryan Lucas marathon. I started from the beginning and am working my way through."

"This is my fourth movie. How long have you been down here?"

"Hours," she admitted. "Though Alex made me fast-forward through most of *Halloween House of*

Horrors. He kept having to come down to investigate all my screaming. By the fifth or sixth time, he was ready to break the DVD in half."

Ryan chuckled and moved on to an actual scalp massage—firm fingers, strong hands, a woman about to propose marriage based on the equal merits of both. "Are you sure you wouldn't rather watch a romantic comedy?"

"Wow. That's quite a sacrifice. You must really hate your own movies."

His only response was to click the play button and resume the show. It *was* awful, the plot holes so huge that not even the highly muscular cop hero could lift them, but she liked slowing the driving scenes down to see if she could catch a glimpse of Ryan. She thought maybe she'd seen his adorably protruding ears in one or two of the shots, but that could have been her overactive imagination mating shamelessly with wishful thinking.

He shifted as a particularly loud car scene started, this one moving improbably through a parking garage that had to have been eight hundred levels tall for it to last as long as it did. "Oh, so this part coming up? Watch when the car slides into that spot behind the Jeep. You can see me get out of the driver's side before they cut to the actor. That happens a lot more in the lower budget movies than in the newer ones."

Sure enough, she caught a flash of his face— young and earnest and clearly proud of his maneuver—as he jumped out. The sight of him hit like a sucker punch to her emotional center. This movie was only about eight years old, but there wasn't even a glimmer of that kind of joy in him now. Or at least not without some major coaxing and bedroom antics first.

"You don't talk much about it, despite it being such a big part of your life," she said between explosions. "What was it like?"

Even though her attention was fixed on the screen, Amy knew the exact moment when Ryan looked down at her, felt the pressure of his scrutiny like weights piled directly on her solar plexus.

"The driving was incredible." His gaze grew lighter as he slipped into a nostalgic tone. "Remember how exhilarated you felt that day in the rental car— after just five minutes? Imagine living that every day. I'll never be the kind of guy who can own the types of cars Mr. Montgomery has, but for a few hours every day, I got to pretend I was. I got to be the badass fleeing from a squad of hit men. I got to be the getaway driver with fifty million dollars stashed in the trunk."

"I knew it! You totally like to play make-believe."

His laughter shook her. "I guess I do. I never thought of it that way."

She could understand the appeal. It was the same as putting on her princess gown and waving to crowds. Losing yourself in someone else's story held a kind of magic few people could appreciate or understand. "So what about the rest of it? I want to hear everything."

"What everything?"

"You know. The parties. The lifestyle. The glamour."

"There was no glamour." His words were flat, but the continual movement of his hands through her hair robbed them of any malice. "There were parties, though. Actually, that should be singular. Party. Just one. A sad, never-ending dance of drinking, drugs and self-indulgence. I walked through the doors one night and never left."

"I saw an old photograph like that once." She nestled deeper in his lap. It was impossible to ignore the fact that her head was encased in great, powerful thighs—that a rotation of about forty-five degrees would have his cock and her mouth in an interesting position. A soft sigh of longing escaped her lips, but that was all she allowed herself. She wasn't messing up this opportunity to peek under Ryan's skin. "It was some old-time dance marathon, and these three couples had been on their feet for like forty-eight hours or something. The party was a mess of deflated balloons and torn crepe paper, but the couples were still standing in the middle of the room, barely able to keep their eyes open, but determined to win. They were literally leaning on one another to stay standing."

He released a soft huff. "I'm not talking about your grandma's sock hop. This was more like a frat party where everyone was in competition to be King Dick. We were all fighting to be the one who could drink the most, the one who could drive the fastest, the one who could take the biggest risks and not get caught. And I lost. I lost everything."

"Maybe that's only because you didn't have someone there to prop you up."

Ryan stopped his movements through her hair, his fingers gripped so firmly in the tangled strands it almost felt like he was trying to hurt her. But she knew, from glancing at the twist of his mouth, that her pain didn't touch his.

"I think you might have missed your calling," he finally said. "You're very good at finding easy solutions to the most complex problems."

"I know, right? I'd have made an excellent shrink. It's because I manipulate tiny brains all day long. They can't handle much more than the easy solution."

"I'm going to take that tiny brains comment as a compliment." He smiled down at her. It was such a soft, gentle smile—so unlike someone who'd hidden behind drunken Hollywood frat parties that she had a hard time reconciling the man in the movie to the one sitting on the couch with her.

"So how much do I owe you, Dr. Sanders? I warn you—I don't have much to give."

"One kiss. Possibly two."

He brought her mouth to his. The kiss he claimed was light to the point of nonexistence, even more meaningful because it was all the payment she'd ever need.

"We don't have to keep watching the movie if you don't want," she offered. "If it's painful, I mean. I just wanted to see how you used to be." *I wanted to see what it is about these movies that holds so much allure. I wanted to see what it is I'm competing against.*

Ryan shrugged. "It's not a big deal. Though I don't suppose we can cleanse the palate with any videos of you dancing, can we? Some obscure European ballet I can use to fuel my fantasies for the next decade?" He'd meant it as a joke, a way to change the subject, but the way Amy frowned indicated that she took it as anything but. Trust him to turn something as beautiful and valued as classical dance and turn it into a sex fantasy. "I'm sorry. I didn't mean for that to come off so perverted."

"No—it's not that." She frowned and then laughed, from one end of the spectrum to the other. "Well, it *was* kind of perverted of you, but that's not the problem. I kind of like your perverse side. But what would you say if I told you there aren't any videos of me dancing?"

"I'd say it's a shame," he said honestly. "And probably not true. Someone, somewhere had to sneak in a camera phone and post a pirated copy of one of your performances. I'm sure I can find one. I'm not just a glorified mechanic. I have exceptional Google-fu."

"Not even the best Google-fu in the world would help you with this one, I'm afraid." She struggled to sit up and brushed a lock of hair from her face, her expression earnest. "Can I tell you something? Something I've never told anyone?"

"Of course you can," he said quickly. Too quickly, like a man no one trusted with secrets, a man who sucked at letting people in. Slower and with more consideration, he added, "I hope you never feel like you have to hide things from me. I know I haven't been very good at this opening up to other people stuff, but I like to think you're helping me be better at it."

She nodded once. "Thank you. That means a lot."

He took her hands and waited, expecting her to launch into her tale, to break into tears, to do anything that would justify the sudden swell of anticipation he felt. Whatever she wanted to confess, it couldn't be any worse than the things he'd done lately.

"You have to promise not to laugh."

"Of course not. I'd never do that."

She cast a doubtful look at him, her nose wrinkled. "I mean it. This is serious. This was my life for almost five years. No giggling."

"I don't giggle."

"You might when I tell you this."

"Amy. I have never, in all my life, felt an urge to giggle at someone else's misfortune."

"Misfortune? You have it all wrong. I *loved* working at the Enchanted Forest."

"The enchanted what?"

"Forest. Just outside Des Moines—you know, *Where fairytale dreams come true-la-la?*"

That ditty sounded awfully familiar…

"I was Fairy Princess Number Three. Do you know how many of us there were? Twenty-five. And I was number three. That's how good I was."

He shook his head as if to clear it. When that didn't work, he reached over and clicked off the television. When that didn't work, he finally gave in and spoke. "I'm sorry—did you just say your big confession is that you worked at a theme park? As a princess?"

She lifted a finger in warning. "Are you giggling right now?"

"No." He clamped his mouth shut. "Mmm-hmm."

"Ryan, you promised!" She sprang to her feet and tossed the bird-embroidered pillow at his face. When it landed square on his nose—that crooked, rugged, as-far-removed-from-theme-park-foresthood-as-you-could-possibly-get nose, she gave in to a profound urge to giggle herself. "I can't believe you. You're such an asshole."

"It's just…I can't…" He really did give in to laughter this time. "Do you know how many times I've compared you to an animated princess in my head? You fended off tourists with a baguette. You delight children in your spare time. I was *sure* that birds landed on your windowsill in the morning to wake you up."

"It's not funny," she protested as he pulled her into his arms and held her there. His chest rumbled as his humor subsided, wiping away any and all negative feelings she'd ever had about her life decisions. It was almost scary, how easily Ryan could make her feel better, this man who didn't laugh at anything unless she made him. "My mom and Mr. Montgomery and everyone—except Jenna, it seems—thinks I was this super great ballet dancer. But I wasn't. I was mediocre at best. I hated almost everything about it. The body shaming and the competitiveness and the being banished from home."

"Hey," he said when her voice caught on that last bit. He tilted her face to meet his, and she could see that the laughter in his eyes had been replaced by a hard glint. "Did they really banish you?"

"Of course not." She buried her head in his chest and spoke directly to the muscles. The muscles understood. "But I was too ashamed to come back on my own. Ballet school was a lot of money, Ryan, and they wanted so badly for me to be successful. You have no idea what it's like to have all these people rooting for you, holding you up and supporting you, and then… boom. Nothing. Failure. Letting them down with a crystal tiara and potted rouge."

"No. I wouldn't know what that's like."

Her mouth fell open. *Oh, crap.* That was a really shitty thing to say to this man, all alone in the world with no one around to care what happened to his career, good or bad.

But he continued on, unabated. "But I *do* know that your mom loves you. And that you deserve to do anything in this world that makes you happy, regardless of what anyone else has to say about it—especially if their last name is Montgomery. And that you were probably the best fucking princess the Enchanted Forest has ever seen."

She choked on a watery laugh. "I was *fantastic*."

"See?" he said gently. "It's not so terrible."

And when he said it like that, things didn't seem quite so bleak. No one *made* her take ballet. No one *forced* her to keep going after that first burst of homesickness when she was nineteen. Her mom might have been disappointed if she'd come home without any accolades trailing behind her, but wouldn't have barricaded the doors against her entry.

"I guess I was too scared to say anything," she admitted. "I got swept up in my lies until it became easier to live with them than to try and correct them."

"No kidding? You? Avoiding confrontation at all costs?"

She shoved him on the chest, intending to be playful but coming across hard enough to knock him backward. He caught her wrists and held her there, his grip hard but his expression soft. She thought she might melt in his eyes, in the understanding reflecting back at her. "Hey. It's okay. I'm not judging you. It's just an observation."

It wasn't *just* an observation, though. It was the truth. Rather than face reality, she'd hide her professional failings behind magical forests. She'd pretend

she didn't care whether or not Mr. Montgomery was
her real dad. She'd tell Ryan it was perfectly fine that
he considered their relationship a pit stop on his way
back up to the top.

Reality was a cold, hard place.

"I *am* a little disappointed about the dancing stuff,
though," he said, not releasing his grip. If anything,
he only tightened his hold on her, bringing her close
enough that she could feel the latent strength rising
off his body, promising untold delights. "I was really
looking forward to seeing you move."

She felt a slow, steady smile creep across her face.
This she was good at. *This* she could do. "Oh, I can
still dance. I took ballet lessons in some form or another for fifteen years of my life, and there was major
twirling every night at the Forest. I've got moves you
wouldn't believe."

His strength wasn't so latent now. Pressed against
him, their bodies flush, she'd never felt so much at a
man's mercy in her life. "Show me."

"Why, Ryan Lucas, you sweet talker, you. I know
just the place."

FIFTEEN

IT WAS A good thing stretching provided so much fodder for the imagination.

If Amy had known she'd be dancing in front of an audience anytime in the near future, she'd have found some time to come down to the studio and brush up on her skills first. Or at least come up with a routine that made it look as if she was still capable of this kind of stuff. It was frustrating—her body remembered every pirouette, every arabesque was sealed into her muscle memory—but the strength wasn't there anymore. This was what it probably felt like for men when the will was strong but the flesh was weak. They knew how to get it up, they remembered performances that rocked worlds, but the physical capabilities held themselves stubbornly out of reach.

Poor men. She'd never laugh at one of those cheesy impotence commercials again.

She'd already spent a good ten minutes squeezing her feet into her old toe shoes, and had lingered over the almost-but-not-quite splits for as long as she could get away with it. Now she was just stalling.

With a sigh, she gave up on the stretching and headed to the sound system built in to a side panel of the studio. It had been a nice facility when she was a teenager, and it remained one despite having sat untouched for so long. The majority of the room was

composed of floor-to-ceiling mirrors without even
so much as a fingerprint to mar the shining surface.
A long barre broke one of the mirrored walls into
twin halves, but not even that impeded the reflections of herself that cast off in every direction, each
one mocking more cruelly than the last.

She used to be so much better at this.

"Are you sure you want to watch?" She leaned on
one leg and pouted. Images of Ryan reflected off in
every direction too, though he looked coolly masculine as he leaned against the door frame, arms crossed
and an expectant pull on his lips.

Expectant and something else. Something hot and
twisty and probably the direct result of those splits.

"You're the one who bragged about all your secret
moves," he said. "I was content to sit there all night
watching my awful movies. What are you afraid is
going to happen?"

*That I'll fall flat on my face in the middle of a move
I'm way too out of shape to attempt. That I'll ruin the
fantasy you've built up in your head of me. That this,
like everything else, won't be enough.*

"I haven't done any of this stuff in years," she said,
picking the first one and running with it. Of the three,
it seemed the safest to put into words. "The last time
I went in for an actual ballet audition, I ran into the
girl next to me. Like, ran into her, knocked her flat
on her ass, had to put myself into the dancer cone of
shame afterward. It was awful."

"It can't be any worse than driving a stunt car into
a freeway overpass."

Well, yes. That was true. "But you were…impaired
at the time. I just suck."

"That's not how I see it at all." He tensed, enough that he wasn't leaning on the door frame so much as the door frame was leaning on him. "I made stupid choices that forced me out of the game. All you did was decide to play a different one."

That was one of the most logical things anyone had ever said to her. And nice. And so much like Ryan it made her want to cry. Because even though they weren't so very different—they were the every-day workers among the rich and famous, lovers of a good old-fashioned game of laser tag—all he seemed to notice were the gaps between them. He wanted the fast-paced life he'd once had. She wanted the slow pace of home.

Maybe he was right. Maybe that was too big of a gap. Maybe there was no bridge big enough to hold them together for long.

She was about to call the whole thing off when Ryan did a pirouette—or what he probably *thought* was one—and stopped right in front of her, his hands coming to rest naturally on her hips. It was this nat-ural fit of him that gave her pause. She'd learned long ago to trust her body to know what it was doing when the rest of her didn't. And the way it reacted to his nearness, flaring like a match the second it catches, screamed at her to hold on as tight as she possibly could.

The feeling only intensified when a playful taunt curved his lips. "This isn't another one of those pin-ball situations, is it?"

"There's no such thing as a pinball situation."

"Oh, yes, there is. It's what I'm officially calling it when you flaunt your nonexistent skills at me, prom-

ising things you can't deliver. That beach volleyball
win was a total fluke, wasn't it?"

Damn the man. He knew very well she was powerless against a challenge like that. She pointed at the
wall. "Sit down, my friend. You're about to eat those
words. I hope you like swans. And lakes."

She wasn't sure what music was in the sound
system, but she doubted Ryan cared whether it was
Tchaikovsky that pounded through the recessed
speakers or the Ace of Base CD she used to play to
warm up before her sessions. When she hit the play
button, the music landed somewhere in the middle—
an upbeat classical remix—so she decided to go with
it. There was no way she remembered all the chore-
ography for *Swan Lake* anyway. This was going to
be a dance done entirely on a wing and a prayer and
the unerring belief that Ryan wouldn't know what he
was watching anyway.

She lifted her arm—wing up. She blew out a long
breath—prayer said.

And she danced.

RYAN WASN'T SURE what he'd been expecting when he
goaded Amy into dancing. He'd never been much of
a one for appreciating the true art of ballet—he had
far too much love of a well-timed explosion for that—
and he also wasn't one of those guys who pretended
to love the highbrow aspect but really just went to
gawk at women in leotards. He'd known his fair share
of guys like that, and he didn't care for the duplicity
of it. If you wanted to go watch a woman dance on
a pole, go watch a woman dance on a pole. No need
to cloak it in classical music and operatic tendencies.

In defiance of everything he knew about dance and women and poles, Amy captured his interest and swallowed it whole. Dressed as she was in tiny jean shorts and a loose-fitting tank top, she was girlish and casual—two adjectives she defined and that defined her right back. The strength of her thighs was visible in each twitch of muscle, the tight, lean curves of her ass cupped and released against the fabric. And as she lifted a leg and spun, and spun again, and kept spinning, he felt a sense of awe and appreciation that had nothing—and everything—to do with sex.

The graceful movements of her arms and legs were breathtaking. So simple, so elegant, that he could only wonder at the strength required to make it look so effortless. At the same time, there was no mistaking that the movements of her body filled him with an irrepressible longing—and not an entirely erotic one. Eroticism was in there, of course—he doubted there would ever be a time when he could look at Amy and not feel the stirrings of desire—but there was more to it than that.

It was sadness. And joy. And a feeling of isolation at odds with the fact that between the two of them, hundreds of their images filled the room.

Fuck. He wanted to fall into the dance with her, stand in the middle of the room and let her whirl around him, binding him with her mesmerizing movements. And when she got so tired she couldn't take another step, he wanted to be there to prop her up until the dance was through.

The realization should have made him elated.

Instead, he just felt crushed. Amy was everything he'd ever wanted, nothing he deserved, and she was tied to this place with so many complicated layers of strings she'd never be fully free of it.

The music came to a crashing halt, and she stopped, breathing heavily, her face red from exertion. "There. Don't say I didn't warn you."

"That you would take my breath away?" Nothing she could have said would have prepared him for *that*. "I take all my doubts back. Every one. That was incredible."

"Really? You thought so?" She wasn't doubtful or falsely modest, wasn't fishing for praise or bringing herself down in that way women sometimes did when given a compliment. She seemed genuinely interested in his opinion.

He strode toward her, feeling the strain on his lower half where the blood had shifted and rendered all movements—except lunging ones—awkward. Taking her outstretched hand, he gave her a twirl. "I can't remember the last time I've seen anything that beautiful," he said truthfully. And before he could think better of it, driven by his urge to make sense of where and why and how they got into this predicament, he kept going. "You're really talented. It's a goddamn shame you ended up at this place."

Where dreams died. And lived again, but only at the expense of people you cared about.

She frowned, her playful twirl stopping as suddenly as it had started. "I didn't *end up* here. This is my home."

He refused to unclasp her hand from his, fearful that their physical separation would equal an emotional one. "You're an amazing dancer, Amy, and an even more amazing human being. You could do anything you put your mind to."

She struggled to pull her hand free, but he didn't let go. "I am doing what I put my mind to. I know the Manor is the last place in the world *you* want to be, but I'm here because it's where I belong."

"Right. You belong. You belong so much you won't even ask about your parentage for fear they'll kick you out."

"I thought you weren't going to push me," she said, her expression growing hurt. "I thought you were going to let me figure this out in my own time."

He was trying. He really was. But she had no idea how difficult it was for him to look at her—free and untainted by the past—and watch her *choose* stagnation. *Choose* to stay grounded when it was so clear she could fly. It was maddening.

"How can you love this place so much when it's obvious you're scared to death of the truth?" The question was harsh and rhetorical, meant to put space between them. But Amy, damn her, only drew closer, became softer, tore at his resolve until it felt as tattered and ragged as the rest of him.

"It's easy," she said. "Can't you feel the ghosts in this room?"

He followed the path of her gaze as it swept over the room, taking in the bright lights above, the warm golden hue of the glistening floorboards below. Even though he'd caught only a glimpse of the outdated sound system, it looked pretty high-end for its time. And it was, of course, nestled in a mansion in one of the most beautiful places on God's green earth.

"No," he said. "All I see in here is hope. I'll never

be Mr. Montgomery's most vocal fan, but if he built you this to help boost your career—" to help get her out of here "—then I think it might be my favorite room in this whole house."

"But he didn't build it for me." Amy took another step toward Ryan, taking comfort from his presence, even as he thrummed with an intense, almost palpable energy. It was so different from her own energy, deflated and tired. When had she gotten so tired? "He built it for Jenna. She expressed an interest in ballet one day, and voilà—a studio was born, an instructor engaged, the nanny's daughter encouraged to take lessons with her to sweeten the deal."

As if understanding how difficult it was for her to confess—to put into words this thing she'd never admitted to anyone, not even herself—Ryan pulled her tight, tucking her head into his neck and allowing one hand to drift to her waist. Their posture meant she was talking into his muscles again rather than to his face, but she found that made the words come easier. And reduced the ghosts to curious spectators. Curious, slightly perverted spectators.

"It wasn't your dream, was it? The dancing. It was never your dream."

"Not even remotely."

"Oh, Amy." He sounded sad for her. Maybe even disappointed. "Didn't you ever tell anyone how you felt?"

Of course she didn't. How could she have, when all she'd ever wanted was to be a part of this family that wasn't her own?

"I never had much opportunity to," she said by way of explanation. "Jenna quit ballet after a few months when she got more interested in horses, but Mr. Montgomery said he'd keep the instructor on for as long as I wanted. I would have preferred to do gymnastics or play soccer, but I was so little at the time—six, maybe seven—and it was the first time I'd had something of my own here. My very own, not just as a bystander to one of the other kids. Even though the studio was a hand-me-down, I liked the idea of having it all to myself."

She could feel Ryan's arms grow tighter around her, and she knew in an instant what he was thinking—what he was feeling. She drew back a little and lifted a hand to his face. "Don't pity me, and don't say that this just means I don't owe Mr. Montgomery anything. I had a lot more than most kids growing up."

One of the ghosts mocked her in the distance.

"So what happened? How did you go from six and a private instructor to sixteen and the professional circuit?"

"My teacher, Madame Pritchard, thought I showed promise, though I don't know how much of that was true and how much of it she was being paid to say. I used to spend hours after our lessons, working the barre, trying to get all the way down in the splits, desperate to learn the grace Jenna had been born with but didn't seem to care about using. I hated it. I was lonely. I wanted to be upstairs with the other kids, riding horses, playing video games, eating cookies. But even more than that, I wanted to show Mr. Montgomery that his gift was appreciated. That I was worthy of receiving it in the first place."

"Amy." Ryan reached down and lifted her chin, forcing her to look up, acknowledge him standing there, bask in his warmth. But she didn't want to. The Montgomery Manor chauffeur was yet another thing she couldn't have for her very own. He was only on loan to her, would be snatched away the moment she let her guard down.

"Ryan." She echoed his tone, that condescension and heat somehow wrapped into one.

"What will it take for you to realize that you're so much better than these people?" he asked. "They have money, yes, and power, sure, but that's all. Nothing they buy or demand or build will ever change the fact that you're worth a thousand of them. I'd rather have one of your smiles than a million of Mr. Montgomery's dollars. I'd trade everything I have to see one right now."

She felt a smile—maybe not a million-dollar one, but one worth at least a few hundred—lift her lips. "Maybe there aren't quite so many ghosts in here now. I think they're scared of you. If you stuck around, I think you might be able to banish them for good."

Ryan's jaw tightened, and the troubled murkiness in his gray eyes signaled to Amy he was struggling not to say what was really on his mind. The compliments might trip off his tongue, the anger at her unwillingness to rip open the wounds of her birth he would gladly share. But God forbid he open up any further than that. They were back to square one. Chauffeur and nanny. Complicated man and a woman so simple it hurt.

She waited, wondering if he'd win the internal struggle not to speak.

He did.

Instead of false promises or soul-searching discussions, he gave her the only thing she'd been promised. A kiss. And she was just stupid enough to take it. His mouth dropped to hers in a slow, almost tentative exploration of tongues and lips.

"I don't care if you never dance another day in your life," he murmured, and pressed another kiss on her mouth before moving on to the rest of her face. Eyelids, cheekbones, jawline, ear. No part of her was left untouched, no nerve ending ignored. "Or if legions of children are bereft at your absence from the theme park. I only care that you do what makes you happy."

"*You* make me happy," she said. "How's that for starters?"

"It's not bad." He growled against her throat, teeth nipping at the sensitive skin, firing her body and causing a warm pull in her belly. "And if you don't mind my saying—that's exactly what you should do right now."

Laughter gave her desire a soft edge. "Wow. That was really smooth. I'm impressed."

"It was, wasn't it?" He didn't stop kissing, now all the way down to her clavicle, where he paid proper homage to the delicate bones there. "I'm swelling up in my own importance over here."

"Oh, you are, huh?" She slipped her hands along the broad strength of his back, trailing the taper of his waist, not stopping until his ass was cupped in her hands and his *important swelling* was pressed against her. "I can tell."

He continued his downward path, his lips lingering where her breasts rose from the low plunge of her tank top. His tongue had just flicked under the lip of her bra, promising more, when he stopped and looked around. "There's not a secret video surveillance system in here or anything, is there?"

"Not that I know of," she murmured, and drew his head back to its more interesting task. "And to be honest, if you keep doing that to my boobs, I don't think I care. In fact, I hope Alex enjoys the show. Wave and smile. He could probably use the fun."

Ryan chuckled and resumed his attentions to her cleavage. Slow and wet, his tongue made demands of her body it was all too willing to give. Weak knees, quivering loins—she was nothing but a collection of parts that didn't know any better than to submit to this man.

"I had no idea you were an exhibitionist, though the contents of your sex drawer should have alerted me to your devious side." He peeked up at her, eyes glinting. "Any other kinky stuff I should know about? I like to know what it is I'm getting into."

"Hmm." She pretended to think about it. She'd hardly call herself a deviant, but she was as much a fan of the occasional maid's costume as the next girl. "I think maybe we should leave some mysteries yet to be discovered. Though I do like the idea of all these mirrors."

This time, when he looked up, his eyes weren't glinting so much as opening up and claiming her. Dropping his hands and his head and his touch, he strode purposefully to the door. With a loud bang, he slammed it shut and turned the lock on the handle.

She didn't wait for him to return before she stripped off her shirt and sent it falling to the floor.

"Jesus, Amy. You could kill a man with those kinds of moves."

"Funny—you don't look near death," she teased. But teasing wasn't what he wanted. Before she had time to register it, she was once again in his arms and being pressed against the mirrored wall. Her back was sticky with sweat from her dance, and she could feel the suction as her body molded to the mirror—which would probably leave telltale sex marks behind. But she found she didn't care quite as much as she should have, not when Ryan's hands moved relentlessly over her body and his mouth greedily took over.

She wasn't a very active partner as he nipped his way back down to her chest, lingering for a while over the boobs that held them both so much at their mercy. She tried to wriggle out of her bra—free the ladies—but he stopped her by dropping to his knees in front of her. She ran her hands through his short hair and looked at him, amused. "What are you doing down there?"

"You wanted to watch yourself in all these mirrors." He tugged at her belt, opening the metal buckle and letting himself in. "So watch."

Oh, dear God. She couldn't move her hands from his head as he jerked her shorts over her hips and down to her knees, her pink cotton panties not far behind. Without giving her a chance to protest or squeal or even breathe, he began kissing down her belly, his path sure and steady and headed right for her core.

Since it didn't appear that Ryan needed or wanted any of her assistance as his warm, wet kisses moved between her thighs, she took his advice and looked in the mirror. The idea of there ever having been ghosts in this room seemed ridiculous when she caught sight of the pair of them. They were hot and human and so very, very real. She, a whimpering body held firmly in place by the hands and tongue of a man who wanted to drive her to madness; he, the living, breathing embodiment of every female fantasy the relevant fifty-one percent of the population had ever known.

She moaned and opened her legs further as he found her wet center. He thrust his tongue against her clit hard enough to wrest a cry from her mouth.

Ryan was not a man who moved in half measures—that was something she'd known from the start. Whether driving his car through a ring of fire or playing with children out in an open field or, God forbid, drinking the pain away, he gave one hundred percent of himself to the task at hand.

Normally, that kind of single-minded intensity scared her. She'd never felt that passionate about *anything*—not work, not play, not even the two kids she'd sworn to devote the next few years of her life to. But when that intensity was directed right at her, as if she was the center of his world, she felt there was nothing better on earth. He buried his face more firmly in her mons, and she gave in to the idea that for right now, there really was nothing better on earth. She was pressed against a mirrored wall, a man suckling at her clit, eating her out as if he'd never tasted anything so delicious.

Yeah. She'd have a hard time topping this moment.

She gripped his hair so tightly he let loose a growl, which rumbled against her in a way that made her legs go numb. Fortunately for them both, his grip was firm enough to keep her standing.

But not for long. She gave herself over to the swirl

of sensations that held her transfixed, caught her own gaze in the reflection across the studio and watched—for the very first time—what she looked like as an orgasm rocked through her body.

It was a beautiful thing, a strange thing, an almost otherworldly thing, and she barely recognized the woman flush with desire and pressing herself into Ryan's face with so much ferocity she was probably suffocating the poor man. The woman in the mirror was so many things she wasn't. She was Orgasm Amy, strengthened by desire and adrenaline and the heady scent of sex that surrounded her.

Orgasm Amy wasn't afraid to take what she wanted. Orgasm Amy would walk up to Mr. Montgomery's office and demand answers. Orgasm Amy would tell Ryan that even though she could never compete with a car moving a hundred and twenty miles an hour, she'd sure as hell like to try.

But Orgasm Amy was a fleeting vision. All too soon, the sensations of pleasure ebbed away, taking her power with them. And Ryan rose from his position on the floor, leaving her standing on her own two feet—wobbly ones, she might add—and standing mostly naked in front of the ghosts again.

She caught sight of his satisfied grin and refused to give in to the pull of the macabre. While Ryan was content to remain with her, she'd be happy. Even if it killed her. "I changed my mind. I really hope no one was watching that."

His smile dimmed. "Was it that bad?"

She laughed softly and lifted a hand to trace his lips. Unable to stop herself, she leaned in and kissed him, deep and lingering, enjoying the musky taste that only the two of them combined could make. A magic potion. *Their* magic potion.

"It was that good," she corrected him. "And I don't think I want anyone else to know about this place. If the women of the world had any idea how hot it is to watch a man go down on them in a room of mirrors, there'd be a line out this door all the way to Hartford."

She snaked a hand between them, running over the soft folds of his worn T-shirt, not stopping until she hit the line where clothes met skin. Although he normally wore jeans a little loose in the hips, she could feel the tight strain of the fabric over an erection built and sustained as he feasted on her body.

God, the very idea that he'd been as turned on by that as she was had her body throbbing again, aching for more.

He stilled her hand. "You don't have to."

Maybe not, but she wanted to. She'd never been one of those women who drooled over the idea of sucking down a well-formed cock—found many aspects of a blow job too unpleasant to make the task a regular occurrence. She could never quite figure out how she was supposed to *breathe* while there was a fully erect penis in her mouth.

But there was something about *this* man and *this* room that rendered pesky details like oxygen nonexistent. She wanted nothing more than to drop to her knees and taste him. She wanted to show him that even though she might not admit her shortcomings to just anyone, she trusted him. She was willing to try for him.

"There are four floor-to-ceiling mirrors surrounding you, Ryan." She tugged on his belt. "And nothing to impede the view. Are you absolutely sure about that?"

She could hear his gulp from inches away. "Carry on."

With a laugh, she skimmed her hands down either side of his legs, hooking her fingers in his pants pockets to aid in the act of disrobing. By the time she hit her knees, he was hard and out and ready for her. A surge of apprehension rose anew now that she was eye to eye with his erection. It was bigger than she remembered. Thicker. And awfully long.

"I feel I should warn you," she said, and licked her lips. She wrapped both hands around the base of his cock to hold it in place. "I'm not very good at this."

He groaned as she gave a liberal squeeze. "You're doing a pretty bang-up job so far."

She laughed and squeezed harder. Hand jobs she could do. Hand jobs were just friction. "I'm serious. You're like some kind of cunnilingus god, and I don't even know where to start with this thing. I might need you to walk me through it."

"You want me to walk you through a blow job?"

Sensing now would be a good time to demonstrate her lack of skills, she ran her tongue along the underside portion of his cock, slow and steady, almost like she was licking a lollipop. An engorged, twitching beast of a lollipop.

Sounds that could have been pleasure—or frustration—arose from somewhere deep in his chest. "You really want pointers?"

Well, not if he was going to call them *pointers*. That made it sound like a basketball game. She rocked back on her heels and peeked up at him. "I want you to tell me what you like. Exactly what you like, and in explicit detail. I'll do my best to accommodate you."

Ryan wasn't sure if Amy was being serious or toying with him, but something about the uncertainty that drew her brow tight sent him reeling. As he struggled to get his bearing, he caught glimpses of her from every angle. Down to nothing but her underwear, breasts pushing up from the tightly packed bra, her ass high and rounded, the taste of her still on his lips—yeah, he was pretty much ready to come the moment she said so.

"Oh, and I have a really sensitive gag reflex," she said, frowning. "As in, hair-trigger sensitive. In case that makes you want to change your mind."

Did this woman seriously think that a gag reflex was going to alter the way he felt about her? That he might turn her away for not stuffing his cock in her mouth at the word *go? Jesus.* All she had to do was smile, and the world lay slain at her feet—a truth she had absolutely no fucking idea was set in stone.

He wished he could find the words to show her that her value wasn't hinged on being the perfect daughter or employee or giver of head, but words seemed to fail him when she brought her tongue once again to the length of his erection.

There was time for talking later. For now...

He groaned. "When you lick my cock nice and slow that way, I feel like I'm going to jump out of my skin."

She slowed down even more. "Is that good?"

"It's good, but there's only so much of that a man can take. Don't be afraid to attack with everything you've got. Lips. Tongue. Teeth. You aren't going to break me."

"You want me to use my teeth?"

"Okay, maybe not teeth. At least not—" The scrape of her incisors, gentle but firm, almost catapulted him from the spot. "Oh, God. Yes. Exactly like that."

She planted herself more firmly between his legs, and he could feel her smile spread against the underside of his cock. Looking down, looking around, everywhere he turned, there she was. Kneeling before him, head bowed. Intent. Sweet. His.

"Okay," she said coyly. "What else do you want? I told you to be explicit."

She wanted explicit? He wasn't sure he could. Too many of his senses were already engaged—locked and loaded—as it was.

"Fuck. You have no idea, do you? You could just sit there and breathe on me, and I'd never ask for anything more."

Her eyes lit with laughter and something more—something he wanted to explore, but wasn't sure he'd have time to. She began kneading his testicles as her tongue continued its eager assault.

He gave himself over to her ministrations. He'd meant what he said—that he could stand there for hours, his cock in her hands, her tongue swirling around until all touch lost meaning except for the tight, hot buildup in his balls that made him want to scream. But that floor was hard, and sleep would eventually overtake them both.

"Take the tip into your mouth," he growled. At her startled look, he moderated his tone to that of a normal human being. "Don't worry—you don't have to go any further than you're comfortable with, and you can use your hands to make up the difference. Everything about this feels amazing."

Taking him at his word, she wrapped her mouth around the head of his cock and clenched his shaft between her fists. Her saliva made the friction smooth and easy, and the heat of her open mouth seared him.

She was fire and ice, sweet and hot. She was everything.

Unable to keep his hands off her for another second, he tangled them gently in her hair and let her direct their movements. Even shallow and tentative, the feel of her mouth sliding over his cock was more than enough to satisfy him. And when he caught sight of the pair of them in the mirror, dozens of their reflections, all of them sucking and fucking, he pulled sharply away.

Hoisting the weight of his dick in his own hands, he pumped long and hard. Amy watched, mouth parted in a perfectly rounded O as his body clenched and his orgasm came to a roaring head, spilling hot and sticky over his hand.

He barely had time to enjoy the last ebb of release when he felt Amy draw near, a gym towel in hand. He tried to take it from her, but she smiled softly and said, "Let me."

As if cleaning him off was the most precious act in the world. As if the spent remains of their passion was a gift. The more time he devoted to Amy, the more her rose-tinted version of the world seemed to take over.

"You were wrong about not being good at blow jobs." He pulled her in for a kiss, cementing the moment, refusing to let it slip entirely away. "That was amazing."

"Yeah, it was." She smiled mischievously. "But I was totally right about the mirrors, wasn't I?"

Ryan tipped back his head and laughed, feeling good about himself for the first time in what felt like years. Yes. She was absolutely fucking right about that.

SIXTEEN

RYAN ALMOST DIDN'T hear the garage phone over the twin roaring sounds of Whitesnake and his pneumatic impact wrench. In all the time he'd worked at Montgomery Manor, he could count on one finger the number of times that phone had rung. And it had been a wrong number.

He took his time getting to his feet and wiping off his hands, assuming the ringing would eventually stop on its own. It didn't. He tucked the phone under one ear and leaned across the table to turn down the volume on the radio. "Hello?"

"Psst."

He shook the handset, wondering if the connection was bad. The black plastic phone had to have been in here since the eighties. "Hello?"

"Psst." More enunciated this time—though still spoken in hushed undertones "You have ten minutes to meet me upstairs. Bring coffee or you won't get past the nursery door. You wouldn't believe what time the twins got up this morning."

"Amy? How did you get this number?"

"Nine minutes and forty-five seconds. Seriously, Ryan—this is an unprecedented aligning of the stars. They're both asleep *at the same time.* For the love of all that is sacred, bring me coffee and your adorable face. Stat."

He checked the clock on the far wall. As usual, he'd gotten most of his required work done well before noon. Mr. Montgomery was out of town for a few days with Serena at his heels—as she often was when Paris was on the itinerary—which left him with very little to do. Especially since Amy had been on night duty for the past forty-eight hours. It was amazing and slightly pathetic how quickly she'd become the center of his world. In the absence of alternate plans the night before, he and Beauregard had spent a quiet evening at the park, chasing squirrels and wondering what to do about the mess that life at the Manor had become.

Before Amy came into his life, his biggest problem had been boredom, the endless waiting for life to start happening to him again. Now, he was dealing with secrets and lies and great sex and clandestine deals and the overwhelming feeling that he was drowning under them all.

"Coffee. Nursery. Check."

"Bless your heart. And when you get here, be sure to tiptoe. If you wake these two up, I swear to all that is good and holy I'll walk out the door and leave them to your care."

Fierce words, but not ones that had the power to scare him. "The twins I can handle." *It's you I'm not so sure about.*

He hung up and made his way to the kitchen, where Holly had two stainless steel mugs of coffee primed and ready to go.

"She called me too," she said when she saw the surprise on his face. "Hers is the one on the right. Vanilla and cinnamon, no cream. I wasn't sure what you took in yours, so…"

"I usually take it black, but whatever you have in there is fine."

"That's what I figured." She flashed a warm smile and tilted her head. Her dark brown hair, pulled into its customary thick braid, was coiled around her head. "And I'm happy to have my suspicions confirmed. I know the dietary habits and restrictions of just about everyone who lives and works and occasionally visits here, but you've managed to elude me thus far. I'll have you pegged soon. Coffee black. Quinoa upon pain of death. I'm guessing you're a strictly pepperoni and sausage man when it comes to your pizza."

"I think I'm being unjustly accused here. I thought your quinoa was delicious."

"Except I saw your face when you tasted it." She laughed and pressed the cups into his waiting hands. "No worries—it's not for everyone. I'm just glad you're finally spending more time with the staff. We're not such a bad lot once you get to know us."

He knew that. It was what he'd feared since the beginning.

"Thanks for the coffee," he said, turning to leave before he said something friendly that he'd later regret.

But Holly stopped him with a carefully worded "So, you and Amy...you're a thing now?"

His shoulders slumped. He should have known that not even coffee came without a price in this place. There was a chance it was the workday coffee date that gave them away and not the making out in dark rec room corners, but he doubted it. Amy was subtle like the crash of a cymbal.

"Kind of. There are extenuating circumstances."

Holly's silence shrouded him in recriminations—

all the more stifling because they were justified. He could practically read her thoughts. *Amy is worth a lot more than extenuating circumstances. Amy is worth a lot more than you.*

He knew it. He'd known it since the day she arrived here. And he realized with a surge of anguish that the time had come to make sure she knew it too. There would be no more of this waiting, this hoping, this half-fearing for the day Mr. Montgomery called him up to his office to decide the job was done, his dreams ready to come true.

He was ready to be back in control of his own future—even if that meant driving himself straight off the road.

"We're just not blasting it from the rooftops yet, that's all," he lied. "We'd appreciate it if you kept it to yourself for now."

"Got it." Holly made the motion of a zipper over her mouth, but he could see the accusation lingering in her expression. "Mum's the word—you don't have to worry about me. I'm a ninja at keeping secrets."

Now it was his turn to study her. Leaning one hip on the counter, dressed comfortably in jeans and a chef's jacket, her feet in sensible kitchen clogs, Holly was the picture of nonthreatening friendliness. This was a woman who cooked disgustingly healthy foods and kept a clean kitchen, a woman who could shrug off a broken dumbwaiter with a laugh. But there was a hard set to her angular jaw, a flash in her eyes—cold and flat and almost black—that made him wonder how much of that was a façade.

"It's not a secret. Just complicated."

Holly shrugged and returned to her work. "Where I come from, those are usually the same thing."

"DON'T TAKE THIS PERSONALLY, but I can't decide whether I'm happier to see you or the coffee."

Since the urge to plant a kiss on Ryan's slightly parted lips was stronger than the one to gulp scalding caffeine, Amy could only assume he pulled out ahead. If he actually cared how much seeing him standing outside the nursery door made her heart leap, he could probably stay ahead for the rest of his life.

She stopped herself from making the mistake of saying that out loud. He did care. Just not enough.

"And before you make the mistake of coming any closer, let me inform you that there's a firm No Funny Business rule once you cross these nursery doors. I'm halfway convinced Serena had a nanny cam installed before her trip to Paris."

"Really?"

"Well, it's the only explanation I can find for that monstrosity." She led him into the nursery and pointed at the giant teddy bear in one corner, so tall its head brushed the ceiling, its limbs like couch cushions. Amy could have sworn its eyes followed her as she moved around the room. "Isn't it awful?"

"It has quite a presence. But aren't nanny cams usually smaller? More understated?"

"Have you ever spent any time with the lady of the Manor? Understatement isn't something she worries too much about." Then, since she wasn't wasting her precious nap moments on Serena or the possibility of surveillance, she dropped to the rocking chair and indicated for him to sit nearby. "I missed you."

Since most of the furniture in the nursery was built for butts no wider than a few inches across, Ryan settled on the floor, one knee casually bent so that he looked like a lounging demigod. A lounging, slightly scowling demigod, but based on what she knew of Greek mythology, that seemed about right.

"I missed you too," he said.

"Then why are you wearing your curb-stomping-puppies face?"

She'd meant the words to be a joke, to lighten the mood, but then she recalled that the last time she'd seen this face was when she'd asked him to close his eyes and replay the worst moment of his life. The worst moment for him had to be the drunk driving accident, when his world had changed and everything he knew and loved was taken away.

Oh, God. That wasn't about to happen again, was it?

"Ryan?" she asked, her voice small. "Are you okay?"

He looked up, and his eyes softened when they landed on her. "I'm fine. But Holly said something that got me thinking."

"A dangerous pastime."

"But a necessary one." He shifted so that he leaned close enough to play with the bottom hem of her jeans, touching but not touching. "I don't think she likes the idea of us sleeping together."

"She's protective of me." Amy took a drink of her coffee, made exactly the way she liked it. "I get the feeling she's the sort who doesn't think anyone is good enough for the people she cares about. You should see the way she hovers over Serena. She jokes about her with the other staff members, but you can tell they have a deep bond."

"She's right to be wary of me."

"I think you're being a little dramatic."

"I'm not." The puppy face was back again. "I'm just the right amount of dramatic. The truth is, I wasn't completely honest with you that day we went for a walk with the twins. And I need to be. I'd like to be."

"You mean Incest Day?"

"Jesus. You named it?"

"May thirteenth will forever be known to me as Incest Day." She placed a reverent hand over her chest. "I'll celebrate by listening to banjo music and gouging out my own eyes."

Before Ryan could stop himself, he found himself relaxing again. Goddammit—she was killing him with her sunny disposition. Here he was, trying to confess his ignominy, struggling to find a way out of this mess, and all she did was make him want to chuck every reservation out the window and ravish her on top of a stuffed floor-to-ceiling nanny cam.

"I mean it, Amy." He would stay firm. He wouldn't be derailed by benevolence and an almost see-through white tank top. This had to be said, if only to free him. To free them both. "The deal between me and Mr. Montgomery that I told you about—the one where he asked me to keep you away from Jake in exchange for my job—there's more to it than that."

"I don't understand."

No. Of course she didn't. Why would she think for even one second that the men she trusted—the men she cared about—would descend to such depths to get their own way?

"You're worrying me, Ryan. Why do you look so grim? What are you talking about?"

He swallowed heavily and braced himself for the worst. "I told you that Mr. Montgomery allowed me to keep my job on the condition that I separated you and Jake, right?"

"Yes. And I still think it was shitty of you not to tell me right away."

"You might want to reserve your swear words for what comes next. The part I didn't tell you was that he also implied he might be able to get me my old job back." When she didn't respond right away, Ryan said the words he'd barely allowed himself to hope might come true. "What he offered me in exchange for keeping the two of you apart was a way out of here. For good."

"He can do that?"

"It certainly looks that way." He had the money and the power and—most important of all—the motivation. "But that's not the worst part in all this. The worst part is that even though I knew I'd have to lie to you and manipulate your relationship with Jake and cause you pain to make that happen, I didn't say no."

She still didn't say anything, just kept looking at him with a soft, almost perplexed expression—like she either couldn't or wouldn't allow the words to sink in. In that moment, he feared she might find a way to twist this around, to give him the same excuses she offered all the people in her life who took advantage and wronged her and otherwise treated her like crap.

He couldn't let that happen.

Gripping her hands tightly in his, he strengthened his tone. "Do you understand what I'm telling you right now, Amy? *I didn't say no.*"

IN AMY'S OPINION, there were no words on the face of the planet more condescending than "Do you understand what I'm telling you."

That simple phrase, dropped from Ryan's lips with a pained grimace, implied so much—that Amy couldn't possibly know what kind of dark, twisted torment kept him up at night, that she was incapable of grasping what went on in the world around her.

But she did know. And she was capable. She might enjoy the company of children and princesses, but that didn't make her blind to the realities that existed around her. Mr. Montgomery had been so desperate to keep her from finding out the truth that he'd recruited Ryan's help, offering the one thing there was no way she could compete against.

So, yes. She understood what Ryan was telling her. He didn't say no. He wanted to go home.

She put on her brightest smile, spread so thin it became brittle. "Well, then. I guess the only question left is when do you leave?"

Ryan's eyes clouded with suppressed emotion. "What do you mean? When do I leave for what?"

"I assume Mr. Montgomery is satisfied with your performance," she said, pushing the words out one by one, a labor of—if not love, something very close to it. "Jake and I are apart. Romance is the last thing on my mind when I look at him now. You did your job exceptionally well, and you deserve to be rewarded for it. So that's it, right? Hollywood or bust? The golden ticket home?"

Ryan placed his hands on Amy's shoulders, squaring her to face him, his fingers pressing so hard they felt like prongs. She fought for only a few seconds before realizing how fruitless her attempt was. The brittle feeling had escalated, and she was afraid that if she struggled too hard, she might break.

"I'm not accepting his stupid prize." Ryan's mouth was firm, his eyes going from turbulent to outright thunderclouds. "Think about what it would mean, Amy. He went to extreme lengths to bribe me with this—extreme lengths to avoid coming out as your father. The second you approach him with our suspicions, the deal is off. Why would he reward me with Hollywood when I led you straight to the truth he was trying to avoid?"

Oh. She hadn't thought of that. But it was obvious Ryan hadn't been thinking of anything else. *He's thought long and hard about how to accept this deal without hurting me. He wants this so much he'll do almost anything to get it.*

And she'd do almost anything to help him.

"So I'll never know," she said quickly. "I'll go through life believing I'm nothing more than the nanny. You know how scared I am of upsetting the balance anyway—it's not that big of a sacrifice."

"It *is* a big sacrifice, and I won't let you make it."

A whimper from behind the door indicated Amy's duties were about to interrupt the conversation just as it was reaching its crux. Ryan could have thrown something or punched a wall or ripped a giant stuffed bear apart with his teeth. There was *always* a fucking Montgomery in the way. As long as she lived under this roof, their desires would always trump her own, their demands be the center of her world.

"Before you go in, please listen. As soon as Mr. Montgomery gets back from Paris, I'm going to talk to him. Not because I plan on cashing in on my prize, and not because I'm going to tell him what we know, but because I want him to know that under no circumstances will I consider his deal. I don't want my old life back—not at that cost."

"Not at *that* cost," she echoed, blinking rapidly.

That was the wrong way to put it. "Not at any cost," he amended, but it was too late. Reality lay stark and exposed between them, a live wire dangerous to the touch. He might balk at the thought of using Amy to get his career back, but the truth was that he'd already taken much more than that. And they both knew it.

The look she gave him, one hand on the doorknob to attend to the twins, halfway in his world, halfway in theirs, was difficult to read. "You know, I wonder if maybe we're missing a really obvious solution here."

There's a solution? Other than turning back the hands of time and actually listening when his goddamned common sense told him not to get involved?

"Don't do anything drastic yet, okay?" She paused just long enough to offer him a smile—wobbly but bright, powerful by virtue of being hers and hers alone. "I'll swing by your apartment after work. I think I might have a way to fix this."

"You do?"

"Of course. Easy solutions to complex problems, remember? That's my specialty."

SEVENTEEN

THE ONE GOOD thing about the Montgomerys being out of town was that there were no family fires for Amy to put out, no last-minute requests for her to feed Evan this or sing Lily that or please keep them entertained while we have guests for dinner.

It was almost as though Ryan could pretend they were normal people with normal jobs and a normal relationship. He'd get off work first and head home to walk the dog that wasn't his. He'd clean up a little so he wouldn't be ashamed when his girlfriend came over. They'd go out for Chinese and hit the mini-golf course and return for hours of mind-blowing sex.

A light knock stopped him in the act of the second one, a quick run-through of his apartment to make sure there weren't any dirty clothes tossed on the floor or other wayward items that would shame him in front of a woman he didn't need to impress but desperately wanted to.

But as he pulled open the door, he realized that with Amy, normal would never happen. It wasn't even a remote possibility. He wasn't confronted with a girlfriend in need of a foot rub and a good laugh after a long day at work, or an angry lover who'd recently learned she'd been used by the man she cared about. Oh, no. Not him. He got a woman in a trench coat.

A woman in a trench coat—unbuttoned and pulled open—tall black heels and absolutely nothing else.

"What are you doing?" Grabbing her by the wrist and pulling her through the door, he looked furtively up and down the hallway to determine who might be gawking at her, but all he could see were rows of closed doors, the muffled sounds of life going on all around him. "Are you insane?"

Her lower lip came out in a pout, but not the kind that signaled grief. This was the other kind. The *sexy* kind.

As the door shut behind them, she allowed the coat to fall open once again. It was just an ordinary coat as far as he could tell—to her knees and khaki-colored and slightly shiny in that way fabric had when it was designed to repel rain. Who the fuck was he kidding? It was a coat. What really mattered were the parts underneath it. His gaze wandered over her exposed body. Up and down. Side to side. Up again. And definitely down once more.

His hands moved forward, drawn to the soft, naked flesh that beckoned underneath the fluttering fabric. He stopped just short of cupping the weight of her breasts, reaching instead for the tie of her jacket and cinching it tight around her waist. "Jesus, please tell me you had all this buttoned up on the way over here."

"No." She frowned down at her now-covered body. "I drove stark naked down the street and got out of the car to pull this coat out of my trunk—but not before the mailman and I chatted about the squirrel problem for a while. Of course I buttoned up. You don't like it?"

"No." He took a step back, thinking distance might

help him clear his thoughts, but it only presented a more complete picture. Even with the coat pulled closed, he could still see the plunge of cleavage underneath, the impossibly long legs ending in heels that made him want to run his hands and tongue and teeth over every flexing muscle of those calves. He swallowed. "I fucking love it."

Amy didn't waste another second. She dropped her hips and rolled them as she walked forward, her full seduction mode on. She didn't have very many moves, if she was being honest. Showing up naked—or nearly so—at a man's house just about exhausted her store of resources when it came to eliciting desire. Everything she'd ever been taught on the subject had included pretty much just being ready and willing.

She was ready. Clearly. She was willing. Clearly.

But it didn't seem to be working. Rather than lolling his tongue slavishly out and pinning her against the wall, Ryan was backing away, a horrified expression on his face.

She stopped her forward movement, her rolling hips stopping along with it. "If you love it so much, why do you look as though I'm about to ask you to remove both your testicles with a rubber band?"

He laughed and then grimaced, proving in an instant how ineffective her attempts at wooing a man were. Duh. Castration wasn't one of the most ideal topics when attempting to entice a lover.

"I'm trying to remember what it was I wanted to say to you. For some reason, my brain seems to be running on empty here."

Good. That had been her intention. Distract and awe and enjoy him for what might be the last time.

She deserved a nice parting gift—especially once Ryan heard what she was willing to do to earn it.

"You were going to tell me I look pretty?" she guessed.

"*Pretty* doesn't begin to cover it."

"Hmm. Maybe you were going to suggest a restaurant for dinner?"

"No. I'll be damned if I'm taking you anywhere if that's all you have to wear."

"Oh, I don't know." She dropped her voice and drew closer, determined to stomp his restraint under her six-inch heel. She'd had to borrow the shoes from Jenna, whose closet was half business maven, half sex kitten. These came from the sex kitten half. "It might be fun. Maybe you can meet me at the restaurant. Or you can meet Lola Bullocks—the mysterious, golden-haired vixen sitting all alone in the corner. She's got secrets only the right man could pry out of her. But he'll have to use his *bare hands*."

The smile Ryan flashed her, slow and deep, pulled at her insides. "Lola Bullocks? Really? That's the best you could do?"

What? She rather liked Lola Bullocks—though not as much as she liked Orgasm Amy.

"How about Tiffany von Hefflewaithe?" she suggested. "She's a runaway from a bad high society marriage—nothing to her name but the diamond ring and pearl necklace she has to pawn to pay her way. Or will she have to uncover *another* kind of currency?"

Ryan chuckled and unwound even more, going so far as to take her by the hand and wrap an arm around her waist. His arms were no longer strong and friendly—they were strong and determined. And they felt fantastic. "Do you have a story for every name?"

"Of course." She ran her hands over his chest, not stopping until she felt his nipples harden to pinpricks under the thin cloth of his T-shirt. "Haven't you ever played this game before?"

"I can't say that I have," he murmured, a hitch in his voice. "Do I get to be someone else too?"

"Of course you do." She slid her hands lower, not stopping until she had her palms under his shirt and was skimming the hard, hot lines of his stomach. "This is a world with no rules. Just mysterious strangers and the promise of sex. Who would you be, Ryan Lucas, if you could be anyone you want?"

He paused long enough to give the thought serious consideration. She was afraid he was going to say something to pull them out of the game and back to the real world she was so patently trying to avoid, but he disarmed her with a lopsided grin and the promise of sex sparking in his eyes. "I'd be Dirk. Dirk Hardcore."

She pressed her face to his shoulder to keep from giving herself away—the laughter and the tears, the overwhelming sensation of loss most of all. She was going to miss hilarious sexytimes Ryan when he left. She was also going to miss flustered Ryan of the red-tipped ears and reserved Ryan who wasn't quite sure where he fit in the world. She was going to miss every part of him.

But that didn't change her mind one bit.

With a deep breath, she schooled her features into what she hoped was a mask of saucy disinterest and pulled away. She sauntered over to one of the metal barstools that sat propped against his kitchen island and took a seat, being careful to cross her legs slowly, the coat splitting over one naked thigh.

Although sitting naked under the trench coat in her car had felt slightly perverted, as though she was planning on stopping at the nearest street corner to frighten away schoolchildren, being in Ryan's apartment half-dressed was a delicious sensation. Feminine and strong. Seductive. Really freaking hot.

Someday, they really would have to try this at a restaurant.

Then she remembered what she'd come here to do and shook her head, allowing her hair to cascade in its carefully fabricated curls down her back. Someday would probably never come.

Swiveling on the stool, she extended a hand. "It's lovely to meet you, Mr. Hardcore. My name's Candi Cumberbottom. That's with an *i*."

"How interesting," he said coolly, his eyebrow raised as he took the seat opposite her. "You spell Cumberbottom with an *i*?"

Her lips quivered as she tried to keep her Candi face on. God, this man was fun.

"You tell me what brings a stranger like you to a place like this, and you can spell it any way you want to." She uncrossed and recrossed her legs, taking her time with the middle part—the part where there was nothing standing in the way of her and Ryan but cold, delicious air. She let loose a whimper when his eyes flared, as drawn to the throbbing between her legs as she was.

"Oh, didn't you know? I own this place." Instead of taking a seat, he swaggered around the kitchen island and dropped a glass to the surface. Without losing stride—or character—he pulled open his fridge and extracted a pitcher of iced tea, pouring it in a long, flourishing stream before gliding it across the cheap laminate to her waiting hands. "I won it in a poker game. Staked everything I owned on a lucky pair of deuces."

She hid her laugh behind her glass. "So I heard. Rumor has it that's not all you won."

"Oh, yeah?" He leaned over the counter, eyes locked on the press of her cleavage over the top of her coat. She pretended to adjust to a more comfortable position, allowing the coat to fall open enough that a hint of nipple peeked over the top. "Where'd you hear something like that?"

"Let's just say I knew the previous owner."

"You mean you fucked the previous owner. You were his girl, weren't you?"

She whimpered again. The growl of possession in his voice felt almost real—almost as though he meant every gruff undertone. "So what if I was?"

"Then that means you're the other half of the stake I won." Fisting the collar of her coat in one hand, he yanked her over the kitchen island and planted a deep, openmouthed kiss that left her gasping, groaning, straining for more.

When he was done, he pushed her back down to her seat, and she realized one of her breasts had popped entirely out of the coat. When she made a move to adjust everything back in place, Ryan gripped her wrist and pulled it away. "Not unless I say so."

A shiver ran through and implanted itself firmly

between her legs. Ryan wasn't just playing the game, he was running away with it. And winning.

Her lip quivered as she struggled to get back on track. What were they pretending? Oh. Right. Poker. Sex slave. "I hate to disappoint you, Mr. Hardcore, but I wasn't his property to stake in the first place. I belong to no man."

"That's not true." This time, his words were lacking bite—soft and hesitant, almost as though he meant them. "You belong to me."

She had no glib response to that, so it was just as well that he chose that moment to pounce around the island and whisk her into his arms. Thrusting one hot arm inside her coat, he had her manacled around the waist and seated up on the bar top before she could emit so much as a whisper of protest. One hand ran long and lovingly up her leg, skimming under the material so that the pair of them became nothing but *his* hands and *her* skin, sparks of desire springing up with each movement. Her shoe was in danger of slipping right off her toes and falling to the linoleum below, but he stopped his upward movement to secure the heel back in place, his fingers lingering reverently over the delicate bones of her ankle.

It wasn't what you'd call a Cinderella moment, but she was definitely seeing balls in her future.

He yanked the tie on her coat—the coat he'd tied in the first place—and pulled it down off her shoulders, trapping her arms in the fabric, pinning her in place with her chest thrust out and at full attention. "Those are the only things I want you wearing when I fuck you over this table."

"Are you talking to Candi now, or are you talking

to me?" She regretted the words the moment they left her mouth. They ruined the moment, took the game from fun to *real*—and that was the last thing she wanted right now. There would be no serious discussions of what came next or meaningful glimpses into the past or future. It would be just the two of them and some hilarious sex before she buckled down and made all his dreams come true. Like a fairy princess. Like a boss.

"I only ask because Candi-with-an-i is partial to countertop sex," she said, covering her tracks. "Candi-with-an-i is partial to a lot of different kinds of sex, actually. She's quite insatiable. I think she might have a sex addiction."

"Candi-with-an-i talks too much," he said, and prevented another word from leaving her mouth. After about sixty seconds of furious kissing, it no longer mattered who she was—or, in fact, who *he* was. They were just a pair of bodies, struggling to break free of their clothes, determined to get as close as they possibly could without crawling into one another's skin.

Ryan wrested her out of her coat before laying her out over the cool laminate countertop. It was one of those moments when she'd have normally cracked a joke about becoming body sushi or the hygienic properties of all meals to be prepared in this kitchen from here on out, but Ryan prowled over her with such intensity that he ripped the words—at least the lighthearted, happy ones—from her mouth before she could form them. Firm hands held her legs open, forcing her to feel every movement of air and skin and lust in the heated center of her. His mouth pressed damp, insistent kisses wherever it landed, lingering on her breasts and clavicle, laving a slow, sensuous path down her belly, nipping inside her knees and thighs.

Once again, Ryan was consuming her whole. It was an incredible thing—to be so cherished by a man that one taste wasn't enough for him, to know that he delighted in each movement of his lips over her skin as much as she did.

He kept moving downward, stopping only when he got to her ankle, where, as promised, the shoes remained the only item to grace her body. He lifted her leg slowly, his kisses soft, sending shivers of delight up and down the limb.

She gasped as he gave her ankle a firm tug, pulling her to the edge of the counter. She was spread before him, totally vulnerable, his to command.

So when he said, "Wait here and don't you dare move," she had no choice but to comply. She wasn't sure her legs would work even if she wanted them to.

It seemed an eternity before he returned again, this time with his shirt off and his cock out. A brief flicker over his supremely naked body revealed that he'd put on the proper protection—and then she lost track of all sensations but him.

The mechanics of on-the-counter sex were new to her, but she got the gist of it when he climbed up to join her, settling himself over her body and leaving her to absorb the hard and uncomfortable surface. It was almost as though he wanted her to suffer—a fact reinforced when he gripped her ankle yet again and lifted her leg, testing her flexibility as the limb moved higher.

"Fuck, Amy. When do you stop giving?"

She relaxed her muscles to deepen the stretch and

purred in response. She was happy to be back to Amy, happier to hear the note of desperation in his voice as he strove to break her. She was probably going to feel the pain of the stretch tomorrow, but she didn't care as her knee approached her shoulder and his cock nudged against her now totally open, totally parted, panting, wet-hot core.

"I don't ever stop." *Not when it's you.*

He pushed into her so slowly she thought she might scream. Her body stretched to accommodate him, and she felt every delicious inch as he went farther, drew deeper, lifted her leg up even more. Although she'd always tried to use her flexibility to her advantage during her relations with men, none had ever pushed her this far, and with so much intensity that she felt they were walking on a wire. And when he was finally all the way inside her, his body suspended over hers, he leaned in and kissed her—deep, slow, the melding of so much more than their tongues.

He moved, slowly at first, gaining speed as the physical sensations took over. Each thrust took him deeper and deeper, touching some part of her long neglected. He kept his grip on her calf firm, holding her aloft, but by that time there was no real need. She would stay open for him as long as he wanted.

It was too long and not nearly long enough.

Her body shattered around his, and she released a cry that was only partially due to the wave of pleasure that rocked through her. She felt the pulse of his own release a few seconds later, and his grip on her leg tightened enough that she was sure he'd leave bruises behind.

Not that she minded. As he lowered her leg and

pulled away, it seemed nice to think that there would
be some mark to look back at. Some proof that this
had happened.

"That was rather…hardcore." She sat up and
swung her legs off the edge of the counter. Hopping
down was a mistake, and her legs wobbled unsteadily
beneath her. Luckily for her, Ryan was there waiting
to hold her, his grip firm on her elbow as he helped
her to the ground, a soft kiss on her neck rendering
the action sweet enough to prick tears behind her
eyes. "That Dirk fellow knows what he's doing. I'd
love to see what he can do with a pair of aces up his
sleeve."

"You may not get the chance."

She sucked in a sharp breath. Was he also making
plans for his departure? Had he beat her to the punch?

But he just laughed. "Next time, I think I'm going
to be Fabian Hunter. A lone wolf with vengeance on
his mind—and a hell of a grudge to pay."

She cupped the side of his face, running her thumb
along his lip, loving the way the gentle scratch of the
five o'clock hour nuzzled his jawline. "You're a lot
of fun, you know that?"

"No one ever accused me of being fun before I
met you."

She wanted to protest, but he moved toward the
bedroom, presumably to clean up. "Grab me something to wear while you're in there, would you?" she
said. "I think you ripped Candi's coat. You can't expect the poor woman to go out in public like that. You
know how possessive Dirk gets."

"You still haven't given me my Metallica shirt

back," he complained as he disappeared from view. "But I'll see what I can do."

R<small>YAN TOOK HIS TIME</small> pulling on clean clothes before grabbing a button-down for Amy. Even though the evening thus far was every sexual fantasy he'd ever had all rolled up into one, he knew, without question, that everything would change once he walked out that door and rejoined her.

They'd come too far, too fast. They'd reached the end of the road before he barely had time to get going.

And when he entered the living room, he could detect the shift in the air—could almost taste it, bitter and sweet, smelling of sex gone cold. Amy leaned one hip against the kitchen counter, her fingers coiling nervously around a lock of her hair. Her nudity now seemed almost vulnerable, so he helped her into the shirt.

She reached for the buttons.

"No. Let me." He reached for the one in the middle, pulling the fabric tight over her breasts before slipping plastic through cloth. He took his time with each button, enjoying the soft rustle of the fabric over skin almost as much as the hasty act of disrobing in the first place. Her pulse fluttered wherever his touch landed, ripples of sensation that traveled straight through her to him. "There. Now you're perfect."

"I'm hardly that," she said, a hesitant smile lifting one corner of her mouth. "But I'm not without my uses. Come. Sit with me."

His heart dropped ominously at her words, but the smile reassured him, leaving him conflicted and adrift. "I'm assuming this is about the Montgomerys?"

She nodded and made her way over to the couch. Ryan's stomach rumbled a warning, reminding him that he had yet to eat dinner, but also that he wasn't fully prepared for what she had to say.

The sex had been a good distraction—a *great* distraction—but no amount of role-playing could forestall the inevitable. He took a seat on the opposite side of the couch, close enough to see, too far to touch. "What is it?"

She waved a hand in his direction, annoyingly vague. The buttons on her wrists hung open, so he scooted closer and began carefully rolling the sleeves up to her elbow, lingering over the soft, downy hairs of her forearm. She put her other arm out, allowing him to repeat the gesture on her other arm. It was a comforting act, one that spoke of a familiarity that surpassed anything else they'd done together.

"I haven't been able to stop thinking about everything you told me," she said. "About the deal Mr. Montgomery offered you and how you might be able to get back on your feet again and what I might be able to do to help. And I've come up with a plan."

"No. No more plans." No more manipulations.

"Just listen," she pleaded. "If what you told me is all true—"

"It is."

"If what you told me is all true, then the only thing that's needed to complete your quest is the final act. The showdown. The slaying of the dragon."

Quest? Act? Dragons? "I think Dirk might have fucked the sense right out of you."

"Oh, it's going to take more than a Dirk to do that. I'd need a Ryan to really lose it." Sobered, she grabbed his hand. "Please at least hear me out on this. I know you hate the idea of feeling like Mr. Montgomery controls you—and I get that, I really do. You're not the sort of man who...you know."

He waited. He had no fucking clue. Played well with others? Deserved anything else?

"You're not the sort of man who does well driving under the speed limit," she said. "The regular rules don't apply to you. I've known it since the first day I got here. I took one look at you, leaning over the engine of some fancy racecar, your ass all perfect in your little mechanic jeans, and thought *that man doesn't belong here.*"

"You liked my ass?"

"I'm beginning to think there's been a severe shortage of compliments in your life. I swear, you latch on to the tiniest things."

"Only when they come from you."

She licked her lips as if tasting them for the first time. Maybe the flavor of him lingered there. Maybe she was holding on to him as desperately as he wanted to cling to her.

"I mean it," she said. "I sought you out because it seemed like you needed a friend, like maybe you had yet to find your place here at the Manor. I thought I could help you feel at home. But the truth is that you don't have a place here. Not because one doesn't exist—because you so obviously don't want one. And that's not a bad thing, Ryan, I swear. I'm the last woman on earth who will push you to embrace a life you don't want. I know what it's like to try to live according to someone else's expectations. It's isolating and it's disappointing and I wouldn't wish it on anyone."

"You understand." Of course she understood. Of course Amy would be the one to offer to smooth the rocks from his path.

"So you see where I'm going with this."

"Not really."

The incredulous look she gave him made him feel like a jerk and a fool. "Yes, you do. You just don't want to admit it. We have to stage a showdown."

"A showdown?"

"A coup. An incest intervention."

"An incest intervention is not a thing."

"It is now." She actually laughed. An encroaching emptiness was taking over him, and she was filling it with her laughter. "And it's exactly what we need. Think about it—if Jake and I run away together, slipping off into the night, we can set it up so you're the one who stops us. Mr. Montgomery will be so grateful that he'll have no choice but to uphold his side of the bargain, even if the truth has to come to light in the process."

"You want us to force his hand."

"Exactly. It's the best way for you to get your life back and for me to finally be able to start mine. You know I don't have the guts to approach him myself, so this is the push I need. And if we plan it big enough, raise the stakes, maybe we can even find a way for Mr. Montgomery to get you a promotion. What's better than driving stunt cars? Stunt tanks? Bear wrestling? I have no idea what kind of hierarchy you people operate under."

"Amy." Her name came out harsh and cold, as it always did when he was overwhelmed by her. "I appreciate the gesture, but there's no way it would work."

"Why not?" She shifted to face him, the shirt lifting up her thigh so far he couldn't help himself from reaching out and gripping the soft, tensile strength of her leg. "It's win-win. You get to be the hero and go back to Hollywood on a white horse. Mr. Montgomery will be forced to come clean. No one gets hurt. It's what you've wanted right from the start."

Yes, but was it what he wanted *now?* Looking at Amy, seeing her bright smile, realizing what she was doing for him, he wanted to cast all the rest of that crap aside and tell her the only thing he wanted in this world was her.

But he wasn't sure it was true. He didn't know if she was enough.

Even under the best scenario of life in Ransom Creek—marching up to Mr. Montgomery's office tomorrow, telling him where to stick his job, picking up shifts at the gas station on Fourth to make ends meet—Ryan would still be surrounded by the Montgomerys every day of his life. They'd still control Amy. And by extension, they'd still control him.

But what was the alternative?

"*If* this works—*if* I agree—you do realize what this will mean, right?"

Him, leaving. Him, going home. Him, never setting foot in this place again. It would mean the end of *them.*

Her smile only burned brighter. "Of course I do. It means you get to do the thing you love most in this world."

"It'll never work, Amy. It's too crazy, too complex. The best thing to do here is come clean—"

"I was afraid you were going to say that." She rose to her feet, her legs unfolding and holding her firm.

"Why do I get the feeling I'm not going to like what happens next?"

"Because I don't really need your permission to put this plan in action, and you know it. All I have to do is grab my favorite trench coat over there and head back to the Manor. I have it on good authority that Jake is home tonight. I'll just saunter on up to his room, tug on the belt, and…"

"You wouldn't dare." He was on his feet in front of her in an instant.

"Oh, wouldn't I?" She gestured over her body. "Everything I need to pull this off is right here and ready to go. And who knows where things might lead after that? He and I could have our very own *Flowers in the Attic* moment. I'm getting all aquiver just thinking about it."

Ryan was forced into a reluctant laugh—the kind only Amy seemed able to elicit. "Now you're riling me up on purpose. You're some kind of messed up, you know that?"

"I do." She reached up and planted a kiss on his cheek. "But I really think this could work. Why shouldn't we make this push to get you what you want? You know you'd do the same for me."

He stared at her, his throat aching as he struggled to keep the words in and somehow keep breathing at the same time. If anyone had asked him to do this a few months ago, he'd have jumped at the chance. Hell—that was exactly what he *had* done, pushing those pesky things like morals and decent human behavior and Amy's feelings aside in pursuit of his own goals.

That was what he did. Lost himself in his own vices, numbed reality until it was easy to bypass.

"Ta-da!" she said, triumphant. "I can practically see you coming around to my side of things. I think I might have a gift for this evil plotting stuff."

Seeing her standing there, unyielding and resolute and so fucking beautiful he'd never deny her anything she asked for? Yeah. He could see how that evil part might be true.

"You've got me backed into a corner here, and you know it. You're a lot more like the rest of the Montgomerys than you realize."

She squealed and wrapped her arms around his neck. "I'm pretty sure you meant that as an insult, Ryan, but I'll take it. It sounds an awful lot like a yes."

It wasn't. But it wasn't a no either.

EIGHTEEN

"I REALLY DON'T see why we have to tell him at all."
Amy barred the stairwell door. "The fewer people
who know about this, the better. And I'm pretty confident I can handle him. Don't forget—I've known
this guy since before I started walking. He won't cross
any lines unless I let him."

Ryan stared at Amy, wishing he could give in to
the urge to lift her by the arms and forcibly remove
her from the door. How could someone so sweet be
so annoyingly stubborn?

"Did it ever occur to you to consider Jake's feelings on the subject? Speaking as a man who's ben-
efitted from the pleasure of your company, I'd say
it's needlessly cruel to throw you at his head only to
yank you right back again."

"Ohh. I get it. You like him."

"What?" He felt his ears grow warm. "Don't be
ridiculous."

She took a step forward, her eyes wide and lit with
laughter. "You do. You totally care about his feelings."

"Refusing to stoop to his level isn't the same as
caring. I never liked this plan of yours in the first
place—I'm not going to add crushing a man's romantic hopes to my growing list of sins."

Amy's arms twined around his neck. "You like
him."

"Stop saying that."

"Jake and Ryan, sitting in a tree."

"Stop it right now."

She tightened her hold. "K-I-S-S-I-N-G."

"I can still back out, you know."

"No, you can't." She brought her mouth to his, sealing his fate. "You're too far in it now. You're too close to the finish line."

Don't remind me. He'd always felt a little dejected at the end of a drive, knowing the exhilaration of the chase was nearing a close and that the only thing waiting for him at home was another party, another bottle of Jack. This drive's end felt all the worse because he was going into it with his eyes open and his head clear.

"We could still back out," he suggested, almost pleadingly. "Confront Mr. Montgomery head-on. Stop playing these games."

"Fine."

"Really?" Relief warred with panic in his chest. He wasn't sure which sentiment shamed him the most. "I can go see him right now?"

"No, I mean *fine* as in you can tell Jake about the plan." She sighed and dropped her arms. "You're probably right about it being needlessly cruel. But promise me you won't tell him about the other thing."

"The other thing, meaning...?"

"You know," she said quietly. "I don't want to say anything to him or Monty or Jenna about being siblings until we know for sure whether or not it's true. Can you at least give me that?"

He reached up and traced the line of her lips, which were pulled into a frown. He might not ever be able to understand why it was she hated the idea of confrontation this much, but he knew how much her pain affected him. And that was enough.

"Okay. I promise."

"Thank you." She kissed his thumb, which he'd been having a hard time retracting from her mouth. "And let him down easy, okay? Buy him an ice cream or a pony or something to soften the blow."

Yeah. Ice cream. That was what every man wanted in a situation like this.

THE TOP OF the tallest tower of Montgomery Manor had a roofwalk that was purported to provide a view all the way to Hartford.

Ryan had never been up there before—there was no need for a man who rolled around under car engines to raise himself up so high—but he'd been told Jake had a habit of taking refuge up there. Probably to hide from his father or work on his tan.

He climbed up the ladder access panel and poked his head up. Sure enough, there was Jake—though he was neither lounging nor hiding.

Thwack.

"Nice hit." Ryan climbed the rest of the way through and glanced around. He couldn't see any cities in the distance, but that was one hell of a view. Patchwork fields in green and gold, the surreal blue of a late spring sky. There was a reason rich people built things like this. "Four iron?"

Jake didn't seem surprised to see him. He didn't look up from his position on the far end of the walk, where a portion of the railing had been cut away and replaced with a spiky patch of fake green turf. "Six. You play?"

"Me? Nah." Ryan folded his hands under his armpits and watched as Jake nudged a ball into place with his toe and lined up for another spectacular swing. *Thwack.* The ball flew in a wide arc up and over the hillside, so far it would be almost impossible to find again. But then, why would he bother collecting his balls when he was done? He'd probably just buy more. "I've always lacked the finesse."

"Oh?" Jake said innocently. "And here I thought you had plenty of that. Enough to win the girl, at any rate."

Ryan laughed. "Hurts, doesn't it?"

Jake slid the golf club into a bag resting against the white wood slats of the house's exterior and slowly removed the golf glove from his left hand, never once losing eye contact with Ryan. "My pride, maybe. And my plans. But I would have never played along in the first place if I'd thought she was serious. I wouldn't have hurt her."

"I know." And oddly enough, he did. He might have started off hating Jake, but the man had proven himself a good sport and an even better loser—two qualities never to overlook in a foe. "What would you say if I could help you make up that second one?"

"My plans?"

"Yes. That is, assuming your plans still include thwarting your father."

"They always do."

"I should probably mention it would be at the cost of the former."

A glint in Jake's eye—such an odd combination

of humor and anger—flashed. "I'm living at home, cut off from my income, not even allowed to take a car out without the chauffeur's permission. You think I'm worried about my pride at this point?"

"Fair enough. All we need is for you to go on another date with Amy."

"*We* need that?"

He ignored the sarcasm, so thick he could taste it. Of course no man with a modicum of decency or self-respect would allow the woman he cared about to put herself in this position. But Ryan didn't have decency. Or self-respect. Or any freaking control over her. He'd relinquished that the moment he agreed to this plan, the second he put his own desires in front of hers.

"This time, it'll just be the two of you going solo—but don't worry. The plan is for me to come in and rescue her before you have a chance to get your evil clutches in."

"Do I get to ask why we're doing all this?"

"No."

"But it'll make my dad mad?"

"He'll be livid."

Jake's smile spread slowly. "I can feel myself warming to the idea already. But there's a little something I'd like for you to do for me in return, Ryan the Car Man."

Fuck. Of course there was. "What the hell is wrong with you people? Why can't anyone in your family do a man a favor without having to strike a bargain first?"

Jake flashed his teeth and laughed, gesturing for Ryan to lead the way down off the roofwalk. "How do you think we got so rich in the first place? Not even the Virgin Mary gets free room and board at the Montluxe. We'd have been sure to get the rights to her firstborn ahead of time." He dropped a hand on Ryan's shoulder as he started to move down the ladder. "But don't worry so much—I think you might actually like this one."

Ha. Ryan wasn't counting on it.

"I DON'T UNDERSTAND." Ryan stood looking down at the frame of a Triumph TR250—stripped and rusty, but fully intact. It had to be worth about five grand even in this condition. "Where'd you get this?"

Jake ran his hand over the spot that used to be a windshield but now showcased nothing but an empty frame. "Oh, I salvaged it from my dad's garage years ago. He sometimes buys up old lots from dealers or collectors who need fast cash—he picks out the gems and sells off the rest."

"Yeah, I know. He did that last year. It's where he got his '54 Bentley. But what the hell am I supposed to do with it?"

Jake looked at him as though he were a few gallons short of a full tank. "Fix it."

Ryan fell into a short laugh. "Just like that? You want me to change the oil and give it a tune-up? You're insane if you think this is going to take anything but six months of labor and ten thousand dollars in parts." He found himself circling the frame, making an assessment of what it might need. Even six months and ten thousand dollars was pushing it.

The car was housed in a dilapidated barn so far on the edge of the Montgomery property he wasn't even sure they were on the family land anymore. Rusty rakes and a pile of broken wood boxes arranged in a circle were the only other things inside unless you counted the dirt and nesting bats.

"So you can't do it," Jake said flatly.

"I didn't say that." He wasn't all that familiar with the TR250, a sixties model most noted for its tiny frame and curricle-like convertible top, but there had to be fewer than a thousand of them circulating in the world. Parts would be tricky to come by, though he might be able to cross over from the more popular Triumph models. It was doable—provided a man had the means and the motivation.

"How did you get this out here?" he asked, perplexed. "And why?"

"I had it towed. Dad's never been interested in fixing up the cars—he only likes to own them and show them off. Possession and pride, nothing more. *You* know."

He did. Regular oil changes and twenty-five miles an hour every day of the week to keep things in shape.

"He said I could have it if I managed to remove it from his garage without fucking it up. So I did. And it's been sitting here ever since."

Ryan examined Jake carefully. "So why fix it now? Why me?"

"It's not some dastardly plot to put you in the middle of me and my dad, if that's what you're thinking. He knows it's out here." Jake shrugged and turned to walk out the barn door. "I thought you might enjoy the challenge. You seem bored out of your mind in this place, and it's a sweet car I wouldn't mind driving, that's all. Forget I mentioned it."

"No, I—" Ryan stilled Jake with one hand. Jake

raised an eyebrow at the physical contact but didn't pull away. "I *do* appreciate the gesture. It's just..."

Jake waited, motionless while Ryan struggled to find the right words. "No worries, Car Man. I'll still play the villain so you can rescue Amy. This one comes with no strings."

"It's not that." And it wasn't. He looked back over the car, feeling the thrum of anticipation in his veins. He *would* love to restore this car. In this place where money was no object and he had nothing but time on his hands, there was no limit to what he could do to finish it. Sure, it wouldn't be *his* car, but at least he'd be building something, working toward a tangible goal. And Jake wouldn't pansy around the block in that car. He'd floor it. Hell, he might even let Ryan borrow it sometimes.

But he wasn't staying in Ransom Creek. The whole point of this plan was to free him from obligations to this family. Not add to them.

"Ask me again," Ryan said quickly. "Next week. If you still want me to do this for you the same time next week, ask again."

Jake straightened the cuffs of his sleeves. "Why? Will your answer be any different?"

"No. But your question might." He angled his head toward the door, tearing himself from the car and the promise it contained. "Come on. It's time to go tell Amy the good news. Though I should probably warn you she didn't want to let you in on the plan in the first place. She was going to use you and toss you aside without ever saying a word."

"And I would've let her." Jake placed a hand over his heart and gave a mock sigh. "The things I do for that girl. She's had everyone in my family wrapped around her little finger for years."

"Even your dad?" Ryan couldn't help asking.

Jake looked at him askance. "You really can't tell? *Especially* my dad."

NINETEEN

"No. I CHANGED my mind. We're not doing it."

Amy laughed and gave a shimmy. "I do look pretty fantastic, don't I? Jenna's got impeccable taste when it comes to this sort of thing."

On its own, the white dress, which was so small and composed of so much Lycra it barely counted as a tube sock, would have been too scandalous for the evening she and Jake had planned. But the delicate lace overlay, which overlapped the hem and came up over the arms in adorable cap sleeves, elevated it from trashy to classy. Or so she hoped.

Ryan's hands dropped to her hips, halting her movements mid-grind, and she gulped when she saw the expression on his face. He *really* didn't like this dress. "No. It's not because you look fantastic."

"Gee, thanks," she said, ignoring the pitter-patter of her heart in her throat. "You really know how to make a girl feel special."

She didn't doubt for a second that Ryan approved of her appearance—his tongue had fallen a little *too* far out of his mouth when she'd walked in for that— which meant that his reservations had more to do with the rest of it. The date. And tricking Mr. Montgomery. And—oh, God—the fact that if all went well, he'd be on the first plane out of town.

Now her heart wasn't pitter-pattering in her throat.

It had stopped beating and lodged there, threatening to choke her.

So she did the only thing she could think of—she turned on the laughter and the flirtation, ignoring the way he glowered like a man facing the worst day of his life. Again.

"Relax, Ryan. It'll all be over in a couple of hours."

He didn't relax. He frowned so hard she could tell he wanted to take relaxation between his teeth and grind it until it was nothing but dust. "I don't like it. Of all the stupid, reckless things I've done in my life, at least the only person I did them to was myself. There are too many others involved in this, and—"

She grabbed the front of his T-shirt and pulled him close. "Dirk Hardcore likes it. He likes it so bad. He wants to march into that hotel, slam Jake against the wall and demand justice. He wants to save Candi from the biggest mistake of her life—and then slam her against the wall too." She lost some of her steam and giggled, ruining what was turning out to be a pretty effective argument, if you asked her. "A different wall, naturally. And a different kind of slamming."

He didn't smile. *Shit.* Why wasn't Ryan smiling?

"It isn't a game this time."

"No," she agreed. "But we're going to play anyway."

She was saved from the agony of his response by Jake's brief knock on the door. After calling a cheerful "Come in," she was saved from all kinds of responses. There was nothing for any mere mortal to say when Jake Montgomery entered a room wearing a tux. On those occasions, speech was rendered irrelevant, admiration all that was required.

My brother, she thought, finding the idea less difficult to digest with each passing day, *dresses up crazy good.*

"Don't look so quick to murder me, Lucas." Jake strode forward and offered Amy a chaste peck on the cheek. She was happy to report there was no fizzle whatsoever. "I promise to be on my best behavior."

"He's chickening out," Amy informed Jake, feeling a familiar twinge of guilt getting ready to perform somersaults in her stomach as she pitted the men against one another. *You're doing this for Ryan's own good. You can't be the reason he stays. You'd never be happy knowing he sacrificed himself for your sake, that he always has one eye on the door.* "He's not so sure he can hack it."

"Is that so?" Jake asked coolly. "Why am I not surprised?"

It was such a perfect response Amy could have clapped. Ryan took one look at Jake's smirk and bristled. "I'm not chickening out. I'm second-guessing. It's different."

"Is this where I have to start clucking?" Jake asked. "Because I can tell you right now—I've never been very good at farce. Amy, be a dear and start making barnyard noises for me."

She didn't dare. She knew when she'd pushed Ryan far enough.

"You're an asshole, you know that, Montgomery?"

"So I've been told."

Ryan tossed Jake a set of keys. "Don't you dare drive a single mile per hour over the speed limit. Keep your hands to yourself at all times. And if it comes down to me or Amy taking the blame for this, it was one hundred percent my idea. Got it?"

"Hey, now." She looked back and forth between the two men, hands on her hips. "I can take care of myself. And it was *my* idea."

She might as well have been invisible for all the attention they paid her, but she couldn't find it in her to be more than mildly irritated. She could practically smell the love in the air as they shook hands and shared a stern man-smile. They were totally friends now. She knew it.

And she was glad. In the fallout of this day—whatever happened—she wanted Ryan to have a friendly face to turn to. She wanted him to have someone else who would be on his side.

"Let's go, Amy." Jake offered her his arm. "If I have to drive at a snail's pace the whole way, we need to get moving."

After checking to make sure Ryan wasn't nearing a Hulk moment, she took the proffered limb, her fingers light on Jake's forearm. She would have liked another minute alone with Ryan, an opportunity to reassure him that everything would turn out okay in the end, but it was too late. She was out the door and into Mr. Montgomery's favorite Rolls Royce before she knew it, about to head out for a night on the town with a man who was probably her half brother.

Maybe.

Possibly.

Definitely.

Oh, man. It didn't matter what she thought. In about four hours, she'd know for sure either way.

RYAN DIDN'T BOTHER knocking on Mr. Montgomery's office door. It was late enough that Katie had already left for the evening, so he didn't have to worry about getting her in trouble. It was just him and the man he'd come to despise in ways he'd never known was possible. Just him and the man who'd given Amy life but not his name, his money but not his love.

"We have a problem." He strode inside the wood-paneled, gleaming room, expecting to find his employer in his customary position, head bent over his mess of a desk in a pose of industriousness. What he got was the exact opposite. Two oversized leather club chairs had been angled in one corner to showcase a pair of middle-aged men relaxing amid a cloud of cigar smoke, tumblers of amber-colored liquid in their hands.

"Oh, I'm sorry for interrupting." The apology rose automatically to his lips. So did what came next. "Len Brigand?"

Mr. Montgomery laughed and rose to his feet. "I see my guest needs no introduction. Come in, Ryan, come in. Have a seat. We were just talking about you."

"Oh, I couldn't," he stammered. They were talking about *him?* After hours? Over drinks and cigars?

"I insist." Mr. Montgomery turned his chair so that the worn mahogany leather beckoned, taking a spindly hard-backed seat in the corner for himself. "Len, this is the young man I was telling you about. My driver, Ryan Lucas. Ryan, I believe you know— or at least know of—Len Brigand. Len is one of my oldest friends from college."

Overpowered by the cigar smoke and the feeling that he was rapidly sinking out of his depth, he took

Len's hand and shook it before falling into the chair. A glass of something cold was pressed into his hand. In a moment of panic, he shoved the drink back, splashing Mr. Montgomery in the process.

"It's okay. It's ginger ale."

Ryan looked up sharply, but he was met with nothing but a kind smile from either man.

"Mine is too." Len held up his glass in a one-sided toast and winked. "Eighteen years sober, each one a touch easier than the last. You'll get there."

"Oh." Ryan didn't know what else to do except drink. The sticky-sweet soda almost made him choke, but that might have just as easily been the sense of panic that was taking over. This wasn't supposed to be happening. He wasn't supposed to shoot the shit and swap war stories with Len Brigand, of all people. He was supposed to storm in here and send Mr. Montgomery flying after Jake and Amy in a cathartic outrage.

"I hear you've been trying to return to the stunt circuit," Len said easily as he leaned back in his chair. His ferrety eyes seemed to pierce through the fog of Ryan's thoughts, extracting the essence and leaving a scooped-out hollow behind. "How's that going for you?"

Ryan set his glass aside. The act of moving cup to mouth as a balm wasn't one he remembered with much fondness. "As well as you might expect, sir."

Len smiled. Inside the friendly creases his cheeks made, Ryan could see the straight pearly white teeth that only Hollywood seemed able to perfect. "It's an unforgiving business, I'll give it that."

Unforgiving. That was one way to put it.

He struggled to calm himself, finding it difficult to know where to look, where to land. This was really happening. There was a real chance they could make this work. Except...he had to rescue Amy first.

He cleared his throat, determined to stay focused on the task at hand and not the drum pounding inside his chest. "I'm really sorry to do this, but would it be possible for me to have a few minutes alone with Mr. Montgomery? There's, uh, a pressing issue I need to discuss with him."

Len's surprise was evident in a forehead that wrinkled all the way up to the crown of his bald pate. "Of course. I'll wait outside, shall I?"

"If you wouldn't mind," Mr. Montgomery said, looking a question at Ryan. "I'm sure we'll just be a moment."

"Don't rush on my account." Len got to his feet, leaving his ginger ale on the side table. "And take your time. Family comes first."

"I'm not family," Ryan said quickly.

"We appreciate it," Mr. Montgomery said just as fast.

It seemed Len took all of the air out of the room, because the moment the door clicked behind him, the walls began to spin and Ryan had to grip the arms of the chair to keep from bolting to his feet and following him out of there. Mr. Montgomery, annoying under the best of circumstances, outdid himself by merely sitting there and letting him struggle.

No questions. No nudges. Just a calm, forgiving patience.

"It's about Jake and Amy," he finally said. Almost

all of the steam had left him by that time, and the words sounded flat to his own ears.

"Oh?"

No less-helpful syllable existed on the face of the planet. "It's just…they're gone. I thought you should know."

"Gone where, exactly?"

"My best guess? Hartford." Specifically, to the Montluxe. Even more specifically, to the lounge for drinks and dancing before slipping upstairs to the penthouse. That was assuming Ryan and Mr. Montgomery didn't get there first. "He took the Rolls."

"You begin to interest me. How, exactly, did he get it?"

Ryan had to fight the urge to cover his flaming ears with his hands to prevent the man from seeing his lies. Dammit. This wasn't how this was supposed to go at all. Mr. Montgomery was supposed to fly into a fury, fall into a panic—take on some sort of action other than smiling calmly at him.

"I must have left the key chest unlocked. I went to close up for the night, and they were gone."

"And you immediately deduced the car was taken by Jake and Amy? You're much quicker on your feet than I gave you credit for. I wonder why they were so careful to keep it a secret from you."

"Well, when you mentioned you'd like me to keep a close eye on them, I, uh, took it upon myself to pay more attention to the cars, and…" Fuck this. He was done. There was a reason he drove the cars in the movies, not starred in them. He sprang to his feet. "Don't you even care? Regardless of how I know or where they've gone, the fact of the matter is that Jake and Amy are together. On a date. Alone."

"I hate to be obvious here, but shouldn't that bother you a lot more than it bothers me?"

He swiveled his head to stare at Mr. Montgomery. "Are you fucking kidding me right now?"

"There's no fucking or kidding on my side of things, I assure you."

"You asked me to keep an eye on them."

"And I thought you did admirably well at it."

"You wanted to prevent them from dating."

"I still do. Which was why I was so pleased when it came to my ears that the two of you seemed to be forming a romantic attachment of your own."

Ryan's head swam. There was so much to process in that statement, he didn't know where to start. So he focused on the one thing currently causing the vein in his temple to throb. Even though it ruined all their plans, even though Amy would probably never forgive him, he couldn't stay quiet on this subject another second. He was so tired of being tempted and trapped and yanked around. At least one person in this house needed to step up and lay out the truth.

"But she's not here with me. She's out there. With him. Even you have to admit that the two of them being related to each other makes that a big fucking problem."

Finally, finally, he got a reaction out of the man. The glass slipped from Mr. Montgomery's hand, landing on the table with a clink. "What did you just say?"

"We *know*," Ryan said through his teeth. "Between your shady deals and her mom's excessive worry, it wasn't hard to put the rest together. At what point will you finally care enough about Amy to tell her the truth? How much longer does she have to be a partial member of this family before you finally accept her as your daughter?"

Mr. Montgomery turned unnaturally pale, the white color such an extreme departure from his normal fleshy hue that Ryan dropped his anger and hurried to his side. "Can I get you a glass of water? Should I call in Len?"

"No, no. I'm fine." Mr. Montgomery began choking, so Ryan ignored his response. He poured a glass of water from the sideboard pitcher and, kneeling in front of him, pressed it to the older man's lips. Mr. Montgomery sipped and immediately sputtered, sending an alcohol spray all over the front of Ryan's shirt. "And that wasn't water."

"Oh, shit. I'm sorry." He stepped back. "But you were so pale. I don't think my career can handle a murder charge on top of everything else."

Mr. Montgomery waved his hand. "It'll take a lot more than this family of mine to kill me. If they wielded that kind of power, I'd have been forced to cock up my toes decades ago." The vodka seemed to help, and he took another deep pull, this time swallowing the liquid. "Tell me, Ryan—is Amy aware of what you just told me?"

"She is."

"And she believes herself to be my daughter?"

Believes? He hesitated. "She does."

Mr. Montgomery's lips drew together tightly. "Take me to her."

"I told you, I don't know—"

"Young man, I've come to grow quite fond of you

over the past two years, but if you don't take me to where the pair of them are hiding right this minute, I'll take you out back and show you firsthand just how difficult it is to kill me."

Despite the harshness of Mr. Montgomery's words, Ryan's lips twitched. "Are you offering to fight me, sir?"

"Don't think I can't do it. You might be half my age and in a hell of a lot better shape than I ever was, but I've got a few tricks up my sleeve. It was how I disciplined my boys for years. I imagine you could benefit from a few right jabs yourself."

Ryan felt his ears growing warm. Not "You're fired." Not "Get the hell out of my sight." It sounded an awful lot like Mr. Montgomery was offering him the exact opposite.

"I'll get rid of Len while you bring the car around," he commanded. Ryan sprang to his feet and rushed to the door, happy to be back in the action again. "And, Ryan?"

He hesitated, his hand on the knob. "Yes?"

"Something fast, please. As fast as you're comfortable handling."

Oh, sweet Jesus. Forget Hollywood. Forget alcohol. The thrill of the ride was what Ryan really felt burning in his veins.

"Must we speed quite this drastically?" Amy's mom spoke up from the backseat of the Ferrari FF, her voice small. "I understand you're upset by all this, John, but they won't do anything drastic in the next thirty minutes. They're just kids. They're probably at the bar trying to drink each other under the table.

Don't you remember when they did that for Amy's seventeenth birthday? I *still* don't know where they got that bottle of gin—but I do know she wouldn't touch the stuff after that, even to this day."

Even though Mr. Montgomery shook his head to indicate that Ryan could maintain the ninety-mile-per-hour pace he'd set since they'd pulled onto the interstate, he eased up on the gas. Since Amy had promised to be able to keep Jake in check, there really wasn't any need for haste, and he didn't want to give Amy's mom a heart attack on top of everything else.

He'd done enough damage as it was.

"I wish one episode of overindulgence was all it would take to cure Jake of his excesses," Mr. Montgomery said. "I honestly don't know what I'm going to do with him, Linda."

"He's young. Give him time."

"I was running a multimillion dollar company at his age. Had already started my family. Youth is no excuse."

"If I remember correctly, you weren't a complete paragon back then. There are one or two indiscretions I can think of—"

Ryan gave over to a fit of coughing. *Indiscretion?* Is that what they'd call it?

"Not *that* kind of indiscretion." Mr. Montgomery looked over at him and frowned. "Amy's not my daughter, Ryan, much as I might wish otherwise."

He almost swerved off the road in his struggle not to slam on the brakes. What the fuck? If she wasn't his daughter, why were they zipping toward Hartford like someone's life was on the line? Why had they stopped to get Amy's mom? "But you said…"

He paused, trying to recall Mr. Montgomery's exact words. He'd never confirmed or denied his paternity—just turned that awful shade of white.

"I said nothing, which was probably my first mistake."

Linda's hand moved between the two front seats, and Mr. Montgomery wasted no time in grabbing the appendage and giving it a squeeze.

"It was my mistake too, John. If I'd have thought for one second she'd get this idea into her head, I'd have come clean long ago. The poor thing. What must she have been thinking of us?"

Out of the corner of his eye, Ryan saw Mr. Montgomery get that white, scary look again. "She probably thought I was some kind of monster, keeping that from her."

Ryan swallowed heavily. "That might be my fault. *I'm* the one who put the idea in her head. If anyone should take responsibility for this, it's me."

"Don't be ridiculous," Linda said. "No one blames you."

They'd reached the turnoff for the city, so Ryan slowed even more, adhering to local speed limit laws and feeling sadly deflated. The momentary lift of sliding behind the wheel of this car and seeing what it could do was giving way to a much stronger feeling of fear.

Fear and doubt and the overwhelming certainty that he'd done nothing over the past few months but dig his own grave. And now he was sitting in it. Alone.

"But you *should* blame me," he said. "I haven't

done you enough justice, Mr. Montgomery—in fact, I've done the exact opposite. I assumed the worst of you and forced Amy to see it too. I understand if this means you'll want to terminate my employment after this."

"Would you stop trying to get me to fire you?" The cold steel was back in Mr. Montgomery's eyes, the command back in his voice, but Ryan was quickly coming to learn that this man wasn't nearly as ruthless as he'd originally thought. His bark was much worse than his bite. "If you want to leave my employ, of course you're free to go. But do it on *your* terms, not mine. And be sure to let me know first, because Len's been pestering me for weeks to lend you to him for his next movie—he's got some dangerous rooftop thing we both think you'd be perfect for. I was hoping to offer you a time-share situation, but I understand if that's not what you want."

Ryan opened and closed his mouth again, unsure what to say. That offer was everything. And nothing. And all the things that existed in the middle.

"Oh, good. We're here." Linda was the first to break the oddly buzzing silence that followed Mr. Montgomery's speech. Ryan pulled up in front of the hotel, his usual spot when he had important guests to drop off.

"I'll just, uh, park and join you inside." Ryan was surprised when Mr. Montgomery merely nodded and took him up on the offer. Surprised, but not offended. He was back in the role of subservience, chauffeur to a powerful man.

And that, he realized, was how Mr. Montgomery wanted it to be.

He wasn't the man's friend, but he wasn't just his employee either. He was treated like an equal one moment, an errant child the next. He was valued and tested and put in his place all at the same time.

For the first time, he realized that Amy might be right about Mr. Montgomery being a decent person. She might be right about everything. If he didn't know any better, he'd say this felt an awful lot like being part of the family.

"WHAT IF YOUR dad freaked out and had him killed? What if he has him buried out behind the pool house?" Amy gnawed on her fingernail, which tasted considerably less delicious than the mai tai she'd just polished off. She didn't dare drink another one, even though Jake was on what had to be his fifth glass of whisky by now.

Not that he appeared the least bit intoxicated. While liquor loosened other men, it only caused Jake to button up, his movements tighter and more controlled, his conversation less expansive. And less helpful. He was definitely being less helpful here.

"It wouldn't be the first skeleton hiding somewhere on our grounds." He kicked back the rest of his drink.

"Or maybe they rushed over here to stop us and crashed in a fiery wreck. We should check the news channels for information."

"Ryan didn't crash."

"But they should have been here at least an hour ago." Amy checked the clock on her cell phone. "We've dined. We've danced. We're drinking. The only thing we have left to do is slip upstairs and look scandalous, but I was hoping things wouldn't get that far."

"They won't."

She threw a wadded-up cocktail napkin at him, her anxiety blossoming into full-on irritation. Jake was much less useful in these sorts of situations than Ryan. Ryan wouldn't have sat there being purposefully obtuse. He'd have laughed with her, however reluctantly. Played along. Turned it into a game. "Would you stop arguing with me for no reason other than to argue?"

"I'm not," he argued. He lifted his glass and pointed. "They're here."

She turned her gaze toward the double French doors to find Mr. Montgomery surveying the room. It didn't take him long to locate them—they had the best table in the spot, as it was a Montgomery prerogative to be seated under the peacock-shaped Tiffany chandelier that had been hanging there for over a hundred years. Nor did it take very long for his normally calm face to fall into a frown.

Good. Let him frown. He should frown. For all he knew, she was about to diddle her brother.

"Mom?" She got to her feet the moment she saw her mother emerge from behind Mr. Montgomery, her slight form hidden neatly behind his own. Why had they stopped to bring her mom? And where was Ryan? "What are you doing here? You didn't have to come all this way."

"Of course I did, sweetie."

Before she could respond, her mother enveloped her in a hug, holding her with a strength she didn't know the woman still possessed. It was a mom-hug, one of those tight, painful, soul-wrenching embraces that made her feel as if she were a kid again and had just found out the tooth fairy wasn't real.

She'd been twelve when she'd learned that—always slow to catch on to what everyone else had known forever. Obviously, this was a trait she had yet to outgrow.

"I'm so sorry it had to come to this," her mom said as she relinquished her tight hold. "I never thought you would push things this far."

Amy bristled. She'd done a decent job of not holding her mom accountable for all this, but that comment hit a long-dormant spot in her gut. No one expected her to push about *anything*. That was the problem. She was the happy-go-lucky nanny, the cheerful and dependable daughter. No one cared that being left out of the loop for twenty-six years of her life might actually hurt.

No one except Ryan.

"Yeah, well. There's a lot you don't know about me."

"And you." Her mom pulled away and glared at Jake. It was a real nanny glare—the kind Amy was sure no amount of practice would allow her to duplicate. But then her mom pulled Jake into a similar hug, holding him until his stiffness melted away. Amy didn't know of anyone else on earth who could accomplish that. "You should know better than to try and kidnap my daughter. I'll find you, young man. Every time."

"Where's Ryan?" Amy asked, searching in vain for the last member of the party to join them. The most important member of the party. The reason all this was happening in the first place.

"He's parking the car," Mr. Montgomery said. "I thought he could use a few minutes to compose himself."

Compose himself? Into what?

"Maybe we should all sit down. I think there are a few things we need to discuss."

Amy realized—belatedly—that she was totally ruining Ryan's chances of making a grand gesture here. She and Jake were supposed to have been caught in a scene of questionable morality, where fiery passions and illicit conversations required a timely intervention. Sitting down and sharing a plate of shiitake canapés was hardly the stuff of high drama.

"I don't think there's anything I care to discuss with you," she said stiffly and turned to Jake. "Our room is ready by now, don't you think?"

Jake lifted a brow but nodded. The man was a good sport, if nothing else. He hadn't even once tried to ask her what all this was about. She wasn't sure if it was because Ryan had warned him against trying to pump her for information, or if he simply didn't care.

"Sit down," Mr. Montgomery said again, this time with much less kindness in his tone. Last month, last week—heck, maybe even yesterday—Amy would have dropped without a second thought. But even though Jake sat with a heavy sigh, Amy remained on her feet. She was tired of doing what she was told. She was tired of being the girl no one wanted.

Everyone at the table turned to face her, their eyes expectant but not concerned, waiting for her to fall in line just like she always did. "I'll stand, thanks," she said.

The wide-eyed, watery look her mom sent her way almost had her giving up her long-overdue obstinance, but it wasn't until Ryan materialized at her elbow that her knees actually gave way.

"I think you should sit, Amy," he said, looking grim. His mouth was a firm line, his body resonating with tension where it very clearly didn't touch hers. "We were wrong. Jake isn't your brother."

Jake looked up, startled. "Was that ever a possibility?"

Oh, dear. Amy gratefully sank to the seat Ryan pushed closer to her, savoring the press of his hand on her shoulder. His hand stayed long after she was seated, and she felt rather than saw him arrange himself right behind her. Literally behind her. He had her back yet again.

"Um. A little bit?" Amy was afraid to look around the table, so she studied the grain of the wood instead. "I know it sounds crazy, but Ryan and I had this theory—"

"That we're *related*?" Jake raised his voice before realizing they were in a public place. He leaned across the table and hissed, "Are you serious right now? You went out with me thinking we might be siblings? On purpose? Shit, Amy. I almost kissed you."

"I know." She dropped her head to the table, all those wood grains beckoning. "But that was before we found out about the… Or before we thought the… Yeah. It's awful. I quit."

"Don't look at me like you want to stab me with your swizzle stick, Jake," Ryan said. "It turns out

Amy and I may have been a touch overzealous in that
arena. You aren't related after all."

Mr. Montgomery interrupted with a long cough.
"That isn't strictly true."

A stunned silence settled over the table, almost
comforting in how it chilled Amy to her bones.

"But you said you aren't her father." Ryan squeezed
her shoulder—though whether for comfort or because
he needed something to demolish, she couldn't say.
"In the car. You told me—"

Amy's mom reached across the table and nudged
her head up, forcing her to confront the whole tab-
leau around her. Mr. Montgomery, his brows pulled
together in concern. Her mother, about to break into
tears at any moment. Jake, struggling to hide his horrified expression behind his usual mask of disdain.
He didn't fool her, though. She could see him making the same mental calculations she had that first
day. *Did we ever...? Have we ever...? What about
that one time...?*

If he ended up remembering something her own
memory had wiped away, she prayed he'd keep it to
himself. She was just starting to feel clean again.

"Sweetie, I owe you an apology," her mom said.
Her eyes flicked to Mr. Montgomery. "John and I
both do. We thought it would be best if we gave you
a normal life—as normal as possible, under the circumstances. A home, a family, any opportunities you
wanted in life. But I think we underestimated how
important it would be for you to know about your
father. I think we underestimated how strong blood
could be."

Amy was no closer to understanding what was

going on than she'd been weeks ago. So she *wasn't* a Montgomery?

She looked up over her shoulder where Ryan stood resolute. As soon as her eyes met his, she knew he understood the pain that was shooting through her, starting in her solar plexus and bursting out in every direction. Supernova. This was what if felt like to go supernova.

She wasn't a Montgomery. She wasn't a part of this family. She was back to being the odd woman out, the reject, the outlier.

"I don't understand. What do you mean *a normal life?* Why shouldn't my life be normal? What am I?"

"You're a Hawthorne," Mr. Montgomery said.

Hawthorne? She wrinkled her nose, trying to recall where she'd heard that name before. It was familiar, but only in a vague, fleeting sort of way, like a dream that refused to hold on after the morning coffee settled in.

"She's related to Mom?" Jake's voice cut through the fog, cementing her in the present. "How?"

Nancy Hawthorne. The first Mrs. Montgomery. A woman she remembered as being cold, hateful and very, very tall. *Tall like me. Tall like Jake and Jenna and Monty.*

"Mom?" she asked, her voice wavering as she looked to her mother. If someone didn't start explaining soon, she was going to pass out right here on the table. And despite all her fairy princess airs, Amy was not a fainter.

"I don't know if you know this, but Nancy had an older brother," her mom said gently. "A very charming, very handsome, very married older brother."

"Uncle Christian?" Jake demanded. "Uncle Christian is Amy's dad? She's our *cousin?*"

She felt the loss of Ryan's hand from her shoulder like the loss of the ground underneath her feet. She opened her mouth to ask why he was leaving, where he was going, how he could possibly leave her at a time like this, but he reappeared by her side. He took a seat next to Jake, his solid presence a comfort to them both.

"I think maybe it's time someone starts from the beginning," he said.

So Mr. Montgomery did.

The story of her birth didn't start out with *once upon a time*, and there weren't any evil stepsisters to move the plot along, but the cast of characters felt familiar just the same. An older married man visiting his sister and brother-in-law for a few weeks. A pretty young woman stopping in town for a few days on her way to the Big Apple. Her mother's part was a little bit sad and a little bit sordid. Yes, she'd known he was married. No, she hadn't intended to sleep with him. But there'd been too much wine from a bar that hadn't checked her ID and too much flattery for a girl straight from a Minnesota farm. Amy had been conceived in the back of a Montgomery family town car.

It was that, more than anything, that drove the rest of the story to its current climax. Her fairy godmother turned out to be a fairy godfather—one who couldn't bear the idea of anyone affiliated with his family abandoning his own flesh and blood. When Christian refused to have anything to do with the pregnancy or the young woman he'd foisted it on, Mr. Montgomery had stepped admirably up to the plate. He'd offered to pay Linda enough money to live the rest of her life in comfort, and, when she'd refused his charity, offered her a position as nanny in his home instead.

"'You'll raise the children together,' he told me," her mom recounted, smiling warmly at the man in question. "'Whatever she wants, whatever she needs, it's hers for the asking. We're her family now.'"

Amy would have burst into tears at that part if Ryan hadn't grabbed her leg under the table and run a warm hand right up her naked thigh. Her outrage at being molested was secondary only to a feeling of gratitude at the distraction.

"That explains so much." She sat back. Ryan's hand moved to clasp hers, their fingers intertwined. It was a simple gesture, but one that made her feel much stronger than she would have been facing this alone. "Mrs. Montgomery—my...aunt, I guess?— always hated me so much. She couldn't even look at me without breaking out in a shudder."

"No, Nancy never did come around the way we'd hoped." Mr. Montgomery frowned. "Don't blame her too much for treating you unkindly. It wasn't a great position for her to be in. You were a constant reminder of her brother's transgression, proof that he was a man who would willingly seduce an eighteen-year-old and refuse to face the consequences afterwards. He never was invited back to our home. And he never will be—not while I'm there."

Jake pushed back from the table and got to his feet, his movements jerky. "I'm glad you can all sit around and turn this into a Kumbaya moment, but I'm having a hard time seeing the sunshine and roses. Christ,

Dad. Amy's our cousin. An actual member of this family, not just some sweet kid we all used to dote on in our spare time. How is it possible that, in an entire twenty-six-year span, you never once stopped to think we might like to be apprised of those facts? Doesn't anyone else see this situation and realize how fucked up it is?"

"I do."

Amy was surprised to see Ryan's look of intense anger, directed primarily at Mr. Montgomery and her mother, who were arrayed as allies on the opposite side of the table. She'd thought he was okay, that he was merely listening and supporting, the gruff chauffeur they could all rely on. But he wasn't being supportive. He was *pissed*.

"Maybe the two of you thought you were doing Amy a favor, raising her surrounded by luxury, giving her a taste of this life, but did you once stop to consider how it might feel to a little girl? To never quite be one of the family? To always run along a few steps behind the curve, and never know why?"

"I never intended to impart that feeling," Mr. Montgomery protested. "I'm not sure you realize, Ryan, the exact nature of her place in my household."

"Don't talk to him like that." Amy's voice was barely distinguishable above the hum of conversation, but the shock of her having spoken so firmly, and so much in opposition of Mr. Montgomery, worked like a moment of stop, drop and roll. "He understands it perfectly. He understands it better than anyone else."

"Sweetie?" her mother extended a tentative query.

She turned to face her mother—this woman she loved so much, this woman she thought she knew so well. "He understands me because he's the only one who knows the truth."

"The truth about what?"

"About how my place in this household has affected me. About what I've been doing away from home all these years."

Amy expected her words to fall like a bombshell, shocking her relatives—all three of them—and giving her a chance to be the one driving the family drama for a change. So she was the illegitimate offspring of Jake's uncle, was she? Big deal. So she was the accident no one wanted to publicly claim, huh? She could cry about that later.

But wouldn't they be sorry once they realized she'd spent almost a third of her life wandering the woods, with none of them the wiser? Wouldn't they feel bad knowing they'd driven her away?

"Do you mean the Enchanted Forest job?" Mr. Montgomery asked. She could tell, from the crinkle in his eyes, that he meant to be kind. She knew, from all he'd just confessed, that he was on her side.

But that wasn't how she felt. She felt manipulated and alone. She felt even more like nothing in this life had ever been truly hers. Not even her secrets.

"You knew?" she cried.

"Oh, Amy. Of course I did." There were those crinkles again. Those damnably kind crinkles. "Why do you think I asked if you wanted to be the twins' nanny when your mom's health got in the way? You were the first person I thought of. I wanted to make sure you weren't just hiding out because you were scared of letting me down. I wanted to give you a way to come home."

Amy promptly burst into tears.

That was the best and the worst thing she'd ever heard. These were the best and the worst people she'd ever known. She hated them and she loved them and she was pretty sure someone was going to have to carry her out of here before the night was over.

But most of all, she just wanted them to leave her alone and let her cry.

TWENTY

ALMOST EVERYTHING RYAN knew about families, he'd learned from the big screen.

Large families set the scene for a lot of showing off—usually because there was a big-name ensemble, with every actor vying for the most screen time. Small families usually signaled a drama like killing or kidnapping. Rich families hid their quirks behind big houses and fancy cars. Poor families hid theirs behind caustic wit. Hollywood had a way of breaking down the most complex family relationship into easily definable roles.

But the Montgomerys—or Montgomery-Hawthornes, he should say—flabbergasted him.

"You should have said something about not wanting to be a dancer." Linda was mostly angry. "Why didn't you tell me? Why am I only finding out about this now?"

"I don't know, Mom. Why didn't you think to tell me that the man *who gave me life* is also a scumbag millionaire? Don't you think that's a pertinent piece of information?" Amy was pretty angry too.

"It was my fault." Mr. Montgomery wore a mask of contrition. "I thought knowing the truth would hurt you, but I see now that I did more damage by keeping quiet. I'm so sorry for making you feel left out of the family, Amy, or like you had to prove yourself to me. I never meant to do that. I've always loved you as if you were my own daughter."

"Oh, Mr. Montgomery." Now Amy was crying again. Why was she crying again? "I love you too."

Ryan slipped away from the table and took a step back, thinking now might be the time to make a discreet exit. He'd done his part, slayed the metaphorical dragon, reunited the princess with her family. No one wanted the knight to hang around in the messy emotional aftermath.

"What do you say, Car Man?" The metaphorical dragon was right behind him—not quite slain, but definitely with a spring or two loped off his step. "Want to slip away with me to the bar? They've got a top shelf Macallan that will make this day seem like less of a travesty."

Ryan shook his head. "Your fancy liquors are wasted on me. I don't drink."

"Oh, that's right." Jake led the way to the bar anyway and turned the wheel of an invisible car. "Crash, crash, bang, bang. No alcohol for you."

He actually laughed. Two years he'd lived with the shame of that car wreck, the knowledge that nothing had killed his dreams but his own folly, and no one had been able to make him laugh about it. Not even Amy. "I promise you, Montgomery. The old me could drink you under the table five times over."

"You think so?" Jake signaled to the bartender and sat at one of the stools before turning his attention to Ryan. "I guess we'll never find out, will we?"

"I'm not going anywhere yet."

"Save your growl for someone who cares. I only meant that if you want to keep dating my cousin, you better cling to that sobriety wagon for dear life. Or you'll have me to deal with." His gaze was sharp but not unkind. "My cousin. Who's been working at a theme park. *Fuck*."

"You think you're upset?" Ryan shrugged, but he was far from feeling calm. Not even that top shelf Macallan would make it go away. He doubted anything would. "Amy's had her entire world turned upside down, and she's still standing. We could all learn something from her."

They both looked over to the woman in question, who was bouncing between tears and accusations, between a sunny smile and a more serious, inwardly directed expression. Ryan thought she'd never looked better. Sure, the dress she wore was designed to appeal—and appeal it did—but it wasn't her exterior so much as the way she was glowing that drew him.

She was happy.

These people—her family—made her happy, even when they made her furious.

"The offer still stands, by the way." Jake's drink had arrived, and he turned his back on the family reunion taking place behind him to attend to it. Ryan recognized the telltale signs of a man who was choosing the wrong way to cope with his problems, but he didn't think he'd reached a point with Jake where that kind of conversation would be welcomed. "About the car. I'm not exactly flush with cash while my dad holds the purse strings, but I think I can manage that much. It'd be fun. Maybe you could even teach me a few things in the process."

Ryan wasn't fooled. "You want me to teach you rebuilding engine things, or how to take a turn at eighty mile an hour things?"

"Let's not be silly." Jake kicked back his drink. "The second one. I don't create valuable items. I only enjoy them. And I sense most of my enjoyment is about to come to an end."

Ryan opened his mouth to ask what that meant, but he felt the heavy press of a hand on his shoulder and knew the worst was yet to come.

"Amy has asked for some time to sort things through." Mr. Montgomery nodded to where Amy sat alone at the table, twisting and untwisting a napkin between her fingers. "She's also asked to talk to you."

Ryan nodded, a heavy sense of foreboding replacing his earlier joy at the sight of her.

"You'll always have a job at the Manor. I hope you know that. But if, after all this, you decide to take Len up on his offer full-time, let me know. I can have you booked on a plane out of here tomorrow—and I'll personally back any insurance policy the studio requests. All you have to do is ask." He paused. "The time-share is also still an offer. If it's what you want, we'll find a way to make it work."

"How will you get back home?" the chauffeur in him couldn't help asking.

Mr. Montgomery just laughed. "Are you kidding? I've been dying to get behind the wheel again. It's been far too long since I took a pretty girl out for a long drive." He crooked his arm for Linda to take and, with just one meaningful glance at Jake and the bartender, issued a command to clear the entire bar of its two dozen or so patrons.

Damn. That was power.

Ryan approached Amy's table cautiously, feeling uncertain of his surroundings and of her. The hum of quiet in the now-empty bar—the French doors shut tight, not even a busboy in sight—felt oppressive and indulgent at the same time.

He wasn't used to being so pampered. He wasn't used to existing in a world where he stood on the inside of the money and power.

"Hey," he said softly, stopping at the table's edge.

Amy looked up with a half smile and cast a meaningful glance around the room. "Hey, back. Seems we have the whole place to ourselves here. It'd be a shame to waste it."

He couldn't tell—was that a hint? Was he supposed to take advantage of the setting to fall into a role, play a game? Dirk Hardcore. Fabian Hunter. A thousand other men who deserved this woman a hell of a lot more than he did. The possibilities were endless and fraught with sexual promise.

Fuck it. He didn't want to be anyone but himself. He sat opposite her, his hands placed carefully on the tabletop.

"How are you doing?"

Her smile wobbled. "Oh, you know. Found out my parentage. Learned my whole life has been a big, fat lie manipulated by Mr. Montgomery. Discovered I've been hiding behind my fears for no reason at all. Your typical night on the town."

His heart ached—for her, for everything she'd suffered, but mostly for himself. Because despite everything that had happened, Amy still had a home to turn to, people who cared about her without question.

All he had waiting for him was a city of drunks

and opportunities, where he'd spent years assuming speed and danger were somehow capable of replacing love. What a stupid, reckless waste that had been.

"I'm sorry it had to happen like this," he said.

"Are you?" She shook her head, a few strands of hair falling free of the careful swirl that completed her upscale look. The locks glinted in the lights of the chandelier overhead, honeyed gold and tempting. "I'm not. Better to get it all out at once than drag out a series of confessions over weeks and weeks of drama. Though I'm still not convinced this confrontation stuff is all it's cracked up to be. I mostly want to take a nap."

"Then why don't you?"

"Take a nap?"

"Sure." He gestured toward the ceiling. "You and Jake bribed your way into the penthouse, didn't you? Why let it go to waste? A few hours in a Montluxe bed should do wonders."

She played with her bracelet, a delicate band of white gold, as she pondered the idea. "They *do* have really nice beds here. Soft and fluffy. Decadent. Big enough for two."

He froze. It wasn't the response a man liked to give when he was being propositioned, but he was afraid that any movement at all would have him tearing upstairs like a starving man. Which he was. He was starved for human affection. Ravenous for a taste of her. Desperate to know what came next.

"Amy."

"I know." She sighed. "I can tell you're getting exasperated when you say my name in that tone of voice. You should have become a nanny. You're really good at it."

"I'm not exasperated. I'm terrified."

"Of me?"

"Of the future." He reached across the table and grabbed her hands, unwilling to go any longer without touching her. The forward movement caused their knees to bump, and neither one of them backed away. Over and under, they were connected, if only by touch. "In a weird, convoluted, Amy sort of way, your plan actually worked."

"My plan?"

"Mr. Montgomery offered me that job in Hollywood—or, rather, a way into it. He said I could leave whenever I want."

"Ryan, that's fantastic!" Her eyes flew open as she jumped up out of her seat, taking even the tiny comforting touches away. "Even though I kind of hate him at the moment, I still believe Mr. Montgomery is a decent man. I hope you can understand that now. He's so good at taking care of his work and the people who depend on him that he sometimes forgets about what his actual family might be feeling in the meantime."

"Amy…"

"He'll see his side of the bargain through to the end. He always does. And if he tries to back down, he'll have me to contend with. I won't be afraid to confront him this time."

So that was it. Ryan's fate was sealed, his departure already half-over.

"And you?" he asked dully. Even in the face of her such obvious exuberance, he couldn't muster more than a glimmer of joy. "Are you going to keep working at the Manor?"

She bit her lip. "I think so. Don't be mad—I know it's not what you want me to do, and it's *definitely* not what my mom wants me to do, but I'm happy there. If there's one thing I've learned in all this, it's that I need to start asserting myself more. If I don't want something—say, a career in dance—I'm allowed to say so. If I do want something—say, to live away from the Manor so I can try to have a life of my own—I have every right to go out and get it. My family won't love me any less because of it."

"You're moving?"

"I'm thinking about it. I've always thought your apartment building was nice."

So was his apartment. It was small and over-crowded and way too high-tech for Ransom Creek, but all that could be changed. He could easily make room for her in there. He could easily make room for her anywhere.

But that wasn't what she was asking for.

He gave a nervous laugh. "I'm not sure what's supposed to happen now. Do we shake hands? Should I offer you a ride back?"

"You could always kiss me."

Hell, *yes*. That he could do.

Ryan didn't waste any time getting to his feet and pulling her into his arms. Her body fit naturally against his, yielding to the force that had him gripping her much more tightly than he intended. He couldn't help it, and he wouldn't apologize. If this was the last time he was going to hold this woman, he was going to make it count.

He made it count.

He bent her so far backward over the table they might have been lying on top of it. His lips crashed onto hers, demanding that she acknowledge what they had. Maybe not time, maybe not a future, maybe not anything other than these thirty seconds of heady openmouthed passion, but a connection that would last for the rest of their lives, whether they wanted it to or not.

As he pulled away and placed Amy back on her feet, she released a cry. He couldn't tell if it was a cry of passion or pain, but as she pressed the back of her hand to her mouth, he realized it didn't matter.

"I can't do it, Ryan." She reached for him, grabbing his arms, his waist, his neck, her search relentless until her head was pressed against his chest, muffling the sounds of her tears. "I tried, I really did. I thought if I just stayed strong and focused on the positive, I could be happy for you, but I'm not. I'm not happy for you at all. I hate your stupid hopes and dreams. I hate them more than I've hated anything in my entire life."

He ran a hand up and down her back, soothing and comforting, feeling one hundred percent confused. But hopeful. He also felt hopeful. "Shh, Amy. It's okay. Whatever it is, it'll be okay."

"No, it won't be." She still spoke to his shirt, though some of her shaking had subsided. "I can pretend I'm all assertive now and demand the things I want from the people I love, but it's no good if I let you go without a fight. You're the one thing I want most of all. Don't you know that?"

"Amy, look at me."

She did, her eyes red from crying, her expression so miserable he couldn't help himself from leaning in to kiss each cheek, wiping the pain away.

"Don't go, Ryan. Stay. Stay here with me. I know Ransom Creek is the last place you want to be, but I promise to try and make it better. I won't work so much and I won't let the Montgomerys dictate all my actions. I'll show you the best places to have fun and maybe you can fly into California to do a movie every now and then. You could be happy here, I know you could. Just let me have a chance to show you how."

He silenced her with another kiss, this one soft and sweet, the taste of her tears salty where their lips met. "Yes."

She stopped in the middle of a sob and pulled back. "What did you say?"

"Yes." He firmed his hand around her waist, determined never to let go again. "I'll stay for you, Amy Sanders. And I'll stay for me."

He'd stay for Mr. Montgomery, a man who was generously offering a bridge between his past and his future. He'd stay for Holly and Alex and Philip and Katie and the entire staff at the Manor, all of whom were encouraging him to open up and find a place with them. He'd even stay for Jake, who was promising him a chance to rediscover what it was he loved about cars—not just the speed and not just the finished product, but the process of getting there, of building a future piece by piece.

The whole package.

Car guys were notorious for being attuned to the whole package.

"Do you mean it?" Amy's voice came out as a squeak. "You really want to?"

"Yes." He'd never meant anything more in his life. He hoisted her up on the table and settled himself firmly between her thighs. They'd all better hope those French doors over there had locks. "But I'll think you'll find that Ryan Lucas can be a hell of a lot more demanding than Dirk Hardcore."

"Ohh." She wriggled, her body vibrating against his, powerful and strong. "I like the sound of that."

"You'll have to take weekends off."

He kissed her neck, loving the rapid pulse under his tongue.

"And no working overtime unless it's agreed upon in advance."

Up to her jawline, where he paused long enough to drink in her scent. Blueberries today. He couldn't wait to discover what tomorrow would bring.

"And I'd love it if you'd have lunch with me every day in the kitchens."

Finally, tenderly, on her lips.

"Oh—and you really have to let me do something about your car. I'm getting tired of having to hide it in the corner of the parking lot so no one else can see it."

Her laughter was a whoosh of warm air against his mouth. "You jerk. This whole time, it's really been my Rabbit you wanted to get your hands on, isn't it?"

Not even close. Now that his hands were on Amy, he was pretty sure nothing else in this world could ever compare.

EPILOGUE

"ARE YOUR EYES CLOSED?"

"Sealed tight."

Amy peeked around the corner to make sure Ryan wasn't lying. True to his promise, he had his hands over his eyes and a foolishly expectant smile on his face. He looked gruff and out of place and adorable, especially when a little boy walked by with a giant puff of cotton candy on a stick and swiped a blue-sugar slash across Ryan's side.

The Enchanted Forest hadn't been his first choice of vacation destination, but he was being an incredible sport about the whole thing. Mostly because the alternative—a Montgomery-Hawthorne family reunion in upstate New York—was a trip she'd decided she could do without.

Her blood might come from there, but her heart was exactly where it belonged.

Besides—it was the least he could do after leaving for three weeks to shoot that Len Brigand film, *Fiery Passions.* It sounded a lot more like a soap opera than an action flick, if you asked her, but he'd come home with a huge bruise along his rib cage and the glowing look of a man who'd driven a car off a rooftop or two.

He'd signed a contract for three movies a year. No more, no less. Enough to keep his blood pumping, not so much he'd lose sight of home. They were even talking about Amy taking a few weeks off the next time to go with him.

She couldn't wait to see him in action. To prop him up in the glittering, fast-paced world that had shaped him.

"Okay." She stepped out from behind the oversized concrete tree painted to resemble the real thing. This one had a face on it, which would spontaneously break out in animatronic expressions of serenity and ancient tree wisdom. "I'm ready, but you have to promise there will be no laughing, no mocking and definitely no inappropriate behavior."

Ryan paused in the act of removing his hands. "Is there a chance I might be tempted to do that last one?"

"Well, I do look pretty amazing in this dress." Even though he couldn't see her, she gave a twirl to prove it. "And you wouldn't believe how many secret coves there are in the place. If you bribe one of the security guards, he'll give you a detailed map. There's this one spot, in the Mermaid Grotto—"

He groaned. "You better stop while you still can."

"But I think you'll really like it there. There are mirrors and everything."

"Now you're just being cruel." Ryan dropped his hands and blinked. And blinked again. And once more for good measure.

In front of him stood a vision in pink tulle and fairy wings. He knew, from the stirrings of lust that started in his groin and spiked through every nerve ending he possessed, that it was Amy inside that dress. Amy, corseted up and splashed with glitter and every inch a member of the theme park royalty. Amy, loving a chance to dress up and play pretend, to recapture the joys of childhood that were never very far from her imagination.

But there was no way he was defiling her in this place.

A stream of kids gasped their surprise at her sudden appearance and rushed to greet her. They all seemed to want to touch her dress and pet her hair and get their photos taken—something he could hardly blame them for. *He* wanted to touch her dress and pet her hair, and he wasn't averse to a photo shoot with just the two of them and that particular outfit. And he got to see her almost every day of his life.

Sorry, she mouthed as she was overtaken by requests.

Ryan stepped back and let her fall into her natural role. It was a role he was rapidly coming to recognize as one she would never be able to fully shed. Kids loved her. Adults trusted her. She was the ray of sunshine everyone wanted in their life, if only for the short space of one of her smiles beaming down on them from afar.

And she was his.

Or rather, she *would* be, as soon as the park closed for the night. Then there was nothing but the two of them, the open sky and a week-long road trip in a Triumph TR250 he'd built with his own two hands.

He was finally moving again.

But this time, he knew it wasn't the forward momentum so much as the woman by his side that made all the difference. She made all the difference in the world.

* * * * *

ABOUT THE AUTHOR

TAMARA MORGAN IS A contemporary romance author of humorous, heartfelt stories with flawed heroes and heroines designed to get your hackles up and make your heart melt. Her long-lived affinity for romance novels survived a BA degree in English literature, after which time she discovered it was much more fun to create stories than analyze the life out of them.

Whether building Victorian dollhouses, consuming mass quantities of coffee and wine, or crying over cheesy 1950s musicals, Tamara commits to her flaws like every good heroine should. She lives in the Inland Northwest with her husband, daughter and a variety of household pets, and only occasionally complains about the weather.

REQUEST YOUR FREE BOOKS!
2 FREE NOVELS PLUS 2 FREE GIFTS!

H HARLEQUIN®

Desire

ALWAYS POWERFUL, PASSIONATE AND PROVOCATIVE

HD15

REQUEST YOUR FREE BOOKS!